“WHAT D[illegible], KENNY?”

The boy, locked in hypnosis, cried. Tears poured from the sides of his eyes, over the darkened bruises that surrounded them.

Mrs. Smith managed to pull herself up from the chair. She was at Kenny’s bedside, wanting to hug her grandson, to tell him it’s okay.

And Whit waited, also entranced, but wanting more than anything to hear a name if the boy knew one.

“I see Missie, laying on the floor. I see blood. I see a man laying there, too. More blood.”

“Him . . .”

A.P.B.

Dave Pedneau

BALLANTINE BOOKS • NEW YORK

Copyright © 1987 by Dave Pedneau

All rights reserved under International and Pan-American Copyright Conventions. Published in the United States of America by Ballantine Books, a division of Random House, Inc., New York, and simultaneously in Canada by Random House of Canada Limited, Toronto.

Library of Congress Catalog Card Number: 86-91644

ISBN 0-345-34205-4

Manufactured in the United States of America

First Edition: December 1987

For Elaine . . .

A.P.B.

In official police jargon an "All Points Bulletin"

Prologue

THE CRACKLING HISS of radio static.

The voice of the dispatcher—words clipped, slurred by urgency.

"County to Unit Three. County to Unit Three."

Gil Dickerson—Unit 3—fumbled for the cruiser's mike. "County, go ahead." No sense saying more. He was the only unit working the hoot owl.

"County to Unit Three."

Gil frowned. "I'm here, asshole." The words didn't go over the air because he didn't key the mike. When he did key it, he said, "Unit Three, reading you loud and clear. Go ahead."

"Unit Three, a caller reports a body—a dead person—at the front entrance to the high school."

Gil's frown deepened. The dispatcher, by tradition the most virgin of the county's deputies, had fucked up. He hadn't coded the message. Any son of a bitch with a scanner now knew what was going on. And everyone owned one. If it hadn't been so late, half the goddamn town would reach the scene before Gil. There wasn't much else to do in Milbrook.

Gil dismissed the error as the full import of the radio traffic sunk in. His adrenaline started to pump; his heart galloped. "Who called it in?"

"The guy wouldn't give no name."

"That's all he said?"

"Yeah . . . Uh, affirmative," the voice crackled. "Just wouldn't give me no more info. I tried. I really honest to God tried to—"

"Okay . . . okay," Gil said, again without keying the mike. No reason to as long as the dispatcher was still yapping. When the whining radio transmission ended, Gil said, "Ten four. On the way, and keep my times for me."

Gil was south of Milbrook, patrolling fly-by-night used-car dealers and greasy hamburger stands cluttering the highway to Virginia. Milbrook High sat on the northern boundary of the small city. He whipped the cruiser around.

It was Sunday night—well, actually 1:12 A.M. Monday morning . . . nontraditional Memorial Day. On Sunday and Monday nights Gil patrolled the entire county by himself. Not that much ever happened—an occasional wreck, sometimes a drunk driver, the customary prowler and disturbance calls. Gil hated those two nights of the week. You never knew when something really big might go down. And this was the climax of the first holiday of the summer. So far it had been a quiet weekend.

Maybe the tranquillity had just ended. On the other hand, maybe some drunk was passed out on the high school steps. Most "dead body" complaints climaxed in the arrest of "the body" for public intoxication.

"Unit Three to County." He waited for an acknowledgment. When it came, he told the dispatcher to call the city police. "See if they have a unit to back me up."

"Ten four."

The city cops had no jurisdiction beyond the city limits, but they were willing to lend a hand if the call was on the fringe of town.

He flipped a switch to engage the blue light and ignored the one that sounded the whooping siren. Department policy required him to use both—never one without the other—

but Gil wasn't driving fast, and the streets were deserted. No reason to roust the whole town. Like most officers, Gil figured policies were a matter of interpretation. The pavement glistened from a brief rain around midnight, just a splash-and-dash shower. Gil had noticed flashes of lightning on the far side of Tabernacle Mountain. The storm must have glided up the mountain ridges, passing east of the county.

A body.

More than likely a prank call.

Television made police work look more glamorous and exciting than it really was. Once in a while, reality fused with fiction, and something exciting did happen. Gil dreaded and craved those rare moments of action.

"County to Unit Three."

Gil gripped the mike, ready to answer. "Go ahead."

"The city unit is tied up on a domestic matter. They'll come your way when they wrap it up."

Shit. Never around when you need them. "Ten four, County."

He rolled down the city's main street. Vapor lamps cast an amber aura over the damp streets. A haze of moisture floated in the night air. The day had been a scorcher, a record high temperature for the date. Perhaps it foreshadowed a hot summer. Gil hoped so. Inside the cruiser the air conditioner kept it crispy cool, but, with the potential of the call in mind, Gil's sweat dampened his summer-weight uniform. The cool air made him chill.

Nothing much stirred, just the squadrons of insects circling the high streetlamps. He left the business district behind, entering an area of upper-middle-class homes, all of which were dark. Their inhabitants slept, secure in the knowledge that guys like Gil kept them safe.

If only you knew . . .

Gil lived two blocks west of the main street. Not that he

considered himself upper-middle-class. He and his wife worked. They were frugal. They sacrificed to own a house nicer than their level of income should permit.

A vision of his wife formed inside his head. The look on her imagined face urged him to ease back on the accelerator—to give the city officers a little more time to clear the domestic complaint. Cops lived longer if they played it close to the chest, and Gil wanted to live a very long time. He was getting to the high school much too quickly. DeeDee Dickerson was just too young to be a widow. And Gil hadn't purchased that extra life insurance policy, which he would do on Tuesday, if he didn't forget it once again.

He brought the mike to his lips. "Unit Three—County."

"Go, Three."

"How about that city unit?"

"Stand by."

Gil reached in his shirt pocket and pulled out a nearly consumed roll of Rolaids. He popped two in his mouth.

"County to Unit Three."

"Go, County."

"The cities are still tied up."

The hell with them then. "Ten four. I'm there. Stand by."

Gil eased the gray and black cruiser into the parking area fronting the school. Its headlights flashed across the empty lot. He rolled down the window and adjusted the cruiser spotlight. As the vehicle crept through the lot, Gil played the thick beam of light over the grounds. Wet grass twinkled at him. Two bright, sparkling eyes made Gil stomp his brakes. The eyes vanished. In the light beam Gil caught a glimpse of a furry object darting for cover.

A fucking possum.

He mopped away brow sweat, then allowed the cruiser to roll forward. The searchlight beam reached the corner of the brick high school. Its beam flashed back in his eyes as it touched the panes of floor-to-ceiling glass that enclosed the building's breezeway. The glitter of shattered glass, lying on the front walk, sent his heart throbbing. The circle of light danced across the glass walls.

"Holy shit!"

The body lay half in and half out of the breezeway, bent double over the lower half of the fractured pane. The upper portion of the panel lay in pieces all over the concrete.

No prank call or drunk this time. Gil ran his hand over his face. "Just what I need," he said aloud.

His hands turned clammy on the steering wheel. Things had to be done at the scene of a homicide. The state police academy had trained him to secure a crime scene, but that had been several years ago. *Now what do I do?* He ached for a drink of water.

The cruiser pulled into a spot in front of the body. The headlight beams laid a spotlight on the gory scene. Before jumping from the car, Gil scanned as much of the surrounding area as the spotlight would reach. He released the hammer guard on his .357 service revolver. Almost as an afterthought, he picked up the mike. "Unit Three to County. We do have a ten-seventy here. I repeat, we do have a ten-seventy."

"Come again, Unit Three."

The green asshole didn't even know the call codes. Thank God he'd be going to second shift soon. "I said we do have a ten-seventy. Check your codes!"

"Oh, the codes! Oh . . . Oooh! Ten four!"

"Dumb bastard!" Gil snapped just before keying the mike. "Call and advise the sheriff—"

"Ten four."

"—and get me some assistance."

"Gotcha."

Gil doubted it.

With his right hand on the butt of his gun, he exited the

cruiser. His left hand wielded a large, black flashlight. Blood smeared the intact pane to the left of the body. The flashlight beam paused on the blood. Gil squinted at it. It looked like—

Not a smear at all. He edged closer. *Words, written in blood. A message . . . reading, "NO. 1."*

Gil wondered if it was his imagination, but he let it go, forcing his attention to the body. It had been thrown into the glass. The body had then sliced down on the lower two or three feet of the pane. Some of the glass had popped to the exterior of the building. The exposed, naked buttocks bore deep gashes from the cascading slivers of glass, and blood pooled on the concrete, spreading out in a wide halo around the body.

A woman, he thought. The buttocks, disfigured though they were, appeared soft, feminine. He could not see her face. To reach her, Gil had to step into the pool of congealing gore. He hesitated.

At that instant headlights flashed over him. He looked to the entrance and saw a city police cruiser. "Thank God," he said aloud, no longer feeling so helplessly alone.

His courage reinforced, he stepped into the slippery stain, careful not to fall, and moved toward the body. Glistening gashes marred her smooth back. She had worn her hair long. The soaking blood obscured its color. Gil reached down and grasped the sticky hair, lifting up her head as car doors slammed behind him.

The head snapped free of the torso.

The two city officers—Cpl. Jay Sanchez and Patrolman Stan Kilgore—saw him reach down. They both knew Gil, Sanchez the better of the two. The Sanchezes and Dickersons socialized. They were casual friends.

For a second Gil stood there, gaping at the head. Sanchez noticed the deputy start to shake. He hurried toward the scene.

"What is it?" Kilgore asked.

With quivering and caring hands, Gil lowered the severed head to the concrete. He settled to his knees in the gore. When Sanchez reached him, Gil was sucking in air, blowing it out, in fast, violent breaths.

Sanchez looked back to his partner. "He's hyperventilating."

Gil's whole body quaked as his breath came faster and faster. "Easy!" Sanchez said, his hand clutching the shoulders of his friend. "Take it easy. You've seen worse."

Gil's mouth and lips moved to form words, but only air came out.

Sanchez glanced at the victim. It was bad, no doubt about it. "Watch him, Stan."

Sanchez leaned down to inspect the corpse. He touched the head. It rolled over to the side, the face grinning at him.

"Sweet Mother of God!" Sanchez crossed himself.

"What the shit is it?" Kilgore cried, growing angry because he didn't know and no one was rushing to tell him.

Sanchez backed away. "It's . . . it's DeeDee. It's Gil's wife!"

At the sound of his wife's name, Gil found his voice. His soul-deep pain escaped in a cry that echoed over the lonely grounds of the high school.

In dark shadows not a hundred yards away, the hunter smiled, lifted a bloody hand to his nose to smell the woman's gore, then hurried away.

It had begun.

ONE

WHIT PYNCHON GAVE passing thought to going to bed. He shrugged off the idea; sleep wasted time. Instead he visited a desk in his living room, opened the center drawer, and withdrew a thick, hand-worn manila folder. It contained his dreams. He settled into his favorite chair, lit a menthol cigarette, and pulled a handful of the colorful pamphlets from the folder. Each one of them advertised a condo or resort community along South Carolina's Grand Strand.

No matter the design, each of the resorts boasted a typically tropical name. Pirate's Cove or The Reef or whatever. He shuffled through them with little interest. Whit wasn't certain why he kept them. Not because the plastic buildings interested him. He did enjoy the photos, filled with green palms and sand and blue ocean vistas. They offered a touch of the Carolina Low Country that he loved and to which he would retire—very, very soon.

Whit wanted a small house on the landward side of an inlet. The beach houses, even the huge condos, were careless offerings to the first strong hurricane that decided to make landfall along the Strand. It wouldn't take much of a storm surge to undercut most of them. Whit had been vacationing there when Diana danced by a few miles off shore. A 135-mile-per-hour whirling dervish, she'd made a believer of him. The September storm had eventually beached itself near Wilmington, North Carolina. Whit, anxious to experience something new, had raced her north, fighting the torrential feeder bands of rain that she had whipped over the Carolina coastal plains. He'd rented a motel room just beyond the evacuation area.

Big, tough Whit Pynchon, investigator for the office of the Raven County prosecuting attorney, had suffered twelve dark hours in a howling nightmare. The storm's eye, knocked askew by ten miles of land that separated Whit from the coast, passed right over that little motel. The walls of his room had vibrated under Diana's assault. Wind squeezed water through the tiniest fissures around the door and windows. The lights had flickered, dimmed, then died, leaving Whit a cigarette lighter and the frequent flashes of lightning by which to see.

Weakened or not, never again. The banks of an inlet were plenty close enough to satisfy his love of the ocean—and not so close as to be threatened by it.

The cop ached to retire, to bid goodbye to West Virginia. The weather in the Mountain State was atrocious. If it wasn't raining, it was about to. He despised it. Maybe its residents didn't have to worry about climatological disasters, but for Whit the constant mediocrity was much worse.

He leaned his head back in his easy chair and lit another cigarette. So what if he was just past forty? People hiked their eyebrows in shock when he told them he planned to turn in his badge and gun at forty-two.

A year and six months away.

In a year and seven months Whitley Francis Pynchon would be a bona fide resident of Georgetown County, South Carolina.

The phone rang.

Its shrill warbling jolted Whit, sending an emotional shock coursing through his body. *Christ!* How he hated phones. He glared at it for two . . . three rings, hoping it would stop. When it didn't, he answered it.

"It's after one," he said as the handset reached his mouth. "You'd better have something damned important to say."

A moment of stunned silence on the other end.

Then, "I was gonna apologize for calling so late, but the hell with it." The tart voice belonged to Whit's boss, Prosecutor Tony Danton. "That's a shitty way to answer a phone, Whit."

"It's a shitty time to call. Besides, it's my phone. I'll answer it any way I like."

"Why in the hell do I feel like I work for you instead of vice versa?"

Whit smiled but maintained an irascible tone to his voice. "If you worked for me, you damn sure wouldn't be calling me at this hour."

Tony Danton's voice turned serious. "We got a mess, Whit."

"Who got arrested for drunk driving? The judge again?"

Tony's silence conveyed his disapproval. "Serious up, Whit. And knock off the drunken-judge jokes. We have a murder."

"A domestic squabble, I guess." Most of Raven County's violence resulted from love turned sour.

"Goddammit, Whit! Stop with the fucking know-it-all crap." Tony had been prosecutor for sixteen years, and Whit had been with him for fifteen of them. Whit knew the lawyer as well as anyone, probably better than anyone, including his wife. The short, feisty lawyer wasn't flustered easily, but on this night an uncharacteristic tremor tinged his voice. Usually he wasn't so testy.

"So what is it?"

Tony wasn't through fussing. "You're always Mr. Friggin' Experience. Always so quick with an asshole quip."

"Damn, Tony. I'm sorry. I apologize. I surrender. Whadaya want? A human sacrifice?"

"Smartass." The lawyer paused. "Someone murdered—no, the word is 'butchered'—Gil Dickerson's wife tonight. He made sure Gil got to the scene first. The poor bastard didn't know it was his wife, not until he . . . well, you know what I mean."

Whit's jaw slackened. "You're kidding?"

"Nope."

"Jesus, Tony. I remember her. A pleasant, classy lady."

"Her death wasn't pleasant or classy. She mighta been killed at her home. Or at least badly injured there. And raped. The killer then took her a few blocks to the high school and tossed her into a glass window. Sliced her up to a fare-thee-well. The fallin' glass decapitated her. The sheriff's department got an anonymous tip. Gil was the only one working."

Whit liked Gil Dickerson, which made Gil something of a rarity. Whit Pynchon didn't care a lot for most of his fellow peace officers. Dickerson, though, was a quiet guy, the strong silent type not given to macho displays of nightstick authority. "How is Gil?"

"The ambulance crew sedated him. I gather he lifted up her head. It came off in his hands. That's when he saw who it was."

The story would be told time and again in Milbrook—for years to come.

Whit cringed. "Jesus!" Then his mind went into official gear. "Was Dickerson patrolling alone?"

"Yeah. He always works the Sunday and Monday hoot owl alone."

"Any evidence they'd been having domestic problems?"

Tony's hissing intake of air signaled his exasperation. ''Damn you, Whit! You're a cynical bastard.''

''You pay me to be cynical, Tony.''

''Gil's a nice, easygoing guy—''

''Still waters run deep.''

''Just get your ass over there and take over the case. Jump to your conclusions after you've checked it out, okay? And get a move on. They wanna move the body.''

''Hell, Tony. You know I never let facts influence my opinions.''

''Just go!''

''On my way.''

''Wait!'' Tony shouted. ''Hold on!''

''Make up your mind.''

Tony let that pass. ''We wanna keep a tight lid on this thing for now. You can understand why.''

Whit laughed into the phone. ''You know me. The only good reporters are unemployed ones.''

Two

DEPUTY HANK POSICH grabbed the phone on the first ring. He'd been awake in his bed staring up at the shadows on the ceiling while caressing a coal black cat that rested on his chest. He didn't want the phone to wake his wife, and it didn't. She enjoyed the sleep of the dead, thanks to her pills.

"Hank, this is Bill down at the jail."

"So . . . what's up? This is my night off." The cat's purring was loud and liquid.

"I . . . something happened tonight which you oughta know about."

"What?" Hank was Gil Dickerson's partner and shift commander on the hoot owl.

"Somebody wasted Gil's wife."

Hank sat up in bed. The cat rolled to his lap, its feet pointed up in the air. "Wasted? You mean killed her?" His sharp movement did cause his wife to stir. She rose up in bed, her eyes reflecting the disorientation produced by the sleeping pills. It would be noon before she overcame the drug hangover.

"Who? When?" Hank was asking.

"Got no idea, Hank." The shaken dispatcher told Hank what he knew of the murder.

"Who's handling the case? The state police?"

"No, the prosecutor's investigator is. He's on his way to the scene."

"Jesus fuckin' Christ! Who decided that?"

"The prosecutor, I guess."

"Well goddamn. That dumb ass!"

"The prosecutor?"

"No, Pynchon! Well, hell—yeah, the prosecutor too. He keeps that bastard working for him. Makes more than you and me put together. I'm coming out."

"I thought you might want to."

Hank hung up the phone. He gently lifted the cat to the floor. Its name was Tear Gas. Hank's wife had found it five years before, a small and shiny black ball of fur cowering on their porch. She had brought it inside, but it was Hank's heart in which the cat came to cuddle.

"What is it?" Missie Posich asked, unconcerned that one of her heavy, full breasts hung from the top of her nightgown.

"Cover yourself." He climbed from the bed.

She focused her eyes on a flaccid brown nipple. "So what's going on?" She shrugged the breast back into her nightgown.

"Gil Dickerson's wife was murdered tonight." Hank was fumbling with his pants, trying to put them on as Tear Gas rubbed his legs.

"DeeDee?"

"Yeah. Some maggot asshole drug her outa her house, killed her, and made sure Gil was the one who found her."

"DeeDee Dickerson? She's dead?"

Hank fought with the buttons on the uniform shirt. "That's what I said!"

"Oh, God! Poor thing." Missie slipped back into the bed and pulled the covers up tight around her. "Who did it?"

"Who knows? What's worse, they gave the goddamned case to that bastard Whit Pynchon."

Missie had heard the name often. Even in the fog of her drugged mind, she remembered it. "He was the one that investigated you a couple of times."

"Damned right he was. I can't believe the sheriff went along with that. Pynchon may call himself a cop, but he's a cop hater."

"They got any suspects?"

"Hell, woman. I don't know. That's what I'm gonna go find out." Hank took his holster and weapon off its usual nighttime place on the bedpost. He strapped it on. "The dispatcher's new. He might not have the straight of it."

Missie shivered. "How was she killed?"

"Raped, then taken over to the high school and thrown through a window. Her head was cut off."

Missie paled. "Oh, Hank! I just saw her day before yesterday at the market. She said that she and Gil were wantin' a child."

Hank was dressed. He checked the action on his gun and leaned down to give the cat a final few strokes. "They waited too goddamn long."

A small white towel covered the head of Mrs. Gilbert Dickerson. It rested on the concrete, partially hidden beneath her torso. "Why didn't you cover the body too?" Whit asked one ambulance attendant.

The skinny young man looked to his partner, then shrugged. "I don't know."

His older partner jabbed him. "Hell, don't lie to the man. You covered the head because them eyes was looking up at you."

"Aw, go fuck yourself!" snapped the boy. A severed head wasn't supposed to repulse ambulance attendants. The kid had an image to maintain.

"Well, why don't you go find a sheet to cover the rest of her?" Whit said. "It bothers me."

Several deputies milled around the scene. Sheriff Ted Early stood to the side, talking to Jay Sanchez. Police cruisers and the single ambulance crowded the parking area just in front of the breezeway. Whit approached the sheriff. "Anyone call the medical examiner, Sheriff?"

Early, as tall as Whit and much heftier, nodded. "Sure did. Right after we called Danton. He said he'd look at her down at the hospital."

Whit shook his head. "That lazy son of a bitch. How about a photographer? I want photos of the scene before they transport her."

Early glared over to Miller Foley, one of the deputies who had been called out. "You tell the station to get a photographer?"

The baby-faced deputy nodded. "Yes, sir."

Early waited for a moment. "Well, did they, boy?"

"I don't know."

Early's infamous temper flashed. "Goddamn, boy, find out."

Hank Posich's cruiser screeched to a stop in a niche between Whit's personal car and the ambulance. Hank exited the cruiser and made straight for the sheriff. "Can I have a word with you?"

Early nodded. "Hell, yes. What is it?"

Hank glanced at Whit. "It's 'tween me and the sheriff."

"A secret?" Whit chided.

Early took Hank by the arm. "Let's walk over to my car, Hank."

But Whit waved a hand. "Whoa! No need for that. I have a murder to investigate, anyway." He ambled back toward the body, which was now shrouded with a sheet.

"Why the hell's he handling this?" Hank asked of his employer, nodding at Whit as he did.

"Whadaya mean?"

"I mean, why him? Pynchon? Why not the state police?"

Sheriff Early crossed his thick arms. "I don't care much for your tone of voice, Hank."

"I'm sorry," Hank said. "I didn't mean any disrespect to you, sir, but I don't think it's proper for that asshole to be handling this."

Early eased back from Hank, whose breath reeked of decayed teeth. It always did. Most of Hank's teeth had long since gone, not because of the dentist but rather from rot, pure and simple. Behind his back, the men called him Death Breath.

"Apology accepted, Hank." Early pointed his nose in another direction. "I don't like him any more'n you do, but the prosecutor makes the rules. 'Sides, for all his faults, he's a good investigator. Give the devil his due."

"Sheeet!" Hank said. "The only thing he likes to investigate is other cops—and he ain't too good at that."

The sheriff looked at Hank from the corner of his eyes. "Oh, were you guilty of something he didn't uncover?"

Several yards away Whit inspected the body. The scene itself had already been violated by the time Whit arrived, but he did his best not to disturb anything that might become evidence. He heard the raised voice of Hank Posich, but he kept his eyes to the woman's bloody shoulders. A small flashlight illuminated the area. Beneath the smeared bloodstains he noticed bruises that suggested the pattern of fingers.

Deputy Foley joined him. "Messed her up really good, huh? I didn't know her, but they say she was a real nice lady."

Whit eyed the young, willowy officer. Many years ago, he too had been that thin. He was still tall, six feet exactly, but he had thickened some. Not much, just ten or fifteen pounds, but enough to push him over two hundred pounds. The Foley kid reminded Whit of himself when he first became a deputy, shy and gullible, trying to win the approval of his peers. Whit had changed more than his appearance.

"What about that photographer?"

"On his way."

Whit turned from the body. "Tell you what—uh, what's your name again?"

"Foley. Miller Foley. The guys call me Millie, but I prefer Miller."

"Okay, Miller it is. You search over that way. I'll go this way. Keep your eyes open for anything that might be evidence, but don't touch. Give me a shout if you find anything."

"Yes, sir."

Another vehicle wheeled into the lot, a small sporty truck with flashing hazard lights. It skidded in behind Hank's car, and a young man bounded out, dressed in jeans and a sweater. The outline of the gun beneath the sweater signaled he was another cop.

"I just heard," Tim Franklin said, breathless from his reckless drive to the scene.

Early wasn't overjoyed by the officer's arrival. Franklin was the department hotdog, a phrase passed on to Early by the former occupant of the sheriff's department. "Who called you?" he asked of the young man.

"I heard the traffic on my scanner. I called the station. They told me."

Franklin's upper torso strained the expensive Izod sweater he wore. His chest and arms bulged with muscles, and the officer dressed to highlight them. His hair glistened from a recent shower.

"You been working out again?" Hank asked.

Franklin's obsession with physical fitness got under Hank's skin.

"I had a date." Franklin grinned at Posich, who made a face and turned away.

The ambulance attendants waited near the body. The stretcher was ready to be loaded. Whit waved them out of his way. "You fellas might as well relax. It's gonna be a while yet."

The older one threw up his hands. "Hey, man. I gotta be to work at six."

"You are working," Whit said. He followed the beam of his flashlight, seeking a clue to the killer's identity.

The attendant tagged along. "This is my second job, man. Can't we speed things up here a little?"

"What else do you do?"

"I work at the funeral home."

Whit stopped to stare. "Damn, fella. You live a morbid life. Those stiffs aren't as important right now as this lady."

"So what's the holdup anyway?"

Whit, indifferent to his predicament, went back to his search.

Tim Franklin stood at the edge of the congealing pool of blood. "Look at that!"

Whit saw that it was Franklin. "And how's Mr. Universe tonight?"

"You always gotta smart off?" Franklin asked.

"I didn't mean to smart off. I heard you were entering one of those bodybuilding contests. I thought I was paying you a compliment."

"Yeah. Sure you did."

The sheriff came up to Whit. "Me and Hank are gonna drive over to Gil's house. Check it out, maybe check out the neighbors too."

"With all due respect, Sheriff, I have to object."

Early bristled. "What the hell does that mean?"

Whit clicked off the flashlight. "First of all, I want the Dickersons' house secured so we can get some state lab people down. Second, Danton wants me to handle this case, and that includes interviewing witnesses. Finally, I don't wanna give him"—Whit nodded toward Hank, who leaned against his cruiser—"the chance to screw up this case."

"And that"—Early pointed down at DeeDee Dickerson—"is the wife of one of my men, dammit!"

"All the more reason to handle it right. I'll take Miller there with me. He looks like he's got the makings of an investigator."

"Miller?" Early said.

The young deputy smiled. "It's Foley, sir. The last name, I mean."

"Well, Deputy Foley then. I'll take him along as a representative of your department."

Franklin loomed on the fringe of the conversation. "You gotta be shittin' me."

Foley tried to give his fellow officer a hard look of warning. It only made Franklin smile.

Early shifted his weight from one foot to the other. "Which means you don't want me along either, huh?"

"I'll take Mr. Miller there . . . uh, Mr. Foley, I mean."

Ted Early, his face glowing with anger, clenched his fist. "Okay, fine with me! But you can believe that me and Danton are gonna have a face-to-face over this. I'll see that this place gets cleaned up, hose off the blood and all."

Whit ran a weary hand through his thick, graying hair. "Sheriff, I'd appreciate the opportunity to search the area in the daylight. Just leave it as it is."

Early's mood grew more irascible. "Dammit, man, this is a school. Kids are gonna be here—"

"Tomorrow's—or rather today—is a holiday."

Early had forgotten, but he didn't want to yield too easily. "By God, if that was my wife lying there, I'd want her blood cleaned up before it became a public spectacle."

Whit turned from him. "You heard me, Sheriff. Leave

it as it is. The kid and I are going over to Dickerson's house. Think you and Hank there can handle the photographer?''

''Certainly!''

''Fine. Have him shoot everything that looks interesting. After that, those two ghouls can move her.''

Hank had been listening, growing even more angry than the sheriff. ''You know, Pynchon, you ain't gonna have that job forever.''

Whit smiled as he spoke to Hank. ''It's that thought which gives me the patience to tolerate guys like you, Hank.''

Hank came at Whit. ''That rips it. I'm gonna—''

Early wrapped his huge arms around the charging deputy. ''Forget it, Hank.''

Whit went to his car. Foley slid in on the passenger side. As the car vanished from the lot, Hank glared after it. ''Someday, I'm gonna cut that cocky bastard down to size.''

''And I just might give you a hand,'' Franklin said.

THREE

ANNIE TYSON-TYREE LOOKED not at all like her byline. The name conjured a false image of a drawling gossip columnist. It wasn't strictly a pseudonym since her true name was Anna Tyson (no hyphen) Tyree. Anna had adopted the hyphenation. The publisher of the first newspaper for which she had worked suggested the name Annie. It tempered, he argued, "the ostentatious affectation of the hyphen."

No one who knew her dared to address her casually as Annie. Nor would anyone who knew her mistake her for the stereotypical gossip columnist. No big floppy hats for Anna. No crusty pancake makeup. Anna Tyree, the name on her checking account, was trim of figure, auburn haired, dark complected, and preferred jeans to a dress. Regardless of what she wore, she snagged male attention. Anna was one of those fortunate women who gave no attention to her "looks." The art of cosmetics came about because of such women as Anna, women who needed no makeup yet always looked made up. Heavy eyelashes outlined her azure eyes. The prior year's tan always endured through winter. And the passing years, a month shy of thirty of them, enhanced her beauty.

Since becoming Annie Tyson-Tyree, she had worked for three newspapers. In her first two jobs she had battled to stay away from the society and life-styles desk, managing instead to build a credible résumé as a journalist with strong skills in court and police reporting. With each job change, she had tried to escape the byline. It stalked her like a bad reputation. Even the publisher of the *Milbrook Daily Journal* had balked at the use of the hyphen. At the same time he liked "Annie."

She had been adamant. "I want the job very much, but 'Annie Tyree' isn't acceptable."

He repeated it aloud. "Annie Tyree. You're right. Annie Tyson-Tyree is better."

Anna had pushed her luck. "How about Anna Tyson-Tyree?"

"Hmmm." He was an aging man, squat and bald. "I think not. I like Annie. Good reader identification."

On such terms she had come to the Milbrook paper just three weeks before and was assigned to the courts and the police beat. The tip about the murder came from a young city cop with the hots for Anna. She cultivated his good will while holding at bay his persistent advances. And she made no bones about it. Each time he had phoned with a "hot tip"—the cliché spoken with an obvious double entendre—she always stopped him. "I appreciate the info, but, before you say any more, you know how I feel."

"Yeah, you find me repulsive," he said on this day.

"No, I don't. I'm nine years older than you."

"But you know what they say about young men. I'm in my sexual prime."

"Statistically you're beyond it, but it doesn't matter. Save yourself for a woman who wants a young stud. I don't."

"I'd love to take you to a movie."

She laughed at his determination. "You know the ground rules."

"Just think it over."

"I have!"

"Don't you even feel a little bit obligated?" he asked.

''Not an iota.''

Anna seldom dated, detesting the courtship game, the sexual fencing and transparent ruses. If she liked a man, there was no game, no fencing.

''It's a holiday for me,'' Anna said. She still wore her bathrobe. ''What do you have?''

Silence spoke his disappointment, perhaps his anger.

''I have to go,'' Anna said.

''Hold on, Anna. It's a murder.''

''Where?''

''The 'who' is more important. The wife of a cop, a deputy sheriff. Gilbert Dickerson's wife.''

''I haven't met him, I don't think. How was she killed?''

''They found her thrown into a window at the high school. Her head had been cut off and was just sitting there, staring at poor Gil. Oh, I forgot to tell you. He got the call and didn't know.'' Even cops weren't immune to rash rumors.

''The husband? He found her?''

''Yeah—because of an anonymous call, probably from the killer hisself.''

Anna scribbled notes on a pad. ''Is he a suspect?''

''Who? Gil? Shit, he's straight as a monk. I hear she was raped. Pretty gory.''

''And no suspects yet?''

''Not that I heard.''

''Is your department investigating?''

''Oh, no. The high school's outside the city. Course, they don't know for sure where she was killed or raped. The Dickersons live in the city limits. You see, if she was killed or raped in the city, then—''

''I know all that,'' Anna said. She'd covered police news long enough to understand words like *venue* and *jurisdiction*, probably better than the young officer did. ''Who will be investigating?''

"Whit Pynchon with the prosecutor's office."

Anna screwed up her face. "I haven't heard of him, either."

"You mean you haven't met lovable Whit?"

The childish palaver irked her. "I said I hadn't."

"I can't believe it. You've been here three weeks and haven't—"

"I have a busy day ahead of me. Who the hell is Whit Pynchon?"

"Well, Whit—" her caller spent a few more moments chuckling, "—is the prosecutor's investigator. He's also the most cantankerous person I know."

"What kind of cases does he handle?"

"He's a troublemaker." The cop lowered his voice. "Anytime the prosecutor gets a complaint about a police officer—city, county, or state—Whit handles the investigation. Really pisses some guys off, especially if he reads them their rights."

Anna was nodding her head. "So he's the local watchdog for the cops. No wonder you don't like him."

"Hey, I didn't say that. I never had no trouble with him, and—"

She interrupted his disclaimer. "If he's involved, then maybe Dickerson's a suspect?"

"No way. I told you. Gil's an all-American kid."

"That's what they said about Ted Bundy."

"Wasn't that the guy that shot his wife through the head over in Wickmore Bottom last year?"

Anna rolled her deep-azure eyes. "Never mind."

"The name's familiar."

"What time did all this happen?" Anna extracted all she could from the young officer, then said, "I appreciate it."

"But not enough to go out with me?"

"You got it, kiddo." She hung up the phone and grabbed the phone book, looking for a home number since it was a holiday. It listed two Pynchons—one as W. F. Pynchon and the other as W. J. Pynchon.

Either one could be Whit Pynchon. She dialed the second name, and a woman answered.

"Is Whit Pynchon there?"

"Who is this?" The voice became suspicious.

"Anna Tyree. I'm a reporter for—"

"Whit hasn't lived here for fifteen years, and I don't appreciate the interruption."

Oh, shit. An ex-wife.

"I'm sorry, Mrs. Pynchon. I didn't know which Pynchon to call. I do apologize."

"Try W. F.," she snapped. "And that doesn't stand for 'wonderful fella.' " The phone clicked dead.

Anna laughed. Whoever Whit Pynchon was, he certainly earned no merits for popularity, which meant she could anticipate a hard time from him. That was fine with her. She prided herself on her ability to melt the coldest of hearts. Anna dialed the second number. It rang several times. She was just about to hang up when he answered.

"Whit Pynchon?"

Anna heard labored breathing on the other end, as if the man had chased down the phone.

"Yeah. Who's this?"

"I'm Anna Tyson-Tyree. I'm with—"

"Who?" the voice boomed.

Jesus. Let me finish. "Anna Tyson-Tyree. I'm a reporter for the *Journal.*"

"A reporter?"

The single expression contained such emphasis that Anna had to ask. "Do I detect hostility?"

"I don't talk to reporters."

"You're a public official—"

The cold, biting voice on the other end stiff-armed its

way into her sentence. "I don't care," he said. "I have nothing at all to say. You must be new."

"Well, yes—"

"—because most of the *Journal* reporters don't bother me."

Cantankerous. That he was.

"I hear you're investigating a homicide."

"No comment."

"The information is a matter of public concern."

"Lady, I'm trying awful damned hard to be polite."

"You call this polite, Mr. Pynchon?"

"Next time, save us both some time. Don't bother calling me."

"Fine! I'll quote you as saying that."

"—which is exactly why I don't talk to your kind. Take your best shot."

The phone clicked dead. Anna stared at it. In nine years as a reporter, most of it on the police beat, she'd encountered a lot of sons of bitches. On that day, she found the prototype.

Reporters always made him mad. To a man (or a woman), they acted as if they possessed a divine right to ask questions and get answers. What the hell was it with them? Whit snatched up the coffeepot from the counter and sloshed coffee on the floor.

"Damn it to hell." He reached for paper towels.

The Supreme Court should make reporters read folks their rights, he thought. *You have the right to remain silent, but, if you do, I'll use that silence against you. Anything you say can be misquoted, misconstrued, or paraphrased—and then be used against you. You do have a right to a lawyer, and anything the lawyer says can be used against you too.*

Whit carried his coffee to the deck jutting from the rear

of his small home. He plopped down in a padded chair and tried to put aside the image of DeeDee Dickerson. His eyes burned from lack of sleep. He'd made it home after dawn and hadn't even bothered to lie down. None of Dickerson's neighbors had heard or noticed anything. The front door to the Dickerson home was open; nothing else was disturbed. He'd returned to the high school. In the virgin soft aura of first light, the shattered, blood-smeared glass was a blasphemy. For several moments he had gazed at the message written in the woman's blood, too clearly to be anything but a warning.

The sculptured beauty of his yard, at its floral best in late May, moderated his worst moods. It was his haven, his creation, his Garden of Eden. Maybe it would dilute the horror of the murder. Rhododendrons, their deep purple blooms just beginning to droop, provided a striking border between his yard and the forested foothill sloping up to Tabernacle Mountain. Several winter-hardy azaleas, still flowering bright orange, offered refreshing breaks in the larger, fuller rhododendrons. Broad-leafed ferns, many of them offshoots from the first few he had transplanted, fronted the larger blooming plants. Towering oaks and a huge full maple canopied the center and rear of his yard, providing his plants with the taste of forest shade that they each craved. Enough dappled sunlight filtered through the oaks to keep his lawn thick and green.

The odor of pine, rising from the dew-moist pine bark mulch, mixed with the aroma of the coffee. And Spanish moss, carried by Whit from coastal Carolina, draped from the gnarled, twisted limbs of the oaks. If he couldn't yet move to the semitropics, at least he could bring a little bit of it to West Virginia. Each spring, when he took the first of several warm-weather sojourns at the Carolina coast, he gathered the moss.

Some folks thought him crazy, especially a neighbor who

had complained to the Milbrook City Council, claiming the moss was a parasite that would conquer Raven County. Whit had secured the testimony of a local botanist to clear the moss's good name.

The floral embellishments made his life in West Virginia bearable. No matter that he had to cover and pamper many of his plants during the bitter winter months. No matter that each year one or two succumbed to the bone-chilling Arctic outbreaks reaching down from Canada. And no matter at all, not in the least, what other people thought. Whit found most people insufferable anyway.

All but Tressa, that is. She was the love of his life. Whit Pynchon spent most of his time consumed with the dark side of humanity. Tressa buffered his cynicism.

Tressa was his daughter.

Four

MILBROOK'S OFFICIAL POPULATION barely earned it the statutory honor of "city." It made a difference. Fire insurance rates were lower; the city police department was bigger, its officers minimally trained at the state police academy. But in its ways, its culture, no town was smaller. By ten A.M. Memorial Day morning, most anyone who was anybody knew about the murder. People drove by the high school, disappointed to find that the gore was gone, the window boarded up with a piece of plywood.

The day was bright and cheery, but women alone locked their doors. Husbands cautioned their wives about going out. Parents warned their children that strangers were deadly. The local department store, which was open for five hours on the holiday, sold a few pistols. Not many though; most of Milbrook owned guns anyway.

When two people met, whether on the street or at the local park where the Memorial Day celebration was planned, the death of DeeDee initiated the conversation. DeeDee was a local girl, and her parents—*God rest their souls*—had been popular. Now DeeDee had joined them. In that most profound of Bible Belt beliefs, many Milbrook residents found consolation.

Her death stole the thrill from the first game of the adult summer softball league. Gil was starting pitcher for the Moose Club team. He was missed that afternoon; the

Moose lost 17 to 3. DeeDee had managed the concession stand at the field. There were no concessions that afternoon. A few players, mostly Moose, suggested after the game that it should have been canceled—out of respect for DeeDee and Gil of course.

As the shadow of Tabernacle Mountain, with its twin peaks, swallowed up Milbrook in the late-evening hours, the town's people wondered what sort of monster prowled their darkened streets and backyards. They eyed neighbors with suspicion. Milbrook attracted few strangers. Therefore, they surmised, the killer was one of their own. A blood-lusting sex offender had emerged from a Milbrook home to send DeeDee to the arms of her parents. And more folks would die. Rumor had turned the writing smeared in blood on the high school window into a "blood note," promising more murders. The reality of DeeDee's death, horrible as it was, darkened as the gossip mills ground down that evening.

The sun westered. The shadow of Tabernacle Mountain merged with the sultry night, but, muggy as it was, few people risked the exposure of their front porches. Many, without air conditioners and fearful of open windows, sweltered.

The most anxious people in Milbrook were the cops' wives. They felt like targets because of their husbands. To their men, the murder of DeeDee Dickerson was a gauntlet and a threat. They promised each other that any call from another cop's home would receive gut-busting, siren-wailing priority. Only a few, like Hank Posich, customarily slept with their guns in reach. That night almost everyone found a place near his bed for his weapon.

Miller Foley had to work that night. His wife, Emma, was studying for her night class when Miller handed her a brown bag.

"What's this?" she asked, surprised at the weight.

"A gun."

She dropped it on the couch. "God, Miller! Are you crazy?"

He picked up the bag and pulled out a small black weapon that to Emma looked purely evil.

"It's a twenty-five-cal automatic," he was saying. "See this hammer? All you have to do is pull it back and it's ready."

Emma pushed it away. "I don't know anything about them, and I don't wanna know."

Miller sat down beside her. "If you handle it—"

She jumped up. "Forget it! I'll be fine. I'll keep the doors locked, but take the gun away. You know how I feel about them."

Emma didn't even like Miller's being a policeman and had gone along with it only after he'd promised to try to take some college classes at night with the idea of someday going to law school.

Miller dropped the gun back in the bag. "Okay, but I'd feel better if you had this."

She returned to the couch and put her arms around him. "How long before you go to work?"

"A couple of hours."

"You've got one weapon that interests me. You can show me how that works."

Miller blushed. They hadn't been married long enough for him not to.

At the offices of the *Journal*, Anna pecked away at the final graph of her story. She had sunbathed during the afternoon and had come in to compile the story after dinner. She had the holiday off, but it was her beat, her kind of story. Tony Danton, the prosecutor, had been as helpful as his investigator was brash. He requested she withhold any gory descriptions of the body.

"I can say she was raped?"

Tony paused. "Actually, I haven't seen the report from the medical examiner. Whit went up for the autopsy."

"Does he share information with you?" Anna joked, having already complained about Whit's attitude.

"He's just set in his ways, Miss Tyree."

"Do you believe the woman was killed because her husband's a deputy?" she had then asked.

"I have no reason to believe that."

"I've heard rumors that there was a note promising more murders."

"Again, Miss Tyree, I'd like to withhold comment in that area. We have no clear indications—I should say, no clear threats—of more deaths."

"And no suspects?"

"My office will attempt to correlate the data we have on known sex offenders. We'll contact the state boys and the Feds too. The people of Raven County can rest assured the case is receiving top priority."

"How many known sex offenders does a small town like this have?"

"Not many, Miss Tyree. That we know about."

Anna made notes on the screen of the word processor. "Thanks for the info. Not to belabor the point, but that investigator of yours has the personality of a snake. I don't understand public servants with his attitude."

Tony chuckled. "He doesn't care much for reporters, as you gleaned. Just call me. If there's anything I can share with you, I will."

"In other words, don't waste my time calling Whit Pynchon again."

"I couldn't have put it better myself."

Whit spent the afternoon in Charleston at the lab of the medical examiner. He didn't even pretend to watch the autopsy. He remained in the room, but he leaned against the wall in a distant corner reading, sometimes pretending to read, a magazine on criminal forensics—which wasn't much of an improvement over the autopsy. The editors of the magazine doted on shots of rotting and/or mutilated bodies.

After shooting an entire roll of photos, the assistant M.E., a short and feverish Oriental, delved with ghoulish enthusiasm into DeeDee's innards. "It make it easier with the decapitation," he was saying to Whit.

Whit assumed he was talking about the autopsy and ignored him. As a young cop, he had made himself watch—just to maintain the image. *The stupidity of youth.* Tony had asked that Whit attend the autopsy. The prosecutor didn't want to have to wait on the written postmortem report, and he couldn't understand the fractured English of the assistant M.E. Usually, when Whit visited Charleston, he stopped at a favored steak house for a double cut of prime rib. This time he passed. When he got back to Milbrook, it was dusk. He phoned Tony at home.

"A simple cause of death," he told the prosecutor. "Her throat was ripped out. That's what decapitated her, not the glass. Before that, he raped her, vaginally and anally. The jerk was no gentleman about it. She's covered with bruises, most of them caused by our man's fingers. Our killer is one strong son of a bitch. The M.E. says she was dead when he tossed her into the window."

"How did he rip out her throat?"

"How do you think?"

"Dammit, Whit. No guessing games."

"With his hands. No weapon was used at all."

"Oh, Lord," Tony said.

"We got traces of mud from her body. They're being sent to the CIB lab. It had rained a little that night. Maybe they can give us some idea on the type of area where she was raped. It didn't happen in her house and probably not at the high school."

"This one's going to be bad," Tony said, thinking aloud. "Did he tear off her head?"

"He broke her neck, savaged most of the muscle of the throat."

"My God. Well, *that* we keep out of the papers! By the way, you certainly pissed off that young lady from the *Journal*."

"She pissed me off first. And you said to keep quiet."

"You can be polite and still say no. Oh, before I forget, Tressa called me earlier today, wanting to know if I knew where you were. I told her."

"As soon as I can get rid of you, I'm calling her."

"Okay, I get the message. Tomorrow I want to compile a list of possible suspects, sex offenders and the like, but I think it's a waste of time."

"So you think it was a stranger, someone passing through?"

"Yeah, I do. Dammit, Whit, if we had some guy this sick running around on a full-time basis, we'd know it."

But Whit wasn't so sure. "People snap, Tony—just like a rubber band that's old or worn out."

"Oh, did the M.E. get traces of semen?"

"The M.E. found no semen, but he found what looked to be talc."

"Talc?"

"Yeah. Our killer probably wore a rubber."

Deputy Bill Curtis thumbed through a catalog of police supplies. He paused to study the small offering of ankle holsters. Hank had recommended he carry one as a backup weapon, but on the insulting salary of a deputy he needed as cheap an outfit as he could find.

Curtis had only come aboard the prior Wednesday, taking Miller Foley's place as dispatcher. Foley got to go out in the field. That was the way of it. The new man always got the radio. Foley had spent a few hours training him and many hours telling him how bad it was to be cooped up in the station.

The holsters were expensive, and the department didn't buy such luxuries. Maybe it was good to have a backup weapon, but not important enough to come with the standard-issue leather. So how did he come up with the money without his wife knowing? She managed the family money, which was appropriate since she spent most of it.

To his right, the green and black screen of the teletype flashed a message at him.

''Oh, shit.'' Had he missed something? Then he remembered what Foley had said. Most of the messages, even the ones that flashed with such urgency, were garbage. Still, Foley had told him to get a ''hard copy''—a printed copy—of any messages directed to Raven County. Curtis had had to ask what a ''hard copy'' was.

He squinted at the message. The words ''Raven County'' winked at him in a highlighted box. He moved closer to read the full message. A Raven County resident had ''eloped'' from the state mental hospital.

Eloped.

Curtis laughed. *Who the hell would wanna run off and marry a nut case? Maybe another crazy.* Curtis had heard wild stories about the state hospital.

''Better get a hard copy,'' he said aloud, anxious to use the official-sounding word.

But he wasn't sure how. Foley had told him—once. The keyboard didn't look anything like a typewriter keyboard. It had way too many keys. To Curtis, it was a ''fucking computer.'' Curtis hated computers. He equated them with notes from collection agencies.

The extra keys were labeled with cryptic letters such as "log stor" and "clr eol."

What the fuck is an eol?

His eyes found a key marked "prt."

That's it—prt!

He hit the key. The printer chattered. The cheap teletype paper crumpled up beneath a bar on the printer. The message printed on top of itseif.

"Goddammit to hell!" Curtis was helpless.

He glanced back to the monitor. A green blip ate the name Ferdnand Tipton. Funny name, he thought.

The message was gone.

"Fuck you too," Curtis told the computer.

Besides, some guy running off from a mental hospital to get married didn't seem all that important anyway. And the guy had vanished on Saturday. If it took them until Monday to send a message, then they were probably just giving him a chance to enjoy some nooky before putting him back in a straitjacket.

Best just to forget it, he decided.

Missie Posich tried to be faithful. She really, really did. Just like she tried to stop gnawing her nails to the quick and smoking cigarettes. But just when she thought she had her lust in check, she always met temptation. And temptation prevailed.

On this night temptation appeared in the sleek, wiry form of Kenny Shaffer. He was due at midnight. Hank was working, of course, alone tonight since Gil was off. Missie had made her date with Kenny on Saturday, the same day she had run into DeeDee at the food market where Kenny worked.

Missie stood before the mirror, assessing her body. Not bad for thirty-five. Her breasts still managed to have a little lift in them, no small accomplishment given their ample size. Her waist remained trim, and her hips flared just right. The mound above her pubic hair was a little larger than it used to be, but she had always had the mound. One of her lovers had dubbed it her "love mound." She ran a hand over it.

Not bad at all.

Light streaks of gray highlighted her chocolate hair. Missie refused to color her hair—too obvious a concession to her age. Better to say, as she did, that the gray hair came from her mother. It was a lie. Her mother had died with a head of dark brown hair.

Hank had come home that morning in a fiery, cussing mood, mad over Whit Pynchon. Once he'd settled down, he'd told Missie the details of DeeDee's death.

"So you be careful," he ordered. He'd pulled a shotgun from a closet and loaded it for her—"just in case." What did she know about a shotgun? Besides, she wasn't going to be alone, not tonight anyway. DeeDee's death bothered her, but she wasn't frightened. Missie had liked DeeDee. She was everything that Missie wanted to be. Pretty, upright, happy with her husband. But Missie knew it couldn't happen to her. She could take care of herself. She was tough.

Almost midnight. Almost time. Already she was horny. She lay down on the bed. Her hand discovered the moist heat between her thighs, and her thoughts settled upon Kenny. He always managed to bag her groceries when he was working. He claimed to be nineteen. Eighteen, she figured. That suited her fine. She preferred brave, young men.

And they had to be brave to fool around with Hank Posich's wife. Sometimes she blamed her loose nature on that fact alone. She loved the thrill of it, the danger. Some of Hank's fellow officers were on her list of "priors," a police term that she had appropriated. They were smart enough to keep their mouths shut. Hank had the reputation of a junkyard dog. He'd earned it during the beer-joint campaigns of the old days when a handful of officers waded in one beer joint after another, arresting anyone who even appeared to be under the influence. Hardly a Saturday night passed without at least one major brawl.

Missie wasn't without shame. She despised her urges. So devoutly was she trapped by her bad habits that she honored her good intentions. It salved her shame to know that she really wanted to stop smoking, to let her nails grow, to stop cheating on Hank.

Tim Franklin had been her last lover. Missie smiled at the memory. Tim idolized Hank Posich. Not so much, of course, that he wouldn't fuck Hank's wife. In her catalog of lovers, poor Tim was dubbed "Fast Franklin, Fastest Shot in Milbrook."

"Better a brother cop than a stranger," he had said of their adultery. The kid had a sense of humor. And what a body! She had loved the way his muscles rippled. So what if he was a little strange, kinky even, wanting her to all-the-time whisper to him what a hunk he was? She'd have done just about anything for him if he'd had more staying power.

And hair trigger or not, she respected Timmy for his courage. If Hank ever found out, he'd tear the guy's head off. Hers too probably. The idea aroused her.

It wasn't that she didn't love Hank. She did, though God knows he needed to do something about his breath. She'd grown accustomed to it, but she could see other people wilting under its onslaught. He was good in bed, too, surprisingly tender.

Her fingers moved inside her, their touch stimulating the musky dampness. She moaned and licked her lips. Her other hand caressed and squeezed a prominent nipple.

Footsteps.

The sound came from her porch. Her heart raced. What if it was Hank? What if he had come home to check on her? He never came home during his shift. His buddies might get the idea he didn't trust his wife. But tonight was different. A killer stalked the streets. The idea sent hot pulses through her body.

A door opened; the sound of more footsteps.

Missie's motions escalated.

When Kenny Shaffer entered the bedroom, his eyes bulged. He started to back out at the sight of the woman, nude and writhing on the bed. He thought she was having a fit of some kind.

Beyond the walls of the Posich house, a dense shadow—blacker than the dark woods from which it emerged—wedged its way through the night damp lilacs. The broad leaves whispered in meek protest. Deep purple blooms fell apart, perhaps as much from the evil touch as from the wasting spring. A night bird imposed on the night its shrill, obnoxious song; car sounds from the distant main street accompanied the bird.

The hunter stopped beneath the window of the Posich home, hunkering down in the shrubs planted around the cinder-block foundation. From the open window came the sounds of sex, a woman's moan . . . the galloping breath of a humping male.

He listened for a brief time, then melted into black shadows.

Five

To most of the students of Milbrook High, the young man in the loose, shapeless sweater warranted no attention at all. It was the kind of unintended indifference common to young folks. He looked the norm. The beige sweater, sagging from too many machine washings, appeared seedy, but then, seedy was in. His faded jeans were just as worn as those on the other kids. Kenny Shaffer was one of those people camouflaged by his environment. He snaked his way through the throng of students toward his locker, his eyes downcast, guiding his course without meeting the eyes of those he passed. And the eyes of the other students, most of them, peered right through him.

But not all. A girl standing in the doorway to the chemistry lab watched him approach.

"There he is," she said.

Another girl studied the milling mass of students. "Where?"

"Shhh!" hissed Tressa Pynchon.

Kenny Shaffer brushed by them, unaware he was being watched.

"Him?" Linda Bowman asked.

"I think he's kinda cute," Tressa whispered.

"He's so blah."

"He's just bashful."

"Backwards maybe."

"Linda!"

The other girl rolled her eyes. "You have such awesomely bad taste, Tressa." She disappeared into the chemistry lab.

Tressa checked her wristwatch and saw that she had a few minutes before the class bell sounded. She fell in line behind Kenny Shaffer, catching up with him when he stopped at his locker.

Should she speak? After all, they were in trig class together. He understood such things as tangents and cosines. Tressa was such a dunce when it came to math. Someone had told her that Kenny lived with his grandmother; that his parents had left him or were dead or something. Once she had talked to him at the grocery store where he worked, and he seemed so much older than the other boys at the school. Maybe that was why? Maybe it was because he supported his grandmother?

"Hi, Kenny."

He looked around, his gaunt face shocked that someone—especially a girl—had spoken to him.

"Are you ready for the trig exam?" she asked.

He was piling books in his arms, one of which tilted, then slapped down on the floor. He bent down to get it. "I don't have to take it," he said as he stood.

Tressa shook her head. "You mean you have a ninety-eight average?" That was the rule. If you had managed to garner a 98 average throughout the year, then you didn't have to take the semester final—if you were a senior, that is. Tressa was a junior. She'd taken trig to avoid home economics.

"I got lucky on a couple of tests," he said, struggling to balance the load of books.

"Let me help."

Tressa made him uncomfortable. She could tell. His face seemed flushed, and there were circles under his eyes. What would break the ice? What could get him to ask her out? At least maybe for a Coke. Or maybe even to the prom? Certainly he was going. And probably he had already asked someone.

Ask him!

I can't.

Chicken, go on. Ask him.

She sensed the heat rising to her face. "Are you going to the prom?"

Their eyes met, locked, for just an instant. Then a rough hand latched on to Tressa's shoulder. "Hey, Pynch." The coarse hand and voice belonged to Carl Loomis, "Crude Carl" to his classmates.

"What do you want?"

"What's your old man saying about the killin'?"

"Jeez, Carl. Bug off."

Kenny Shaffer faded away into the crowded hallway.

"Gawddamn, girl. If I had a cop for a daddy, I'd sure as shit know what was going on."

Tressa's lip curled. "You're a jerk, Carl."

"Whatsa matter, girl? It ragtime?"

"Up yours," Tressa said.

Ferdnand Tipton cavorted in the dark mountain wilderness. He had come home. The warmth survived the setting sun. Ferdie wore nothing but a pair of cutoff blue jean shorts and some rubber sandals. Once his feet became calloused from the rough mountain land, he would cast off the sandals.

The cops had spirited him from his mountain in January—a raw winter night, he remembered. The same night they'd gunned down his brother. The memory of that night haunted Ferdie. He had told his brother not to go out the door with the gun. Even Ferdie knew that was just begging to be dead. But Frankie was mad. You didn't stop Frankie when he was mad.

Not unless you killed him—like the cops did.

They'd found Ferdie cowering in the corner of the one-room shack, his ears pounding from the sound of all the gunshots. How many times had they fired? He'd forgotten already, but enough to turn Frankie into raw meat. And just because of a few chickens. It was so cold; they were so hungry. They'd crept into the man's barn and taken two chickens. And the cops had come with guns and killed Frankie and locked Ferdie up in jail and beat him. A day or so later they sent Ferdie to the loony bin.

They said he was crazy. Always he'd been called crazy. He could have told them he was crazy. He could have shown them a card that said he was crazy. He always carried it with him. A pretty nurse had offered it after his first trip to the hospital. "If you have trouble with anyone, like a policeman, show him this," she'd said.

Ferdie couldn't read too well, but he knew the card proved he was crazy.

No way could he return to his house. They'd be looking for him there. So he'd spent the day on the mountain, trying to find an old mine shaft that he and Frankie had played in when they were kids. Late that afternoon, he'd found it, its mouth almost overgrown with brush. Ferdie left the brush in place to conceal the opening. He'd collected pine boughs to make a soft place to sleep. His stomach had been empty, but he'd needed rest more than food. So he slept away the afternoon, rising at twilight to hunt. As hungry as he was, the night forest acted upon him like liquor. It lifted his mood and made him happy and daring.

The smell of the hospital clung to him. Ferdie fell to his knees and scraped at the thick layer of rotting leaves until his hands reached cool dark humus. Like a dog, he rolled in the fertile earth. Afterward he leaned against a large rock and stared into the clear night sky. The bugs soon discovered him. Gnats swarmed his sweating face, and a mosquito supped on his blood. Ferdie didn't mind. They had their place just like he had his. They had to eat, just like he had to eat.

His eyes, black and flat and still night-sharp, tracked a movement in a nearby pine, a dark shadow flitting along a limb against the night sky. Ferdie's stomach rumbled. For two days he had gone without eating. The prospect of raw meat brought saliva to his mouth. At the hospital they forced him to eat meats burned to a gritty crisp, vegetables boiled until they tasted like cloth, and sweets that hurt his broken teeth.

"Cominuts," he called the hospital people. "Dirty cominuts trying to poison me."

At night Ferdie saw the clouds of poison seeping from the walls of his cell. The fumes drifted in the air, and many a night Ferdie spent hours holding his breath, trying to breathe no more than he had to. And he slept on the floor to avoid the poison oozing from his bed.

But now he was free. And his stomach yearned for untainted food. He jumped to his feet, eased toward the tree, keeping to the darkest shadows and knowing by instinct that he was upwind of the tree. The secrets of stealth came back to him. The ways of the forest always were second nature for him. Three times they had locked him away for long stays, and three times he had returned to the forests of the mountain.

He waited under the tree. Minutes stretched into an hour before the creature darted within reach. Ferdie's hand whipped out with the speed of a lizard's tongue. The squirrel gnawed at his hand. Ferdie squeezed.

"It's awesome, Daddy." Tressa held the photo of the sailboat in the candlelight.

"She's hardly big enough to call 'awesome.' Impressive maybe. She'll be christened *Tressa*."

"That's embarrassing!"

"Queen Mary didn't think so. If it weren't for you, I wouldn't be able to afford it."

The evening had started with a candle-lit dinner at the Steak Haus, then several drinks after dinner for Whit and a single wine cooler for Tressa.

Tressa giggled. "I should get another drink to toast her."

Whit smiled tolerantly, but Tressa got the message.

Many times people had mistaken Tressa for Whit's girlfriend. They weren't that far apart in age. In spite of his graying hair, he had a youthful face. She had just turned seventeen, but she had matured early. Her figure was that of a woman, and she dressed and applied her cosmetics in a fashion that enhanced the appearance of maturity.

Tressa admitted her Oedipus complex. If she ever married, she wanted her husband to be like Whit Pynchon. *Well, almost.* Whit could be boringly stubborn and rude, but usually it was just an act—an image he projected.

Whit and Julia Pynchon had been divorced for a dozen years. Since Tressa had become old enough to fathom the concept of a divorce, Whit's child support payments had been a joke between him and his daughter. The amount was ridiculously extravagant when considered with the alimony, but both came to an abrupt end on Tressa's eighteenth birthday.

Tressa shook her head. "Mother'll just die."

"I ask for nothing that drastic," he joked. "A good case of indigestion, followed maybe by intestinal gas."

"Daddy! That's cruel." She brandished the photo. "Have you bought it yet?"

"Still haggling, so to speak—with myself. Besides, I still have a little while to go."

Tressa's face sagged. "Because of my college, I guess."

"Not really. As long as you don't go to Vassar or Harvard—do they accept females? Anyway, I have an insurance policy that is paid up for that."

"Can I come live with you?" Joy sparkled in her face. For some reason her mood had been subdued all evening. He reached across the table to squeeze her hand. Tressa Pynchon possessed the honey blond hair of her mother, the green eyes too, but she had Whit's strong nose and chin. Her beauty made him proud, but beauty was often a difficult gift for a young woman to manage. He hoped she had inherited his common sense.

"Some guy's gonna grab you before long, but until then you're always welcome aboard ship." Whit looked at his watch. "Does your mother know we had this date for dinner?"

"She suspects, but I denied it. I told her I was going to a friend's." They often met on the sly. Not because they had to. It simply made Tressa's life easier.

"So," Tressa said, announcing a change of subject, "how's the job? You haven't said a word about it."

"I almost made it through the night without having to talk about it."

"Sorry, I just thought . . ." She allowed the sentence to trail off.

"It reeks, which is why I haven't talked about it."

"Sometimes you freak me out," she said. "You have it made. You work the hours you want. Tony lets you do what you want."

"So, except for Tony, the job reeks."

Her eyes twinkled. "What about the murder last night?"

"You heard about it, huh?"

She nodded. "On the radio."

"And you've been dying to ask. It's not very pleasant to talk about."

Tressa pouted. "Damn, Daddy. It makes me look real

cool if I have one or two inside tidbits of information. What's the good of having an important father if he never tells you anything?''

''Better not let Julia hear you saying 'damn.' She'll blame it on me. It isn't cultured.''

''You're changing the subject, Daddy.''

''You're relentless. We spent a boring day trying to gather records on the kinda sleazy guy who might be capable of that kind of murder. Frankly, Milbrook's short on deviants. The worst we could come up with was a guy who liked to flash meter maids.''

''Really? We have a guy who does that?''

''Yep.'' Whit raised his right hand. ''And I swear he's the worst of a not-too-bad lot.''

''Not even a rapist or two?''

''Sorry. No rapists.'' Whit rubbed his temples. ''We'd better go before we really do give your mother indigestion.''

Both of them hated to leave the cool interior of the restaurant. The late-May heat wave hadn't ebbed with nightfall. If anything, the humidity had increased. They had brought Tressa's small compact, which had no air conditioner. ''I would come in for a while,'' she said as she let him out, ''but you know how it is.''

Whit looked through the open window. ''We wouldn't want to stir the bile of the fang lady. Dear sweet Julia.''

He put his hand on hers. ''You put up a good front tonight, but what's eating you?''

She jerked her eyes up at him. ''Nothing.''

''Bullshit. I know better.''

''Really, it's nothing. I like this guy at school, and he doesn't even know I exist.''

''Then he's either blind or gay.''

''Oh, Daddy.''

"Things like that work out in the long run," he said, knowing it was a bald-faced lie.

"Sure. Want me to take Mother the photo of your boat?"

"Vamoose, kiddo. And be careful. You going straight home?"

"Of course." Tressa saw the worry on her father's face. She knew it was for her, but also she knew he worried too for all the other people. "If anyone can catch him, you can."

"Thanks for the vote of confidence. Sooner or later I'll nab him, but how many will he kill before I do?"

Kenny Shaffer was in love. Missie Posich had taken his heart and his virginity.

But she hadn't invited him back. "I'll see you at the market," she'd said. "Maybe we can get together again."

Maybe. He fretted at the uncertainty of the word. *Why maybe?*

"Tomorrow night?" Kenny had asked, trying to make a little more of the word.

"No, I'll see you at the market."

He had slipped from the house feeling a failure. She'd acted like she'd enjoyed it. Maybe she was just acting? Trying not to hurt his feelings?

He awoke the following morning with an erection. He didn't want to jack off. That was now kid stuff. He ached for Missie. All day long, at the worst of times, the erection came back. He covered it with his hand, with his book. In physics class he had bobbled an easy question. No matter, though; he was graduating in a week. At the food market he'd dropped a whole bag of groceries. Egg yellows exploded on the floor. Pickles rolled underneath shoppers' feet. The manager had gone berserk.

His father had vanished when he was born. Never even gave Kenny a chance. And his mother had died a long, slow death with leukemia, leaving him to be raised by his grandmother. Grams—that's what he called her—was nearing sixty-nine. She wasn't well, and she went to bed early each night.

At eleven that night, once Grams was asleep, he crept from his bedroom window and started across town. Maybe if he just happened by the front of her house, she would notice him—invite him inside. That hope kept him aroused during the twenty-minute walk. He kept to the back streets. When he reached her house, its windows were dark. *Damn it to hell. Doesn't she feel the same way I do?*

Hank Posich was at work. He knew that, trusted in it. So maybe she just went to bed early? He walked back by the house, clomping his feet on the sidewalk so that she might hear. *Maybe she's with someone else.* The thought boiled his blood. He turned again, went back by the house. His feet made sharp thuds on the concrete.

''Come here!'' the hefty woman said. ''Look there.''

The man had just dozed off. ''Huh? What?'' Their bedroom was dark, but he could see the massive bulk of his wife silhouetted in the window.

''Who the hell you spying on now?'' he asked.

''Come here, I said.''

He threw back the sheets, sat for a moment on the bed, silently damning his misfortune, then went to the window. He saw the young boy walking in front of the Posich house. ''So what?''

''It's the fourth time he's done that.'' She inched open the curtain. ''He keeps pacing back and forth.''

''With the goings-on over there, who cares?''

''Not this time. He's actin' funny. Maybe he's that killer?''

The man had forgotten about the murder. He peered closer. ''Hell, he's just a kid.''

"You 'member that boy that killed his whole family? He was a kid too."

She had a point. "Well, best not to get involved."

"I'm calling the police."

"Oh, shit." The man dropped on the bed. "You best listen to me. Stay out of other folks' affairs."

But she was busy trying to dial the phone in the dark.

Kenny was a block away from Missie's house, heading home, when the cruiser pulled up beside him. He glanced over and waved. The officer glared. It paced him for about twenty yards, then speeded ahead.

Whew!

But it stopped with a short, sharp screech just ahead of him. The door opened. A bright flashlight beam blinded him.

"You're out walking awful late, kid." Officer Jay Sanchez thought the boy looked familiar.

"I—uh, I had trouble sleeping. Thought I'd take a walk."

The other officer held the flashlight. Kenny, holding his hands up to ease the glare, couldn't see him, but he heard him.

"You always walk back and forth in front of the same house?"

"The same house?" Kenny's breath quickened, his bladder suddenly full.

"Yeah."

"I don't understand."

Sanchez moved closer. His breath, bitter with garlic, assaulted Kenny. "We got a complaint. You were walking back and forth in front of a house on Murdock? Casing the joint maybe?"

Kenny thought about his answer, maybe just a little too long. "That's where I decided to turn around."

Before he could finish, Sanchez put a hand in the small of his back and shoved him toward the cruiser. "Okay, punk. Hands on the roof. Assume the position."

"Huh?"

The second officer slammed Kenny against the car. "You heard the man." He kicked Kenny's legs apart. Sanchez frisked him.

"Where you live?"

"The other side of town."

The second officer put the back of Kenny's neck in a vise grip. "Don't get smart, asshole! Where do you live? Address?"

"Three seventy-eight Oak."

"That's a long walk."

Kenny didn't know which officer was speaking now. He was too frightened. He quaked. Panic gained on him. His stomach began to sour. "Hey, I swear to God. I didn't do nothing."

"Wrong, asshole. You did!"

"What? I don't—I don't think—"

"You paraded up and down in front of the wrong fuckin' house."

Strong, angry hands whipped him around. The flashlight was jammed at his face. "Now where the hell do I know you from, punk? Juvie court?"

"I bag groceries down at—"

"Yeah! Now I know you."

The other voice said, "I bet you bag the groceries of a lot of cops' wives."

They know. Hank Posich knows. Kenny retched.

Sanchez backpedaled. "Goddamn you, you puke on me, punk, and you better say your prayers."

"Let's go," the other one said, opening the car door to shove him inside.

On the way Kenny could finally see the two officers. He

knew the one that looked foreign, had seen him at the store. The other one, older and meaner, rode on the passenger side.

"I didn't do anything," Kenny whined.

The older cop, the American-looking one, glared at him.

Kenny started to cry. "I swear it. I didn't do a thing."

It was the driver who spoke. "Like we said, you did the worst possible thing. You were casing the house of a cop."

Kenny couldn't help it. He vomited again, this time on the carpet of the cruiser.

"Fuck it!" growled the older officer. "Do that once more, you pukin' maggot, and I'll rub your sissy face in it!"

Kenny forgot about the charms of Missie Posich.

SIX

THE PHONE WOKE Whit long before dawn. He buried his head beneath the pillow, but the ringing didn't go away. Five times. Ten times. Whit snatched it. "Yeah. What is it?"

"Pynchon, Hank Posich here. We got the killer."

Whit rocketed up in bed. "You what?"

"We got the bastard that killed Gil's wife."

"Where?"

"Casing my goddamned house. That's where."

"What else have you got on him?"

Hank hissed into the phone. "What the hell else we need? The fuckin' kid was marchin' up and down in front of my goddamned house. Works down at the food market. Knows all the guys' wives. 'Sides, he's actin' guilty as hell."

Whit wanted to scream. "Where is he now, Posich?"

"We're questioning him."

"Damn you, Hank. If you've botched this case, I'll have your balls hanging in my office. I'm on my way."

Hank was saying something, shouting obscenities most likely, but Whit hung up the phone. *The friggin' moron.*

He picked up a plastic cigarette lighter, tried to get a cigarette from the crushed pack on his nightstand, then threw lighter and cigarettes across the room. "Asshole," he said aloud. How many times had good cases been meat-axed by a cop who fouled up when he damn well knew better, who played fast and loose with the rules just because he didn't like them, knowing some spineless prosecutor would cover for him?

He got his underwear on backward. He left them that way. He missed two belt loops and let that pass. When he got his shirt on inside out, he took time to correct it.

Hank's gnarled, scarred fist whumped into the boy's soft belly. "I wanna know where the shit you were early Monday morning!"

Doubled over, the boy had no breath left to answer. A pile-driving fist exploded on his back. Kenny crumpled to the floor. The two of them were alone in the shift commander's office. Hank drew back a booted foot. "You better talk, kid—spill it before I bury my toes in your murderin' nuts."

"Home," he gasped. "Home . . . I was—"

Hank leaned down, grabbed a handful of hair, and yanked up the boy's head. "You weren't home tonight, scumbag. You were at my house."

Kenny heard his own wheezing. "Couldn't sleep."

"You just like walking in front of my house, huh?" Hank cuffed him on the forehead with an open hand.

Tell him, Kenny thought. *Tell the dumb shit that you were fucking his wife. It can't get no worse. He's gonna kill you anyway.*

"I wanna lawyer," he managed to say.

Hank's hand stung his face . . . once . . . twice. His head clunked against the cold tile floor.

"That makes you guilty as hell," Hank said. "If you want a lawyer, then you did it."

"Didn't do nothing." A trickle of blood seeped from his nose into his mouth. The salty copper taste gagged him. Tears streaked his face.

''Nothin', huh! You made the mistake of your young life. You did nothin' in front of my fuckin' house.'' Hank drew back his fist, prepared to splatter the kid's nose from ear to ear. The ringing phone stopped him.

''I told you not to bother me,'' Hank said when he answered it.

''Whit Pynchon's here,'' Bill Curtis said. ''He demands to see the kid.''

''Oh, does he?''

''Yes, sir. And he says now.''

Hank grinned down at the kid. Kenny Shaffer hugged himself into a fetal position. ''Give me a minute or two, then send the bastard in.''

He hung up and leaned down to wrap his big hand around the boy's thin arm. Hank twisted skin and muscle. The boy whined. ''I could break it, kid. Snap it just like a toothpick. I'm gonna say you resisted arrest, and you'd better agree. If you don't, then snap! But it'll be your neck, not your fuckin' arm. Got that?''

The boy grimaced but didn't answer.

He twisted a little more. ''You got it?''

The loud, angry voice of Whit Pynchon penetrated the door. Hank hauled the boy to his feet by his shirt collar, slamming him into a chair. ''Say a word about this, and you're hospital fodder.''

The door burst open. ''What the hell is this?'' Whit said.

''By God, Pynchon, you''—Hank pressed in on Whit, jabbing at him with his finger—''don't run this office. I don't work for you!''

''Get it out of my face, or I'll shove it up your dumb ass . . . all the way to the elbow.'' Whit tried not to flinch in the rank miasma of Hank's breath. The cop might read it as a sign of weakness.

''You and whose fuckin' army?''

Bill Curtis loomed behind Whit, wide-eyed and cowered by the ferocity of the confrontation.

Hank's purple face melted into a smile. ''Come in and meet Kenny Shaffer. He likes to rape and kill cops' wives.''

Whit kept his gaze on Hank. ''This case is under the supervision of the prosecutor.''

''I didn't make this arrest.''

''I know who the made the arrest. I just want to be sure that things are crystal clear. The next time you interfere, in any way, I'll come after you.'' Only then did Whit glance toward the young boy. He was huddled in the chair, his whole body trembling.

Whit saw the puffy redness on his forehead, the blood from his nose. ''What'd you hit him with, Hank?''

''He obstructed me.''

Whit kneeled down to the boy. ''What's your name?''

The boy looked at him with red-rimmed, terrorized eyes. ''Shaffer, sir. Kenny Shaffer.''

''Where do you live?''

Kenny told him.

Whit looked up to Hank. ''Where's his rights form?''

''We were just about to get to that part.'' Hank smiled at Curtis.

''From what I hear,'' Whit countered, ''you've had the kid here for quite a while. Were you waiting for someone to get here who knows how to read?''

Hank bloated up with anger, then whirled and shoved Curtis aside as he left.

Whit took a chair at the desk. ''I've talked to the city officers who arrested you. Witnesses did see you walking back and forth in front of Officer Posich's house. Before we go any further, I want to be sure you know your rights.''

Kenny sniffed back mucus, nodding that he understood.

From his coat pocket, Whit withdrew a form which he read. ''You understand all of that?''

"Yes, sir."

"How old are you?"

"Seventeen—almost eighteen."

Whit wondered if he knew Tressa.

"You're sure?"

"Of course I'm sure."

Whit scooted his chair closer to the boy. "Down here on the bottom of this form, it says that you waive—that means 'give up'—your rights, that you want to talk without a lawyer, that you—"

"I wanna talk," the boy said, "but I'm not signing anything."

Whit sighed. "We'd better wait."

"But I didn't do anything."

"If you can prove where you were Monday morning, very early, then perhaps all of this is unnecessary."

Kenny's trembling increased. "Sir, I thought . . ." He shook his head, not completing the sentence.

"Go on, son. What were you going to say?"

The boy lowered his chin to his chest, dropped his eyes to the floor, which was smeared with drops of his blood. "I thought I didn't have to prove anything, that you had to prove it. That's what they taught us in civics class."

"That's what the law books say."

"I was just walking along the street when the police got me."

"Why did you make two or three trips back and forth?"

"I don't have to answer?"

"No."

The boy nodded. "Then I better not."

"Even if it means you go to jail?"

The boy didn't answer.

Whit moved closer to the boy, pushing in on him, trying to rattle him. "Did Posich hit you?"

"I don't wanna answer."

"Okay." Whit got to his feet.

"Do I go to jail now?"

"We'll see." Whit left the room. Hank was talking to the dispatcher. "The boy walks, Hank."

Hank shrugged. "I figured you'd let the little cocksucker go."

"I don't think he's our killer."

Hank's control waned. "The little s.o.b. was casing my house!"

"Walking in front of it," Whit countered. "Maybe he's got bad taste, but it's no crime."

Hank headed back for the deputies room. "Hold on!" Whit said.

Whit hurried to catch Hank and managed to get into the deputies' room ahead of the angry deputy.

"Let's go," Whit told the boy.

"Do I get locked up now?"

"You're going home."

But Hank stepped between Kenny Shaffer and the door. "Punk, I catch you around my house again and you're paid for!"

"It's a public sidewalk," the boy said.

Whit tugged the boy's arm. "Come on!"

"You're a smart-ass punk!" Hank shouted after them. "Remember what I told you—"

They were outside before Whit stopped. "Okay, son. I don't think you killed anyone, but I want the truth now."

Light from a lamp over the door to the sheriff's office illuminated them. Kenny stared into Whit's eyes.

"I didn't kill anyone," the boy said.

"So satisfy my curiosity."

The boy's eyes teared up. He looked up into the light. "I just can't say."

Whit had heard tales about Missie Posich. "Were you there to see Mrs. Posich? Is that it?"

"Not tonight."

"But you have been there to see her?"

The boy's face reddened. He didn't say anything.

"I think I understand, son, but you oughta know better. Let's take you over to the hospital, get them to check you over."

"I'm okay."

Whit took a hold of his arm. "I want you checked."

This time the boy resisted, pulling his arm away. "No! I said I'm okay."

Whit shook his head. "Fine, okay. Then I'll give you a ride home."

"I'd rather walk."

"Forget it, kid. You're riding. Next thing you know, if you walk, you'll be down here again. Then I'll be down here again. I need a little sleep tonight."

Once they were in Whit's car, the boy said, "I know your daughter."

Whit's eyes narrowed. "So?"

"She's a nice person, Mr. Pynchon."

The Milbrook Mutilator.

The Milbrook Monster.

The Milbrook Madman. Or just *The Madman.*

Anna Tyree bounced the names off the walls of her mind, wanting something catchy, something that rolled off the tongue. She said them aloud. One murder does not a mass murderer make. She knew that, but she'd heard the rumors the killer had left a message vowing more killings. She wanted to be prepared. The story might end up grabbing national attention. Not that she wanted more killings. Anna wasn't that ambitious. But if it did happen, no reason to be caught with her page proofs down.

Milbrook's Maniac.

"Well, shit!" She wanted something different.

The only other person in the room was the paper's prim, proper, prudish society editor. Anna's exclamation caused the woman to raise her eyebrows.

The Slayer.

The Womanslayer.

"The Womanslayer. The Womanslayer!" Anna pounded her fist on the desk. "That's it!"

The society editor frowned. "Are you all right, Miss Tyree?"

"Yes, quite all right now."

Anna's first story on the murder made the Wednesday morning paper. It was old news to Milbrook. Most people knew about it by word of mouth or from the local radio. In order to make the story timely, Anna spent Wednesday morning writing a profile on Denise Della Dickerson. Real news had been hard to come by.

The sheriff had refused comment.

Danton had said, "The investigation is continuing."

DeeDee was to be laid out for family visitation that night, burial to follow the next morning. Anna planned to attend both. She had heard that the casket was going to be open. How could they do that with a woman who had been decapitated? Anna made a note to herself to do a feature on the reconstructive art of the mortician—not right now but a few weeks down the road. People like to read about that kind of thing.

The Womanslayer. God help her, she really didn't want another killing to happen . . . really, really she didn't.

The prosecutor ambled into Whit's small office. Files of potential suspects from across the state, compliments of the state police, cluttered his desk. An overflowing ashtray spilled its contents over the paperwork. Empty candy wrappers added color. Whit was flipping through the files, sipping on a Dr. Pepper.

"How goes it, Whit?"

Whit stretched. "Hell, I asked the state police for files on sex offenders. I get files on everything from trespass to murder. I haven't found anything of interest."

Whit leaned back and lit a cigarette.

"You back to smoking?"

"I never stopped."

"Tressa told me you did."

Whit smiled. "She thinks I did."

"Hard-nosed Whit Pynchon, pussy-whipped by a girl."

"She's my daughter, Tony. Watch your words."

"Sorry. For what it's worth, I just finished talking to a cop who worked on the Ted Bundy case. I met him this spring at a seminar on serial murders."

Whit chuckled. "Yeah. I remember. At Hilton Head, South Carolina."

"What's wrong with that?"

"Just seems like a funny place to conduct a seminar on such a gory subject. Detroit or Atlanta would have made more sense."

"I told you. I didn't play one round of golf. Anyway, he told me to be sure and get all the details to that national group on serial murders, just in case our man's mode of operation matches with another somewhere else. He said we might as well expect another one, and to be conscious of the possibility of copycat killers."

Whit laughed. "Copycat killers! In Milbrook?"

"It could happen."

"And maybe it was just a stranger passing through. One of a kind, for us at least."

"Ah," Tony said. "The fellow put an end to that theory, at least in my mind. Our killer's local. Otherwise, why call the station? Why give us a tip? He knew Gil would find that body."

Whit thought about it for a moment. "Good point."

"The guy gave me quite a few ideas. A lot of them deal with complicated computer stuff beyond our abilities. They call it 'databasing criminal records.' It's the coming thing."

"I can see it now," Whit said. "Most cops around here would wanna buy a brassiere for a floppy disk."

Tony shook his head at Whit. "You got no faith. Anyway, he suggested we get a psychiatrist to do a profile on the guy. He gave me the name of one to call. He also said that we should try to collect trace evidence. The FBI lab will work it up for us. If things get really bad, he even offered to fly here just as long as we pay his expenses."

"If I remember the Bundy case," Whit said, "the cops fucked it up. Why would we want him? Besides, we've got one killing. As bad as it is, let's not make it more than that. Next thing you know we'll be calling in some damned fortune-teller or carnival creep to divine a suspect."

"Well, he did give me the name of a psychic—"

SEVEN

WHEN GROVER THOMPSON was a child, his father had given him two rabbits to raise. Soon enough, Grover had more rabbits than either he or his father could handle. In those days, the rabbit market was bullish, but Grover's rabbits saturated the market, which slipped into a depression. The Thompsons, faced with more supply than demand, had started eating more rabbit. Even as a child Grover hadn't the slightest qualm over chopping the furry creatures across the back of the neck with his hand, skinning them out, then delivering the carcasses to his mother for cooking.

Grover grew up, married, and had kids of his own. Once they were old enough for responsibility, Grover bought them a pair of rabbits. Times, though, had changed. Grover's kids were just as good at raising the rabbits as he had been, maybe even better, but they gave their rabbits names. And it was as true as the Gospel: Once you put a name on an animal, there's no way you can put the animal on a dinner plate. The first two rabbits were Andy and Barney, named after Andy Griffith and Don Knotts on *The Andy Griffith Show*.

Barney turned out to be a female. Before long she begot Droopy, Snoozy, Snorey, Sleepy, Boo, and Sleazy. Boo was named by Grover's daughter, who didn't care much about the Seven Dwarfs. Grover got to name Sleazy. Of the six, Snorey passed away one cold winter's night, but the new litter did their share of begetting. Before long Grover's place was going to the rabbits.

On Easter past, Grover had a hankering for rabbit for dinner. They could always tell the kids that a rabbit had gotten loose and run off. The meat could pass for chicken of sorts. So Grover broached the idea with his wife.

"My Gawd," she said, "that's blasphemy. Eating rabbit on Easter! What do you want me to do? Bring poor ol' Boo to the table singing 'Here Comes Peter Cottontail'?"

The Thompsons enjoyed a traditional ham.

The kids fed the rabbits after school, and on Wednesday, because the school year was drawing to a close, they were home early. Bonnie, six years old, and Jimmy, eight, bounded in from the school bus and went out giggling toward the rabbit hutches behind the barn.

Moments later, a frantic screaming brought Grover to his feet. Jimmy came running from the barn. "Daddy! Daddy! They're all messed up."

Grover, slightly crippled by a mine injury, lumbered toward the rear of the barn. Bonnie sat in the grass, cuddling Boo to her chest. Traces of time-darkened blood matted the rabbit's coat. Some of the pen doors were open. Other pens were ripped apart. Rabbit fur drifted along the grass on the arms of a light breeze. Bloody carcasses and body parts littered the ground.

Grover squinched up his face, trying not to cry. No use though. Not with Bonnie sitting there like she was. He leaned down, tears dripping from his rough cheeks. "Let's put Boo down, hon."

She lifted her angel face to him. "What's wrong with Boo, Daddy? Why's he bleeding?"

Jimmy asked, "Was it a wolf, Pop?"

Grover Thompson examined a new hutch that he had just built. He'd used two-by-twos and had painted it white. A smudge of blood leaped out to answer the question, a smudge made by a human hand. "What kinda sick nut would do such a thing?"

Boo rolled from Bonnie's arm. She reached over to touch the crushed, mutilated body of Sleazy.

Grover stopped her. "Come on, child."

Mrs. Thompson turned the corner, saw the massacre, then screamed. Grover rushed to her. "Hush up, woman! You gonna frighten these kids half to death!"

Too late. Bonnie started bawling, then Jimmy too.

He trembled with rage. "It ain't right, dammit! I never done nothin' to nobody. Never! Ain't right to hurt kids like this."

Deputy Dooley Chaffins got the call. He was the closest to the Thompson place. The aging veteran listened to the details, his face turning from pensive interest to offended disbelief. "Rabbits?" he asked of the dispatcher.

"Deceased rabbits," came the reply.

"Deceased rabbits," Chaffins mumbled. "Stupid asshole, trying to sound official." He brought the mike to his mouth. "Are they prize rabbits or something?"

"Just rabbits."

The air conditioner on Dooley's cruiser was on the blink. Sweat seared his crotch. "Are you sending me to investigate the killing of these animals?"

"Ten four." The words were spoken as if it happened every day.

Normally a deputy never questioned a call from the station. He answered it, even if it was bullshit. But this wasn't a usual day. Dooley's thighs were chafed. He had a headache. He really wanted to go home. "Is the sheriff there?" he asked.

The dispatcher's voice sounded belligerent. "Negative. He's at the prosecutor's office in a meeting."

''Well, get ahold of him, and ask him if he wants me to waste time on rabbits.''

There were several moments before the reply came. ''Stand by.''

Dooley smiled. The dispatcher was pissed.

Sheriff Early was pissed too. He was directing his rage toward the prosecutor. ''Gawddammit, we had a suspect in custody, an honest-to-God suspect. Pynchon busts in like some gawddamn legal-aid shyster and lets him walk. It's not right.''

Tony pointed his finger at Early. ''And your man Posich whipped that kid's ass. You want me to do anything about that? Like maybe charge Posich with felony assault?''

''Posich says he didn't.''

''What the hell do you expect, Early? Posich isn't too smart, but he's been around long enough not to confess.''

''I believe Hank,'' Early declared.

Tony catapulted from his chair. ''And I believe Whit.''

Early saw the intensity in Tony's dark Italian eyes. ''I just didn't like his attitude,'' he said, softening his voice.

''Were you there?'' Tony snapped.

''Of course not, but—''

''Then you're just telling me what Posich told you, right?''

Whit sat in the corner of the office, trying to keep silent. It had been a prosecutorial directive. Early's face revealed his frustration. Whit had seen the look many times before, usually from cops who thought their calling was so crucial that the laws shouldn't apply to them.

''But the kid might be the killer,'' Early said.

Tony picked up a file from his desk and tossed it across to Early. ''Read that, Sheriff.''

Early looked down. ''What is it?''

"DeeDee Dickerson's autopsy. No scrawny kid could do what was done to her."

Tony's phone rang. He grabbed it. "Whadaya want? Oh, okay."

He offered Early thc phone.

"I said I didn't want to be bothered," Early said into the phone.

But he listened for a few minutes to his dispatcher, then said, "Jesus Christ, man. What can we do about dead rabbits? Call the s.o.b. back and tell him we got better things to do. He can come in and file a report."

The sheriff tossed the phone back to Tony. "Somebody mutilated a bunch of pet rabbits."

Whit broke his code of silence. "Where?"

"Hell, I don't know."

Whit got to his feet. "You mind if I go check on it?"

The request, or maybe Whit's polite manner, took the sheriff aback. "No. Hell, no! It sounds like your kinda case."

Whit strangled a response.

As Whit entered the control room, the dispatcher eyed him with open suspicion. "Where's the report on those rabbits?" Whit asked.

The young man hesitated.

"I was with the sheriff when you called him, dammit."

"What the hell." He handed a sheet of paper to Whit. "The guy got pissed and said he was gonna call the newspaper or something."

"Oh, hell. Try to get him on the phone."

Whit scanned the terse, hand-scribbled report as the young man dialed the number.

"It's busy."

"Great."

"They'll just think he's a crackpot," the dispatcher said.

Whit headed for the door. ''I doubt it. Newspapers hire smarter people than we elect.''

Anna Tyree took Grover Thompson's call.

''Have you cleaned it up—uh, the mess?'' she asked.

''Hell, no. I thought the law might have the gumption to come out here and look for clues or evidence or something.''

Not a bad story, she thought—a different kind of horror to give their readers. ''Can I come and talk to you? Maybe take a few pictures?''

''Yes'm. You're more'n welcome.''

He gave her directions.

Whit got directions from the dispatcher. The Thompsons lived on the highway leading north out of Milbrook, just as it started up toward the twin summits of Tabernacle Mountain.

A white sports car sat in the driveway to the house. Somehow it just didn't fit the image created by the well-kept two-story farmhouse. No one answered the door, so Whit left the porch and ambled around the house toward the backyard. He kept his eye out for a dog, just in case. At the rear of the house he saw no one, but he heard voices coming from the rear of the barn.

As Whit turned the corner, a young woman was snapping photos of the bloodied remains. ''Afternoon,'' Whit said.

Thompson scowled. ''Who in the hell are you?''

Whit flashed his ID. ''Whit Pynchon—investigator for the office of the prosecutor.'' He offered the man his hand.

Grover Thompson took it. ''I thought you folks didn't have time.''

The camera fell from the young woman's face. She stared. ''Well, well . . . so you're Super Cop.''

Whit ignored her. "The sheriff's department didn't have time. I do."

Anna wasn't so easily ignored. Not even by Whit Pynchon. He had no idea who she was, but he figured she was a reporter. She was more than that. She was a fine-looking woman. The jeans she wore were molded to her trim body. The plaid shirt was open just one button above immodesty. And her face reminded him of someone, a movie star of course. Maybe Linda Evans from *Dynasty*.

She aimed the camera at Whit and clicked off a shot. Because he had been so taken with her, it caught him off guard. "Hey! No shots of me!"

"Sorry, it's taken." She smiled at him. "I'm Anna Tyree."

The name struck home. Whit was as surprised by her as she was by him. "You called me the other day!"

Whit had seen her byline. *Annie Tyson-Tyree.* To him it sounded like the name of some Magnolia Queen. "Well, Miss Tyree—it is Miss?"

"Certainly."

"I'm here to conduct an investigation. I can't do anything about the fact that you're here, but don't get in my way."

"But I was here first. And these poor rabbits"—she went over to Bonnie and put an arm around her—"belong to the children. That one is named—or was named—Boo." She pointed to a small brown-and-white clump of fur.

Whit cringed, imagining the headlines.

Anna Tyree turned her attention to the children. "Bonnie, would you stand over here beside Boo, kneel down beside him?"

"Jesus," Whit whispered. He pulled a notebook from his jacket pocket. He noticed the huge thunderclouds building to the west. They already dwarfed the mountain. A gusting wind riffled the pages of his pad. "Mr. Thompson, do you have any idea what time this happened?"

Thompson pursed his lips, satisfied now that the police had come. "I'd say last night. I didn't get out here during the day. The kids—poor things—found them after school."

"Did you hear or see anything?"

"Nope. I been meanin' to git a dog, but that's kinda tough what with the rabbits and all. Them rabbits'll drive a dog to distraction." Thompson's eyes wandered over the dead animals. "Course, guess it won't be no problem now."

The small boy inched his way between them. "You a cop?"

Whit saw the tear tracks on the boy's freckled face. "Sure am."

"Where's your gun?"

Mrs. Thompson hurried to retrieve her son. The reporter continued to chat with Bonnie, but Whit knew she heard everything.

"Have you had any trouble with predators?"

"Weren't no animal."

Whit spopped taking notes and cocked his head at the man. "How do you know that?"

"Lookee here." Thompson strode over to one of the mangled cages. He pointed to the human handprint.

Whit examined it.

Anna Tyree pressed in close too. Her perfume, wafted by the rising winds, caught his attention.

"I didn't see that earlier," Anna said. She snapped a photo.

A stroke of luck, Whit thought. Fingerprints were mostly TV stuff. Whit himself remembered only two cases that had been solved with prints. Usually the prints were smudged or indistinct. He rotated the piece of wood. This handprint, complete with fingerprints, appeared intact. ''I'll take that with me.''

He turned back to the farmer. ''Has anyone got anything against you, Mr. Thompson?''

At that point Mrs. Thompson chimed in to the conversation. ''Lord, mister. Grover here hasn't an enemy in the world. We're Christian people.''

''She's right,'' Thompson said. ''Not close enough to many folks to call them friend *or* enemy. We mind our own business. I get a little disability because of a back injury in the mines. I manage to raise some crops.''

''Did you sell the rabbits?''

Jimmy answered. ''We raised them. They was ours.''

''That's gospel,'' Grover said. ''The rabbits belong to the kids.''

Whit glanced toward the approaching storm clouds, then bent down to examine the bodies. He moved from one to another. Bonnie and Jimmy followed him. When he reached the last one, he ran a hand over his face. Violent death, even when it befell pet rabbits, did something to a person.

Bonnie stood beside him, almost leaning on him. ''That's Barney. She's the mommy.''

''What's your name?'' Whit asked.

''Bonnie.''

Whit put an arm around her. ''Can I take Barney with me? She might help us find who did this.''

''But we gotta bury her, Mister.''

''I'll bring her back.''

''You promise?'' the little girl asked.

''Yes, but, when I bring her back, you mustn't look in the box she'll be in.''

''But maybe she won't be in there.''

Whit hugged her. ''I'm a policeman, Bonnie. Policemen don't lie.''

He heard the feminine chuckle behind him, then the

words, "And elephants fly." He turned to glare at the reporter.

Bonnie relented. "Okay—so long as you bring her back."

Mrs. Thompson and the children went to find something in which to put the rabbit.

"Something I didn't tell you," Grover said as soon as his family was out of sight.

"What's that?"

"A couple of the rabbits are missing. I don't think the kids really know it, I mean they're so torn up and all."

"How many?"

"Two, I think. Kinda hard for me to tell."

Whit made a note.

"Investigator Pynchon?" It was Anna Tyree. "Do you think this may be related to the death of the deputy's wife?"

"No comment, Miss Tyree."

"I think you must. Otherwise you wouldn't be here."

"No comment."

The children returned with a white kitchen bag. Grover lifted the rabbit's stiff body into it as Whit held it open. The children watched. Just before it disappeared into the bag, Bonnie reached out and patted the cold remains. "Bye, Barney."

It brought a sheen of moisture to Whit's eyes.

Eight

A crowd, moved as much by curiosity as compassion, overflowed the Milbrook Funeral Home. They mingled, chatted, laughed some, and wound their way by the casket of DeeDee Dickerson. The family formed a grieving line for the mourners as they reached the coffin. Most of the family were strangers to Milbrook, relatives of Gil, who was last in line. Gil had remembered that DeeDee had an aunt whom they both usually forgot even at Christmas. He had made arrangements for her to travel from Cleveland.

Whit Pynchon avoided funeral homes. The ritual harkened back to some primeval ceremony, first begun at the dawn of history. He found it abominable, so much so that Tony had in his office vault a letter that stated Whit's preferences regarding his own death. No visitation at all, no open coffin so folks could file by and comment over how good he looked. Whit wanted an uneventful cremation. He came to the funeral home that night in search of a break in the case. A long shot, but he had nothing to play but long shots. Even the good prints on the rabbit cage were a long shot. Assuming the state guys at the fingerprint lab could ID the prints, it didn't mean the rabbit killer had also killed DeeDee Dickerson. It was just a thought, made worthy of pursuit by the lack of other thoughts.

Whit eased forward with the crowd, nodding to those he

knew and dreading the moment when he would have to say something to Gil. *What the hell do you say?*

If there's anything I can do—

I'll miss her. Whit shook his head. Hell, he didn't even know her.

The moment came seconds later. He shook hands with those relatives he didn't know. When he reached Gil, the deputy spoke before he could. "Whit, please get the bastard that did this. I know a lot of guys give you a bad rap, but I'm glad you're handling it."

Gil wore rose-tinted glasses to conceal the emotion of his eyes, but the tremor in his voice was unmistakable. Whit felt his own eyes fill—for the second time that day. "Gil, what can I say? I promise you I'll get him, but that won't make your pain any less."

Gil dropped his head, turning it toward the casket. "Maybe it'll keep someone else from having the same pain."

Whit put a hand on Gil's shoulder. "I'll keep you posted."

As he walked by the casket, he felt better. Why, he really didn't know. Somehow the vote of confidence helped. He paused to look down at DeeDee Dickerson. He'd met her once—at a courthouse Christmas party. She looked peaceful but so plastic. A very high-collared dress concealed her neck.

Someone bumped him. He looked back at a pudgy, elderly woman. She motioned for him to move along. "Jesus," he muttered. As he moved away, he heard the woman say to her companion, "They got her neck covered. I told you they would."

Whit stopped. Again the woman prodded him. He wheeled on her. "Did you get your jollies, lady?"

"What?" The woman flushed. "What did you say?"

Whit moved off.

"Who was that?" he heard her ask.

In the lobby he found Tony. The Tyree woman had him cornered, and Whit had to walk right by them to get to the exit. He turned to look for a rear door, but Tony saw him. "Whit!"

"Shit," he mumbled.

Tony motioned for him. Whit slipped sideways through the thick crowd.

"You been through?" Tony asked.

"Yeah."

"How's Gil?"

"How would you be?"

The reporter grinned at Whit but spoke to Tony. "He's even curt with you."

"I'm used to him." Tony eyed the long line. "Well, I might as well get this over with. I'll leave you two to chat."

"How kind of you," Whit said as Tony, chuckling, vanished into the crowd.

"Nice seeing you, Miss Tyree. I have to be going."

She stopped him with a gentle hand on his arm. "Wait a minute, Whit."

The use of his first name took him by surprise. It showed.

"Do you mind if I call you Whit? And how did you escape being called Pinch?"

"I never tolerated it."

"Can we talk?"

"Not about the case, Miss Tyree. Not about anything if you're going to put it in the paper."

"Okay. Off the record then. And that's something I never do—or at least never did."

The crowd pressed in on them. Whit discovered he was trapped. "I've gotten burned off the record too."

Anna also appeared to be suffocating from the crowd. "Let's go outside, Whit. I need some air."

"Lady, if you can forge your way outa here, I'm right behind you."

And she did, pushing and squeezing and asking in a sweet voice to be "pardoned" as she inched to the wide front doors.

"Whew!" she said once they were out in the rain-cooled night. The thundershower had charged through with violent but brief fury. The temperature had plummeted from the mid eighties to the high sixties. The sun had reappeared around eight, just long enough to create a glorious sunset.

"It's nice out here," she said.

Whit lit a cigarette. "What did you want to talk about—off the record?"

Now that they were free of the stifling crowd, Whit had the opportunity to see that she wore a pleated long skirt, topped with a white blouse. With her heels she stood as tall as he.

"I didn't want to ask anything. I just wanted to say I was impressed today."

"With what?"

"The way you handled those kids. It was . . . well, nice."

"I'm only cross with reporters." Whit felt himself blushing at her comment. He hoped his color was concealed by the semidarkness in which they stood.

Anna was laughing. "The way I hear it, you can be cross with anyone."

"Don't believe everything you hear."

"Anyway, I was impressed."

Whit sucked the menthol smoke deep in his lungs. "I figured I was going to read in the paper tomorrow about the super cop who wasted taxpayers' time investigating dead rabbits rather than a dead woman."

"Oh, no! Absolutely not. I wrote a nice article about that—the rabbits, I mean. I know you won't confirm it, but you went out there because you think there's a link with that poor woman in there. That's why I went."

"You're digging," he said.

Her voice didn't break stride. "And you found those prints. So maybe your hunch will pay off. As I said, I am impressed. And you aren't as irascible as you pretend to be."

A cool breeze lifted her hair. Whit smelled the scent of her perfume, the same scent he had noticed earlier that day, light and fresh and—

"Do you have children?" she asked.

"One—a daughter."

"How old is she?"

"Seventeen going on thirty."

Anna Tyree nodded. "At seventeen I was going on forty."

Whit damned himself. As much as he tried not to, he liked this woman. Her laugh, her voice; they had a musical tone, a sincere quality.

A steady string of people exited the funeral home and passed them as they chatted on the sidewalk.

"You're not from here?" Whit asked.

Careful now. Whit had surprised himself, asking such questions.

"No, I'm originally from Kentucky."

"Well, I'd better be going."

He started to turn.

"Would you like a drink?" she asked. "I could use one."

Whit eyed her. "Lady, am I getting led down the primrose path?"

Anna crossed her heart. "I promise to *try* not to talk shop. Notice I said 'try.' Old habits are hard to break."

"Well, anyway, I don't frequent any of the bars around

here. Oh, maybe for an early dinner at one of the places without a band, but never this time of night."

"Yes, you do have an image to protect."

"A body to protect," Whit countered.

"I'd settle for an ice cream—no, a banana split. From the Dairy Bar. How about that?"

"It's my turn to be impressed," Whit said.

"Why?"

"The women I know spend most of their time worrying about calories."

"Not me. I have better things to do."

Whit considered the idea. "Something tells me this is a mistake."

"I don't bite or claw or even pick my nose in public."

Whit laughed. No woman had ever asked Whit out before, not even for an ice cream. It was unsettling.

"Okay. I could use a milkshake." And he regretted it the moment he said it. The woman was a reporter. So what if she smelled good and was pretty and didn't put on airs? "I'll meet you there."

She hesitated. "You won't stand me up?"

"No, ma'am."

But if he had any sense at all, he would, Whit thought.

Emma Foley needed six credit hours to have her degree in psychology. And once she finished the class she was taking, she'd lack just three. After that she wanted to take a few graduate hours.

The psych class met once a week. She left the class building with a group of other students, all of whom were younger than she. Emma had dropped out of college in her senior year several years back because of her pregnancy. And she had miscarried in her fifth month.

"Your husband told you anything about the murder?" one of the young male students asked.

"He got called out on it. He wanted to give me all the vivid details, but I didn't want to hear it."

"Lotta good you are," a female student said.

"I have a weak stomach."

One gangling youth said, "If I ever get caught smoking a little dope, I hope your old man'll get me off."

Emma giggled. "He wouldn't even get me off."

They reached a Y in the sidewalk. One path led to the Student Union, the other to the parking lot. The group invited Emma to come have a beer with them. The class, a summer session offering, was just getting started, but Emma knew most of them from a prior psych course. She begged off. "I have dinner to cook."

"At this hour?"

"He doesn't get in from work until eleven P.M."

They expressed their sympathies to her, then headed to the Student Union. She moved toward the parking lot. Emma hadn't felt entirely safe since DeeDee's death, but she wasn't about to go around packing a gun. Miller had wanted her to go to the funeral home tonight. She had compromised with him by promising to attend the funeral the next day.

The Foleys' 1980 Buick was parked beneath a towering, thickly leafed maple. The dark parking lot itself was almost empty, just as the campus was. Not a lot of students returned for the summer session. Emma hurried to unlock the door. Once inside, she breathed easier. It was silly, being so jumpy. She inserted the ignition key. It hung. Sometimes it did that, but on this night it seemed especially stubborn.

"Dammit." She leaned down, trying to see in the dark car.

Something moved—just a kind of shimmy.

Emma glanced into the rearview mirror. She saw nothing. She looked around the lonely parking lot. Nothing there either. Just to be on the safe side, she quickly locked all four doors to her car and returned her attention to the ignition. This time it slipped right in. "Bingo!"

Emma cocked her wrist to turn the key. Again she felt movement, this time more definite and pronounced. She glanced into the rearview mirror. Eyes twinkled back at her. Before she could shriek, the piano cord flipped over her head and cinched tight around her throat.

In her last clear flash of thought, she remembered the gun, thinking how absurdly useless it would have been to her. The sounds she made were full of bloody misery as the thin, choking wire sliced through skin and muscle and piping.

Emma Foley had come as close to her bachelor's degree as she ever would.

Whit changed his mind and ordered a chocolate nut sundae. True to her word, Anna had a banana split. They sat across the table from each other.

"Without talking shop," Anna said, "what is it you have against reporters?"

"That question is out-of-bounds."

Anna cocked her head. "Maybe. Maybe not. I'm just curious. Why do you detest us so much?"

"You mean other than the obvious reason?"

"Hey, none of the reasons are obvious to me."

Whit fished for the sugary red cherry. "Reporters have no ethics, no sense of fair play, no respect for the truth. They're only interested in nosing into other people's business."

"Okay, other than a few minor flaws of character, what else?" Anna said, smiling.

And Whit laughed again—for the second time that night.

"Seriously," she said, "a lot of folks think the same thing about cops."

"I don't like cops either."

Anna, who was shoveling a gigantic piece of ice-cream-covered banana into her mouth, almost choked. "Damn, you got me tickled!" she said when she regained control. "I've heard you give cops a hard time."

"You've heard an awful lot."

"I was told that you spend most of your time investigating other policemen."

"That's bullshit." Whit found the cherry and ate it. "Besides, we're talking shop. How long have you been with the paper?"

"Oh, it's okay to talk my shop, just not your shop?"

Whit closed his eyes. "You got me on that one."

"It's okay. I don't mind. I've been here almost a month now."

"And they call you Annie?"

Her eyes narrowed. "*No one* calls me Annie. It's Anna."

"I thought your byline—"

"I don't like my byline."

"Oh, I see," Whit said, even though he didn't. "How come the hyphenated last name?"

"Good question." Anna sucked the plastic spoon clean. The gesture, not lost on Whit, was almost sexual. "In order to get that hyphen," she said, "one simply strikes the proper key on the typewriter—or word processor—or whatever."

Whit dropped his eyes. "I didn't mean to be nosy."

"I wasn't being rude," she replied. "I mean it. Tyson is my middle name, and, before you say anything, it was my grandmother's maiden name. My parents were rather traditional. And I just added the hyphen because I like the looks of it. My bosses like the name Annie. A compromise, I guess."

"And you like your job?"

"I love it." Her eyes twinkled.

A city cop walked into the ice cream parlor. He saw Whit and waved, smiling at what he saw.

"See that?" Whit said.

"The cop?"

"The look on his face."

"So what?"

"Within an hour, the grapevine will have spread the word that I was out with a person of the opposite sex. Worse, a reporter."

"There goes your image."

"Puff!" Whit said.

The cop picked up a bag of food waiting for him and left the restaurant. "Did you see that?" Whit said.

"See what? Damn, do you watch everything?"

"He didn't pay for the food."

Anna thought about it. "You're right!"

"He just accepted a gratuity. A small one, but still a gratuity. It's inbred with cops. Preachers are the same way. For some reason they think society owes them a free ride. It amazes me."

But the cop wasn't gone long. He came back in, marching straight for Whit. "Maybe he reads lips," Anna said as she saw him coming.

"Whit?" The cop came right up to their table.

"Yeah."

The officer leaned down. "We have another murder."

"Where?" Whit remembered Anna, what she did for a living. "Never mind." He got up.

"I'm going too," Anna said.

Whit had been right. He'd made a hell of a big mistake.

Tony Danton stood by the Foley car. "Precisely the same mode of operation. Poor Foley found her. This time, though, the caller said he wanted to report someone too drunk to drive. He told the dispatcher that a guy was passed out in a car parked beneath the big maple here.''

A group of county deputies, aided by several city police, held back the onlookers, mostly college students. Anna, though, was among those being restrained. She was furious she was being denied access. Whit heard her screaming at him.

''Where the hell were you anyway?'' Tony was asking.

''At the Dairy Bar.''

Whit looked at Emma Foley. ''Oh, sweet Jesus.''

Blood soaked the front of her blouse. Her head lay back on the headrest, much too far back. Her eyes were open. The gaping crevice in her throat seeped blood and air bubbles.

''The killer must have been waiting for her in the back seat. The key's in the ignition.''

''Foley? How's he?''

Tony shrugged. ''They'd taken him away by the time I got here. He was sitting down right here by the car, beating his fist on the pavement.''

The prosecutor looked to the crowd. ''Is that the reporter screaming at you?''

''Yeah.''

''I guess we'd better let her at us.''

Whit started to protest. Why not? he thought. ''I'll escort her over here,'' Whit said.

Anna's face was livid. ''You jerk! How dare you—''

''Please join us, Miss Tyson-Tyree.'' Whit motioned for the officers to let her by.

''How dare you bar the press from the scene of a major crime?'' she said as he led her toward Emma Foley's car.

''We had to secure the scene first. Don't touch a thing. Nothing.''

''I know. I know.''

''She's in there.'' Whit pointed to the car.

The headlights from the gathered cruisers illuminated the vehicle. Anna leaned down and peered inside. Whit braced for her reaction. There was none. Calmly she clicked off a photograph.

Tony was stunned. "Surely to God you people won't print that."

"It's up to the editor," Anna said almost offhandedly as she adjusted the exposure of her camera.

Tony's voice softened. "Miss Tyree, could we impose on you for some of the prints? We'll be happy to pay. Might save us from calling out a photog."

Anna squinted at the small white numbers around the lens. "That depends, Mr. Prosecutor. Do I get a story on this?"

"Of course," Tony said.

"And can I quote Whit here?"

"Forget it," Whit said.

"Won't I do?" asked the prosecutor.

Anna thought about it. "I guess."

Tony directed her. Whit got back out of the way, amazed by her composure. Emma Foley wasn't as mutilated as DeeDee Dickerson. Apparently she hadn't been raped, either. Still the scene was revolting. Anna Tyree hadn't batted an eye.

Whit turned to business. He found Deputy Tim Franklin standing behind the car. "I want this thing impounded once the body's transported. We're gonna go over it with a hand sweeper, so try to disturb as little as possible."

Franklin feigned a sharp salute. "Yes, sir."

Whit shook his head in disgust.

Tony gave the sign to the ambulance attendants to move the body. They opened the door and eased it out, careful to hold the head in place. A body bag waited on the ground.

A piece of paper fluttered from the body to the ground. Whit bent down, picked it up with a small pair of tweezers.

Thickening blood obscured the scribbling. He caught Anna looking over his shoulder.

"What's that?" she asked.

"A grocery list."

Nine

The *Journal* awarded the killer his mythic identity Thursday morning. "WOMANSLAYER MURDERS AGAIN," proclaimed the banner headline.

A smaller headline enhanced the information. "Second Cop's Wife Garroted." Several photos, including a distant shot of the body being loaded into the ambulance, centered the front page. A sidebar told of the Thursday afternoon services for DeeDee Dickerson.

Whit read the front page, then looked for the story on the rabbits, finding it on the first page of the second section. Annie Tyson-Tyree—the byline made Whit chuckle—omitted any mention of the prints, but she hinted that the killings of the rabbits might be somehow tied into the killing of DeeDee Dickerson—and now Emma Foley.

He laid the paper down on his deck and inhaled the brisk morning air. The cool front had replaced the taste of high summer with the crispness of late spring. He allowed his eyes to roam his backyard, his mind to travel to the Carolina Low Country. How could life be at once so glorious and yet so dismal? To him it was a lovely day. How did the day appear to Miller Foley, to Gil Dickerson who that afternoon would lay his wife to rest under the clear sunshine? And how many more were to die?

A plump mourning dove landed in the center of his yard to peck breakfast from the grass. Whit checked his watch.

Eight o'clock. Time to leave for work. He ached to stay right where he was. Or better yet he wanted to get in his car and drive southeast until he reached his paradise.

But he had a duty.

Tony Danton was waiting on him when he got to the courthouse. He followed Whit into the coffee room. "We haven't got diddly shit on either of these cases."

"The guy's smart," Whit said as he dumped several teaspoons of sugar into the cup. "He's committed crimes in places where we aren't likely to find much evidence."

Tony's mood was down, which was unusual. Usually he didn't give enough of a damn to let something depress him. "I came in at six and went through those files you had on known offenders. Came up with zilch too."

Whit looked up at him. "Didn't you trust my judgment?"

"I had to do something. That's all there was to do."

"I don't think we have a sex offender, Tony."

"What do you mean?"

"The Foley woman wasn't raped."

"So maybe our guy shot his wad while he was strangling her."

Whit tested the sweetness of the brew. "He wore a damned rubber the first time, Tony. I just think he's looking for shock effect. I think we have a cop hater here." Whit reached into his coat pocket and withdrew a paper bag. "Here's this. Ponder that for a while."

Tony took the bag and looked inside. It contained a bloody sheet of paper.

"It wasn't a grocery list," Whit said.

The paper bore a message in cut-out newspaper letters. It read, "No. 2"—nothing more.

Tony's brow wrinkled. "Why didn't you show this to me last night?"

Whit headed for his office; Tony followed, wanting an explanation.

''Every time I saw you, Tony, you were tagging after Miss Tyree like she was a bitch in heat,'' Whit said.

''Like hell I was. I wasn't the one who took her out for ice cream.''

It didn't surprise Whit that Tony already knew.

''We'll get this up to the lab,'' Tony said.

''It's a waste of time.''

But Tony had stopped listening. He was sniffing. ''What the hell is that odor?''

Whit smelled it too. ''I don't know.'' His eyes caught the white plastic bag beside his desk. ''Goddammit to hell!''

''So what is it?''

Whit lifted the plastic bag from the floor. The odor exploded. ''It's Barney.''

''Barney?''

''A dead rabbit. I meant to refrigerate it.''

''Mother of God! It smells like a dead rat. Get that thing outa here!''

''I can't believe I did that.''

''Why the fuck have you got a dead rabbit?''

Whit reminded him of the complaint yesterday as he tried to tighten the seal on the bag. ''I drove out there. Maybe a dozen rabbits were killed . . . butchered, really.''

''So? The mountains are full of wild animals.''

Whit lifted the wooden piece of the hutch from the floor. ''Animals don't make handprints like this one. The person who left this killed the rabbits. Maybe he killed two police wives too.''

Tony rolled his dark Italian eyes. ''Damn! You're grasping at straws!''

''Well, I'm asking the local vet to do a postmortem. And I'll send the print to the lab. It's worth a try.''

"Just don't let that woman reporter know about this. Imagine what she could with it?"

"Too late, Tony."

"My God, she knows?"

"Yeah. She knows."

Tony paled. "Jesus, Whit, I can read thc headlines now."

"Relax, Tony. Hell, she was at the house before I was yesterday. Didn't you read today's paper?"

"I didn't get by the 'Womanslayer.' "

"Not a bad name. Anyway, she treated us okay on the rabbit story. I was surprised."

Tony's relief was visible. "She's a hunk of woman, Whit."

"But deep down, beneath that sexy exterior, beats the cold and cruel heart of a goddamned reporter."

Tony stared at Whit, filling the doorway as he leaned on its frame. "Someday you're going to overcome that paranoia."

Sara Barnett, the office secretary, tapped Tony on the shoulder. "Can I get by?"

"Huh? Sure."

"I have two messages for you," she said, handing the notes to Whit. "A reporter for the Charleston paper wants you to return his call. Another reporter from ABC also wants—"

"ABC! Oh, my God," Tony said.

"—wants you to return his call."

Sara started to leave. "Oh, I forgot. Anna Tyree wants you to call her too."

"Get Miss Tyree on the phone for me, Sara."

"What about the other two?"

"The hell with them," Whit said.

"But what if they call me back, Whit?"

Whit propped his feet on his desk. "Tell them to go to hell."

"No!" Tony snapped. "Get them on the phone for me, Sara. ABC first. I'll handle it."

Sara vanished.

"Jesus, Whit, you're going to have to learn. One of these days—" Tony left the rest unsaid.

"If you're going to do something to me, Tony, you'd better get on with it. You won't have me to kick around much longer."

DeeDee Dickerson's earthly journey ended at 3:17 P.M. Thursday. Six deputies, commanded by Lt. Dan Linnerman, carried her bronze casket to its grave. Two dozen uniformed officers formed a tunnel of honor for her. The differences in the uniforms created a collage of authority; city officers in blue, the musky green of the state police, and the somber gray and black of the Raven County Sheriff's Department. Even Ted Early, who stood with Gil Dickerson, abandoned his customary rumpled suit for a creased new uniform, trimmed in gold. It was the first time that he had worn a uniform since taking the office.

Whit stood apart from the mourners. His eyes were on the wives of the officers. They stood together, like wagons circled, each of their faces tense with its own kind of fear. The phrase "like lambs to the slaughter" came to his mind; he was at once ashamed of the thought. He couldn't repress the image. They looked so damned much the part. He'd heard by the grapevine that a few of them were leaving, taking their children with them. The local radio station was quick to air an editorial. The station manager concluded by asking, "If the local police can't protect their own, whom can they protect?"

The editorialist had the police up in arms, ready to storm the station, but he had made a good point. Whit didn't blame the wives who were leaving. They were more aware of the limitations of their policeman spouses than the public in general. If Whit had a wife, he'd exile her too. Wonder if the killer was interested in ex-wives? *Shame on you, Whit Pynchon.*

"Hi, Daddy."

"Tressa! You startled me."

"I couldn't get to the funeral at the chapel, but I thought I'd come for the graveside services."

He slipped an arm around her trim waist. "Glad you did."

"I guess there's nothing to report—"

Anticipating her question, Whit grimly shook his head. A dozen times already he'd been asked the same question. And the press hadn't even got to him yet. Gil Dickerson had made it a point to seek him out.

"I have faith in you," Gil had said, perhaps with less conviction than he had expressed the night before at the funeral home.

"We need evidence," Whit said to Tressa. "Sooner or later he'll make that one mistake."

The procession from the funeral home had been long. Some of the cars were still emptying mourners. The preacher and the family waited quietly to lay DeeDee to rest.

Whit studied Gil, amazed at how well the young man was holding up.

"Afternoon, Mr. Super Cop."

Another feminine voice . . . Anna Tyree.

"I tried to call you this morning," Whit said. "I owe you one for the story on the rabbits."

"Well, I'm not all bad. I hear your boss isn't too happy with the name we gave the killer."

"Your idea?" Whit asked.

"Wanna come see me tonight?"

"Uh . . . I . . . I can't."

Missie hiked her darkly penciled eyebrows. "You can't? What's wrong, kid? I thought things went pretty well the other night."

"Oh, I didn't mean—they did . . . really." He fumbled, then dropped a can of soup that went rolling down the aisle. Kenny chased it down, brought it back. "I just . . . I mean, I can't get loose tonight."

"I bet you could if you tried." She pressed close to him. Kenny could smell her, feel the warmth of her body. "You just got a sample the other night."

He felt the tension in his groin.

"It'll be safe."

Should I tell her or not?

"It might be your final invitation," she said, her voice not so sweet anymore.

Again he looked around. A woman stood way down at the dog food, her interest consumed in her study of the can. Funny, how they took longer to buy dog food than peanut butter. "Can I come in the back door?" he asked.

"Sure, hon. You can use both back doors tonight."

"Both?" Kenny didn't understand.

"Never mind. I'll leave it open for you."

His stomach fluttered, but there was no denying her effect on him. It pushed against a can of Chunky Chicken Soup.

She reached down, patted his crotch. His eyes jerked up to the woman at the dog food.

"Now don't go playing with yourself," Missie purred. "Save it for me."

Ferdie slept late into the day. He awoke with the taste of blood lingering in his mouth. Lice tormented his balls. He scratched them viciously. Flies buzzed around the rotting pieces of animal flesh that he stored a few feet from his pine-bough bed. The odor of festering death filled the cave. It comforted him. He was beginning to lose the fetor of the hospital.

According to the vet, someone—a person—had taken a huge bite out of the rabbit. After dropping the rabbit off at the Thompson farm, Whit returned to his office. A meeting was going on in Tony's office. Sheriff Early was there along with two of the three county commissioners.

Tony hailed him. "Join us, Whit."

Whit despised political bullshit sessions, but he obliged his boss.

"The guys here are wondering about the courthouse picnic on Sunday," Tony said.

"I haven't checked the weather report," Whit said.

"Shit, Whit. They're wondering if it's safe."

The president of the county commission, a bumbling wimp who ran a hardware store, wore an expression of severe, practiced concern. "Do you think there's any danger?"

"How should I know? The killer's never struck in the daylight. Elk Run State Park's a long way from town. I'd say it's okay."

The commissioner nodded. "I hope so. It's become such an annual tradition—the people look forward to it so—I'd hate to cancel it."

Besides, Whit thought, you're up for reelection next year.

Early straightened up in his chair. "A few of our guys are relocating their wives, but most of the women are hanging tough. Speaks well for them. I'm sure quite a few of my people will be there."

"We'll schedule a moment of silence at the beginning of the meal for the victims," the commissioner said.

Whit suppressed a laugh. How nice it would be to be honored at a drunken picnic!

''Rest assured, Mr. President. We can keep things under control,'' Early boasted. ''We'll come well armed.''

''On second thought, Mr. President,'' Whit said, ''it might not be so safe after all.''

Ten

Fear soured Kenny's stomach.

"What is wrong with you?" Missie said.

"I just can't do it."

Missie tossed back the bedcovers. She placed her tongue on his nipple, circled it, then moved to the other one. She licked down his stomach, his belly, leaving a moist trail. Her hand reached beneath his timid penis. She slipped it in her mouth.

Nothing.

She tried harder.

"I'm sorry," he said.

Missie swallowed her anger. "It happens to all men, hon. What's troubling you?"

He had come to the house prepared to tell her. Now, as he looked down into her face, he couldn't. Kenny wanted to be a man, and men didn't do what he'd done. Besides, she would get mad that he had done something so stupid, so childish—parading in front of her house like that.

"I just don't feel too good."

"Gawd, I hope you aren't catching the flu or something. You haven't been with someone else, have you?"

"No, ma'am."

"You wanna do something for me?"

Kenny's face clouded. "What?"

She moved up beside him on the bed. "I bet you haven't tasted a woman before."

"No, ma'am."

Missie hissed. "For Gawd sakes quit calling me 'ma'am.' It makes me feel so old."

"I'm sorry."

"Let me show you what to do."

Just as she started to "educate" him, they both heard it. Something thumped against the house. Kenny yelped. Missie yanked the bed sheet over her nakedness.

"What was that?" Kenny waited to die.

But he didn't. They both lay quiet for several minutes. They heard nothing else. "Maybe it was Tear Gas."

"Tear Gas?"

"Our cat. Didn't you see him last time you were here?"

Kenny was still listening. "No, I don't think so."

"Well, it sure isn't anything to worry about. Come on, let's get back to what we were doing."

But Kenny wanted none of it. "I gotta go. It's getting late."

Missie flew mad. "Just who the hell do you think you are?"

Kenny fumbled with his clothes.

"Really, Mrs. Posich, it's nothing to do with you. I just feel bad. I gotta get home."

Missie wasn't aroused anymore. It wasn't so much a matter of sexual satisfaction as it was ego gratification. She felt rejected.

"You just see if you ever get invited back."

Lady, I don't ever wanna come back, he thought, but he didn't say it.

Gathering clouds obscured the moon and stars. When Kenny walked over, the night had been clear. An orange moon had hung low on the horizon. Now, as he looked toward the sky, he saw only the dull glow of the moon through thickening overcast. The smell of impending rain hung in the air.

A cool breeze whipped in from the northwest, rustling the newborn leaves on the trees.

Kenny kept to the back streets. He had left the Posich home at 12:35 A.M. He should be home by one. God, he wished he was already there, safe beneath the covers of his bed. What if the cops saw him out again? He quickened his pace.

The street along which he walked was only partially developed. He kept to the berm. To his right the widely spaced homes were dark and still. The forest on his left, on the side which he walked, stretched all the way to the top of the mountain ridge. If he saw or heard a car, he planned to duck into the trees. The terrors of the dark woods frightened him much less than the idea of facing Hank Posich again.

He heard a car. He stopped, ready to dive into the woods. The car, though, was one street over. The wind paused. In that pause he still heard the rustling of leaves. The hairs on his neck prickled. He looked back toward the forest. Something moved behind the curtain of trees, the gaps between them shot full of inky blackness.

And the wind picked up again.

Kenny hadn't forgotten that two women had died. Some kind of maniac was loose. He hadn't read anything but the headlines that morning.

Sweat popped out on his forehead. He hunched over and started toward home. Something white charged out from the brush—right at his feet. He jumped, then realized that it was just a Hardee's bag, rolling along with the breeze. It didn't lessen his fear. He still heard the sound of something moving along with him, something so ugly and threatening that it hid itself in the black woods.

His walk became a trot.

His unseen companion crashed through the brush.

"Oh, God," Kenny cried.

His sneakers pounded the asphalt. His breath became raspy. The noise paced him for a short while, then stopped. Kenny didn't stop. Not until he had to and then he was only a block from his home. He had entered a more populated area, a part of town that he knew like the back of his hand. As a child he had played through these backyards, often been chased out of them by angry old women who had some kind of crazy affection for flowers.

But he didn't take the shortcut through the backyards. He kept to the sidewalk, to its welcome light. Down the street he could see his house, as dark and tranquil as all the other houses he passed.

"Thank God," he mumbled.

He looked into the shadows of a neighbor's backyard and saw something dash from the rear of one house to another. The panic returned. He ran crying and panting toward home. Once inside, he bolted the door and went to his bedroom, where he spent the rest of the night guarding the single window in his room.

Whit's first break came at 2:48 P.M. Friday afternoon. The phone call came from the State Criminal Identification Bureau.

When big cities decide that they have a mass murderer taking the lives of their citizens, they mobilize. They form task forces. In small towns, denied the luxury of seven-figure budgets, they just hope. And they beg a lot too, as Whit had done when he sent the prints from the rabbit cage to the fingerprint division of CIB. Most of the state's towns were like Milbrook, and every one of them had cases that were important. Small-town cops didn't take the time to send things to the lab unless the case was important. As a result, evidence stood in line.

Worse, there were pecking orders, and little Milbrook wasn't high on anyone's agenda. Usually Raven County waited months for chemical identification of suspected drugs. They waited almost that long on blood tests and reports on "questioned documents" and even fingerprints.

But this time Whit had begged. He had been around long enough to know the fingerprint examiner on a first-name basis.

"What do you have for me, Tommie?" Whit asked. He expected to be told nothing.

"We got a match for you."

"You're kidding?"

"Well, let me rephrase, Whit. I don't think my comparison will stand up in court. The characteristics are consistent. That's as far as I can go."

"Just give me a name," Whit said, his blood starting to course with excitement. "It'll be a place to start."

"Okay. The name's Ferdnand Tipton."

"Ferdnand Tipton?"

"That's it. According to our records, he lives in Raven County."

"I've never heard of him."

"As I said, the prints on the wood are consistent with those of Ferdnand Tipton. I'll send you an official report in a few days."

"Maybe the sheriff's department has a record on him. Hey, I appreciate the rush."

"You folks made ABC news last night. Glad to help. Just remember me if this thing turns big."

"I will, and again many, many thanks."

Whit slammed down the phone. He hurried into Tony's office. Several lawyers were seated around Tony's desk. It was something of a ritual every Friday afternoon, a "shoot-the-shit" session as they called it.

Tony saw the look on Whit's face. "You got something?"

Whit motioned for him to come outside.

"Hell, Whit," said one of the attorneys, "let us in on it too."

Whit ignored him as he led Tony back to his office. "Does the name Ferdnand Tipton mean anything to you?"

"Tipton? It sounds familiar— Oh, yeah. Back in the winter, Tipton was killed. Remember? They went to arrest him for stealing chickens or something, and he came at them with a mowing scythe. Let's see. Maybe Posich shot him?"

"He's dead?" Whit's heart sunk.

"Yeah, I remember it. Wait! Didn't he have a brother?" Tony pondered the matter. "Hell, let me get the file."

He came back with a thin manila folder. "Yeah, he had a brother named Ferdnand."

"That's it! That's whose prints were on that rabbit cage!"

Tony's eyes brightened. "They got a match?"

"Well, the word Tommie uses is 'consistent,' but at least it gives us a place to start. Where does he live?"

Tony checked the file. "The state hospital. He was committed there after his brother was killed. If I remember correctly, these two guys were real weirdos. They lived—"

"The state hospital?" Whit asked.

"That's what it says here. Of course, they may have released him already. That place is worse than a jail, in and out . . . in and out."

"He'd sure have reason to want to get even with deputies," Whit mused.

"If he's out of the hospital. Like I was saying, I remember those two. They lived in a shanty up on Tabernacle Mountain. Both of them were mental defectives. The grand jury found that Posich and''—he again checked the file—''the others . . . which were Chaffins, Dickerson, and Franklin . . . were justified in shooting.''

''Well, Ferdnand Tipton, or someone with almost identical fingerprints, was at Grover Thompson's farm this week,'' Whit said. ''I'm going over to the sheriff's office.''

''Keep me posted on this, Whit. I mean step-by-step.''

''Afternoon,'' Deputy Curtis said to Whit as he came into the control room.

''I need a record on someone,'' Whit said.

''Name?''

''Ferdnand Tipton.''

Curtis's eyes snapped at the name. Whit saw it. ''You know him?''

Curtis turned red. ''Well, I think we got a message about him this week.''

''Message? What kinda message?''

''He ran off and got married or something.''

''He what?''

''The message said that he eloped.''

''Eloped? From the state hospital?''

''That's what the message said.''

''My God, man! Where's the message? When did this happen?''

Curtis toyed with a paper clip. ''Uh, it happened this past weekend, I think.''

''Dammit, man! Get the message.''

''I can't.''

''You can't! You keep all those messages, don't you?''

''Yeah, usually, but I'm kinda new at this. Somehow the printer jammed—''

Whit was livid. "But you didn't tell anyone about it. Is that it?"

"Well, I didn't think it was important. Some guy running off to get married and all. It just didn't seem important at the time."

"Do you know what *eloped* means?" Whit asked, his words biting and angry.

"Of course I do."

"Oh, yeah. It means to run off and get married."

"That's right." No wonder everyone hated the son of a bitch, Curtis thought.

"Find Tipton's record for me," Whit was saying, "and I want an A.P.B. put out on him right now."

Deputy Bill Curtis frowned. "An A.P.B.?"

"God help us," Whit said.

ELEVEN

THE WESTERING SUN spotlighted the twin towers of Tabernacle Mountain. Dooley Chaffins, squinting into the late-afternoon glare, eased the cruiser into a rutted dirt road midway up the highway that sliced through the double summit's crotch.

"We'll have to walk from here," he told his passenger.

Whit cringed. "How far is it?"

" 'Bout half a mile."

Chaffins, a sixteen-year veteran, knew the mountain as well as anyone. Before he became a deputy, Chaffins had served as a constable. Before that, he had made some of the best moonshine in the coalfields. In those days he'd knock heads with anyone, the toughest cop or the vilest criminal. Now as he approached sixty, a bulge hung over his belt, and his face hinted at high blood pressure.

"You can make it," he told Whit.

"I was worrying more about you."

"Shit, boy. You haul your ass and I'll manage mine."

And he did, too, moving up the sloping, weed-filled path at a pace Whit couldn't match. The path, once a logging road, cut a diagonal scar down the mountain face. Wild locust, tall grass, and prickly berry vines clogged the rutted lane. Huge bumblebees, aroused by the locust blooms, buzzed them.

"Watch for snakes," Chaffins said.

Whit swung at a bee. "Hell, I can't watch for anything for these damned bees. I've never seen such monsters."

"They won't do you near as much hurt as a timber rattler or a copperhead. This mountain's alive with them."

"Gee, thanks for telling me now." Whit lowered his eyes to the ground as he plodded up the trail. A sheen of swcat glistened on his face. Chaffins broke the trail through the low brush, leaving a wake of drifting pollen. It irritated Whit's sweat-slick face. He sneezed several times.

"How much farther?" Whit asked.

Chaffins allowed him to catch up. "Whatsa matter, Whit? You can't keep up with an ol' man?"

"I never claimed to be in shape."

"The exercise is good for you."

Whit, now up with Chaffins, stopped to get his breath. "I had a friend who always said that anything that made you feel as bad as exercise does couldn't be good for you."

Chaffins looked around, trying to get his bearings. "Ain't much farther. You can't see it from the road though."

"You call this a road?"

Whit's light blue shirt was darkened with perspiration. Bits of leaves clung to his gray pants. His gun, a two-inch revolver, weighed a ton. It pulled down on his belt. "I'm not dressed for this. You should have warned me, Dooley."

"Well, the road's grown up a mite since the last time I was up here. Come to think of it, that was last winter when we come to arrest the Tipton boys. You know, I would have never figured Ferdie for turning this kinda mean. Fact is, I never figured he had the sense for it."

Whit chuckled. "He probably didn't have. I talked to the doctor today. He said he was better, at least in a medical sense."

"Better?"

"Yeah. He can now think beyond today. That's how that foreign doctor put it. You know why they were three days getting out a teletype?"

Chaffins said that he didn't.

"Because of the holiday Monday."

The deputy was only half listening. "If I recall, there's a big rock and a smaller path beyond the rock. The path goes through a briar patch. The Tipton place is just beyond the briar patch."

Whit looked at the towering pine, birch, and maple that lined both sides of the road. Lesser shrubs and trees created a wall that protected the forest.

"Well, let's get moving. I have an appointment tonight."

"You got your wind?"

"Lead on, old man."

Chaffins belly-laughed. "Old man, huh?" He walked another ten yards, then halted. "There ye be!"

Whit hurried to stay up with him. "What?" He followed Chaffins's pointing finger. "Is that the rock? I don't see it."

"A rattler. Just there, slithering out of that clear patch."

Whit froze, his eyes searching for a snake. "I don't see anything."

"You gotta be quick, boy."

Whit eyed Dooley Chaffins. "You trying to spook me?"

"Hell, no. The fuckin' thing was laying right there in that clear spot, sunning itself."

"Jesus, Chaffins. Unless I'm about to step on one, just don't tell me about them."

"They travel in pairs. You see one and you can just about bet there's another one nearby. Course, they're as afeared of you as you of them."

"Then there's two snakes pissing their pants now."

Chaffins grinned. "The rock's up there."

Whit saw it. He also saw the wall of thorns surrounding it. "Damn, Dooley. We gotta get through that? How?"

"Carefully. That's how."

Chaffins pointed out a smaller path branching off from the logging road. Whit saw nothing resembling a path. The huge stands of briars sprayed up from the ground. Chaffins moved toward them. "Wedge yourself through," he said, stepping into a narrow gap.

"Are you shitting me?"

"That's the path. These berry bushes grow fast. Once we get in the shade of the forest, it'll thin out. Watch for—"

"Snakes," Whit said. "I know, dammit."

"You first, Mr. Investigator. Don't let them briars flip back in my face."

Whit advanced on the small gap.

The noise came from just ahead of him.

Whomp. . . . Whomp. Then the rustling of brush.

Whit fumbled for his gun. His hand snagged on a thorn. "Oh, shit!"

"Easy," Chaffins said, coming up behind him.

"What the hell was that?" Whit looked at the angry streak of red on his hand.

"A turkey. Didn't you see it?"

"A turkey? Christ, it sounded like an elephant."

"It was a big turkey. You're not a hunter, huh?"

Whit shook his head and rubbed the scratch. "No way."

"Well, you can bet your ass I'll be up here when turkey season comes on. That was a nice bird."

Whit's heart still raced. "A turkey," he mumbled.

Chaffins eyed the settling sun. "We'd better move it."

"Then you go first."

Chaffins shrugged. "Suit yourself. Watch them briars."

It wasn't nearly as bad as Whit expected. After pushing a few yards through the clinging brambles, they reached the shaded canopy of the mountain forest. Whit saw the trail winding its way through the towering trees. It turned cooler, more tranquil. Patches of rock dotted the forest floor. A few hundred feet in front of them Whit saw the bright glare of a clearing.

"That's where the Tipton place is," Chaffins told him.

The bees and the bugs were gone. "It's nice in here," Whit said.

"You still oughta watch your step, especially around those rock areas. Copperheads—"

"I know already. Let's go."

To reach the clearing they forged through a low barrier of brambles. The shack itself, a slanting heap of weathered wood, occupied the clearing. Even from a distance Whit saw the dark shapes of wasps buzzing around the rotting front porch. A torn screen door hung askew on a single hinge.

"One of us should go around back," Whit said.

Chaffins looked at Whit with dismay. "You're kidding me! As much noise as we made, you think anyone's still in there? Just cover me from here." Chaffins drew his weapon. Whit followed suit.

When the deputy placed his weight on the first step, it snapped, cracked like a shot. Dust billowed up around the deputy as he struggled to keep his balance.

Ferdie hunkered down behind a granite outcropping a hundred yards from the shack. He had heard their approach as he foraged for food. They were searching for him. *About time too.* It had worried Ferdie that he had seen no one looking for him. Sooner or later he expected them to come to his house, the one that he had lived in. That's why he had made camp in the old mine shaft. Just that morning he'd thought about moving back in the house if no one was going to come up looking for him.

* * *

"You okay?" Whit asked.

"Yeah, fine." Chaffins dusted off his pants. The turmoil had stirred up the wasps. They flew in erratic circles around the two men.

"Ain't nobody been on that step for a while."

Chaffins tested the second step. It creaked and groaned but it held. Then the third . . . it held. He inched his way along the porch. "Look there." The deputy pointed down at the floorboards.

Whit moved closer, trying to see. "What is it?"

"That's the bloodstain left by Frankie Tipton. You never can get them stains out of wood. Funny, huh?"

Whit's gun was held at the ready. "Yeah, funny."

Chaffins kicked the screen door out of the way and peered inside. Then he vanished into the shack's dark interior.

Ferdie knew the older deputy, the one that had just gone inside his house. Not by name of course, but he remembered that he was one of the cops who was up there the night his brother had been gunned down.

The other one, Ferdie didn't know. Maybe he was from the hospital or something? While the cop was in the house, Ferdie took the chance to slip down a little closer.

"Dooley!" Whit squinted into the darkness beyond the door. "You okay?"

Whit's hand tightened on the pistol. He dodged one especially nasty wasp that wanted to hover in front of his face.

Chaffins stuck his head out. "It's clear. Looks like the varmints have taken over the place."

"You took your time."

The deputy exited the building with the same care he

had used to enter it. "The place is ready to collapse. And it's filthy in there."

"No sign of him?"

Chaffins shook his head. He searched around the building's foundation until he found a thick wooden beam. He lifted it from the earth, ignoring the grub worms and crawly things scurrying along its length.

"What are you doing?" Whit asked.

"The place is unsafe." Chaffins grasped the beam like a baseball bat and took a roundhouse swing at one of the bowed pillars supporting the front porch. The force of the blow sent the pillar flying out into the yard. The roof sagged. The building creaked.

"I figured that would do it," Chaffins said, swatting at the squadron of angry wasps. "Better get back toward the woods. I'm making these sons of bitches pretty damned mad. They got nests all over the building."

Whit obeyed.

Chaffins took another swing. The second pillar splintered in the middle. The old building started to shift. Chaffins flung the beam into the house, then darted from the swarm of black wasps. The building popped and cracked. The roof of the porch slammed down against the front wall, which in turn caved in. The entire roof fell with a splintering din. Dust billowed into the rays of the setting sun.

The two men stood in the fringe of the forest.

"It's still half standing," Whit said.

Chaffins rubbed at a red welt on his hand. "Them bastards hurt when they sting. You can go back and finish the job if you want."

"No thanks."

Ferdie Tipton cried.

He'd almost charged from his cover when he saw the old cop hammering his house—the house his daddy built.

He couldn't remember his daddy, but his mother had always said he'd built it with his own hands. His mother—and Frankie too—had loved the house.

Once the two men were out of sight, Ferdie slunk down to the house. Dust still hung thick in the air. So too did the wasps. One of them assaulted Ferdie's naked shoulder, spearing him with its painful sting. Ferdie brushed it off. Just under the edge of the rear of the house, something yellow snagged his attention. He bent down and pulled it from the rubble. It was a plastic cup, his cup when he'd been a kid. Ferdie's tears were muddied with dirt.

"They shouldn't oughta done it," he said aloud.

TWELVE

ANNA FELT SUCH a fool. Tressa Pynchon had called her to say that she and her father were to dine at the Steak Haus at 7:00 P.M. Did she want to "kind of just be there?" Already it was 7:20 P.M., and neither Tressa nor Whit had appeared. It brought back a bittersweet adolescent memory. Anna had had a crush on a boy in her class, and one of her girlfriends had arranged a blind date at the local snack shop. Anna had waited two hours for the boy. She later found out that the friend who had arranged the blind date had ended up going out with the guy that same night.

What the hell am I doing here?

Anna even suspected Tressa. Not that she thought the young girl would do anything intentionally, but maybe she had slipped up and told Whit and he had decided to go somewhere else.

The waitress was growing irritated with Anna's insistence that she wanted to enjoy a drink before dinner. One drink had turned to two and was about to become a third.

"Oh, Anna! I'm sorry." Tressa blustered up to the table.

"Tressa, what happened?"

"He phoned me a few minutes before seven to say to meet him here at eight. He was out chasing a suspect or something. I came on because I knew you'd be here, but I had a flat tire."

''Oh, no!''

''A city cop helped me fix it.''

''Now what was that about a suspect?''

Tressa put her hand over her mouth. ''I forgot you're a reporter.''

Anna laughed. ''Okay, tonight I'm not. Forget I asked.''

''Maybe it worked out better this way,'' Tressa said. ''This way I can already be sitting with you when Daddy gets here. He'll have to sit with us.''

''From what I've seen of Whit Pynchon, he doesn't *have* to do anything. He does just what he wants.''

The waitress reappeared. ''Are you ready to order?''

''I'll have a Coke,'' Tressa said. ''We're waiting on someone.''

The waitress's face creased with exasperation. Anna told her she didn't need anything, adding salt to the waitress's wound.

''What's wrong with her?'' Tressa asked.

''She works for tips. The longer we stay here, the less turnover in people, therefore less tips.''

Tressa saw her father. ''There he is.''

She started to rise, but Anna stopped her. ''I don't know about this. Maybe—''

But Tressa was waving at her father.

Whit approached the table and stopped dead in his tracks when he saw Anna.

''Hi, Dad. Look who I ran into.''

He nodded to Anna. ''Miss Tyree.''

''Please, call me Anna. And if I'm intruding—''

''Oh, you're not!'' Tressa said.

''Of course not,'' Whit said with little conviction.

Tressa saw that his hair was damp. She smelled the soap of a recent shower. ''You look tired.''

''I had a long, rough afternoon.''

The waitress returned with Tressa's Coke. "Now are we all here?" she asked.

"If the ladies don't mind, I'd like a cocktail before dinner," Whit said.

"Oh, I'm sure they won't mind." The waitress glared at Anna as if it were all her fault.

"One question," Anna said, unable to resist. "Are you ready to announce that the murderer is in custody?"

It was a joke—or at least Anna meant it as such. Whit, however, snapped his eyes at her. "You know—"

"Jesus, Whit. I was just kidding. Trying to win a smile."

"Well, we don't know any more than we knew yesterday."

"Is that the official position?"

"You sound like a reporter," Whit said, fencing.

"And you sound like a cop."

"Do I really sound like a cop?" Whit asked.

Tressa didn't like the way the conversation was going. "What do I sound like?"

"A typical teenager," Whit said.

"Tressa tells me you like the beach."

"When did she tell you that?" He looked from one to the other.

"Yesterday—at the funeral," Tressa said.

"Well, yes. I like it," Whit said then. "I hope to move down there before long."

"Just as soon as he can stop paying Mother alimony and child support."

"Tressa!"

"I'm not leaving!" Mary Linnerman stood in the small kitchen with her arms crossed, her eyes fiery.

Lt. Dan Linnerman leaned in the doorway. "It's not just you. What about the kids?"

"Send *them* to their grandmother's if you want, but I'd rather face the killer than your mother. I'm sorry, Dan. That's it. Forget it."

"A lot of the wives are leaving."

She folded a dish towel. "I don't care what a lot of the wives are doing. In the first place, I'm not about to miss the picnic Sunday. It's one of the few chances I have to get out. And what would they do without my baked beans?"

Linnerman didn't think it was funny. "There's talk of canceling the picnic."

"Canceling it! Why for God's sakes?"

The lieutenant lifted the morning paper from the table. "Because of this, Mary!" He pointed to a story on Emma Foley—and the name Womanslayer. Linnerman tossed it toward the trash can. It missed and fluttered to the floor. "This isn't any coincidence, first Gil's wife and now the Foley kid's wife."

"I'm not scared."

"Which makes you stupid, not brave."

She hung the dish towel in its place. "Well, nothing will happen at the picnic. Too many people there." She went to her husband and put her arms around his neck. He stood almost a foot taller than she, and she was pulled to her tiptoes. "I'm not going to be run off from my home, Dan. You know me better than that."

Linnerman kissed her. "Sometimes I think you're the one that shoulda been a cop."

Hank Posich hated going out, at least to someplace like the Steak Haus. And he never went without a fight, which meant that he and Missie ate their expensive meal in tense, angry silence. As he parked his car in the restaurant's lot, the chill between them threatened to frost the car's windows.

Hank exited the vehicle, slamming the car door, and headed straight for the entrance. He glanced around for Missie. She wasn't behind him. She still sat in the car, waiting.

"Goddammit to hell." He returned for her.

"One of these days," he growled as he opened her door.

"Thank you, kind sir."

"Just one drink. No more than that."

Missie Posich couldn't hold her liquor. She contracted the giggles when she downed more than an ounce or so. And the madder Hank became, the more she giggled. The hostess led them to a small table in a tight corner of the crowded restaurant.

"Ain't you got something bigger?" Hank asked.

"We're crowded tonight, sir. If you would care to wait in the bar—"

"Forget it."

Hank scowled at the crowd, as if each one of them had committed a personal offense against him. His eyes stopped on Whit Pynchon. "I'll be fucked."

"Hank!" Missie looked around to see if anyone had heard him. Several heads were turned in their direction.

He ignored her. "Look at that! That son of a bitch got one of the best tables in the place."

"Who?"

"There! Whit Pynchon."

Missie didn't know Whit Pynchon. "So where is he?"

"Right over there. With the two women with him." Hank stood, not even apologizing when his chair clunked into the chair of a patron behind him. The shaken man didn't say anything. Hank radiated an aura that by itself intimidated people.

Missie put a hand on his arm. "Don't, Hank."

He jerked his arm away.

* * *

Whit sipped his drink. His leg muscles were just starting to tighten and ache from the hike up Tabernacle Mountain. The alcohol, which was quickly infiltrating his system, eased the discomfort. Hardly reacting to the heavy hand on his shoulder, he turned to stare into the leering face of Hank Posich.

"Evenin', Whit."

It startled Whit. The Steak Haus wasn't a place in which he expected to find the brash, crude cop.

"Whadaya want, Hank?"

"Just thought I'd come over to say hello."

"Hi and bye." Whit dropped his eyes from the burly deputy.

"Aren't you gonna introduce me, Whit?"

Anna kept her silence. The animosity between the two men was tangible.

Whit turned back. "No, I'm not."

Hank grinned. He extended a hand to Anna. "I'm Deputy Hank Posich. I know who you are."

Anna managed a weak smile as she shook the huge, hairy hand.

Then he leaned over to offer the same hand to Tressa. "And just who might you be?"

"I'm Tressa Pynchon." She kept her hands in her lap, appalled at the rank breath of the man.

Hank, maybe a little embarrassed, jerked his hand back. "Well, I'll be. Last time I saw you was—hell, I can't remember, but you were a little thing. You're a mighty attractive young lady."

"Thank you." Tressa couldn't help it; she felt her face warm with a blush.

"You folks are mighty fortunate. We had to take a little ol' table all the way back there in the corner." Hank's cold defiant gaze settled on Anna. "I didn't think Whit here cared much for reporters, but I can see why he changed his mind.''

Whit knew Hank was digging, jabbing, trying to provoke a reaction from him. ''If you don't mind, Hank, our dinner should be along before long.''

''I don't mind a bit, Whit. What did you find at the Tipton place?''

Anna perked up, her journalistic radar triggered.

Whit noted her reaction. ''Just a nest of angry wasps,'' he said.

''He's our boy. I'll make book on it.''

''Who might that be?'' Anna asked of Hank Posich.

The deputy patted Whit on the shoulder. ''I'll let the prosecutor's investigator tell you the details. Wouldn't want to steal his thunder. Y'all have a good dinner.''

Hank left.

''You do have a suspect!'' Anna said.

Whit boiled. ''That low-down, conniving asshole.''

''Daddy!'' But Tressa knew her father. She knew his anger. Gently Tressa prodded Anna under the table.

But Anna didn't relent. ''Come on, Whit, give me something . . . anything.''

Whit looked around. ''I'm tired. If dinner doesn't come soon, I'm leaving.''

Tressa's poking continued. Anna closed her eyes in self-censure. ''I apologize, Whit. I guess we both are what we are.''

Whit nodded. ''Just like oil and water. We don't mix.''

''I'm glad we came,'' Hank said, swirling the foamy dregs of his beer around in the mug.

''You are?'' Missie almost choked on her drink, a pink frothy concoction, loaded with vodka, which cost almost as much as the dinner she'd ordered.

"Yeah. I am. Glad to see Whit's got a woman there. Maybe it'll soften him up."

Missie had been watching them. "They don't seem too chummy to me."

Anna excused herself to go to the powder room. Once she was out of sight, Tressa clunked her glass down on the table. "You should be ashamed, Daddy. You're being rude, crude, and unattractive."

"You don't understand."

"I understand that you can be polite without giving away your secrets."

"Some things just don't work, Tressa. As long as I have this job, I don't need to be fraternizing with reporters. It puts both her and me in bad positions."

Tressa turned her face from him. "There's still no excuse for being rude. That's something Mother says and she's right."

"Oh, gee! Thanks. I needed that."

"What you need is a good kick in the ass!"

"Tressa!"

"It's true!" People were now staring at the father and daughter. "Mother always said you were a social disaster."

"With that I agree. I thought you women always went to the bathroom in pairs."

"I'm going now." She marched away.

Tressa found Anna standing before the mirror, reapplying her makeup. "I apologize for him."

Anna gaped. "For him? Hon, I'm the one who came on like storybusters. Damn, why can't I for once forget that I'm a reporter?"

"But he's rude, Anna. He doesn't have to be rude. He sits there like some pouting kid."

Anna shrugged. ''He's right, you know. He and I go together like . . . what was that he said?''

''Oil and water.''

''Well, Tressa, he's right.''

The two women were winding their way back through the tables. Anna halted. ''Tressa, he's left.''

''Maybe he went to the men's room.''

''Somehow I doubt that.''

Tressa was saying something about ''prideful and stubborn,'' but Anna's attention was fixed upon Deputy Hank Posich, who was smiling at her.

Thirteen

THE BRAIN TRUST of Raven County law enforcement met Saturday morning in the spacious conference room of the prosecutor's office. Tony chaired the meeting. Whit sat to his left, Ted Early to his right. Sgt. Mel Trevayne of the state police held down the other end of the table. Milbrook Police Chief Thomas Wampler had been invited, but he declined—a previous engagement at the country club, Tony said.

Trevayne didn't appreciate the comment about Chief Wampler. "None of the crimes have occurred in his jurisdiction."

"So far," Whit said.

"And I might add," Tony said, "that the Dickerson woman was abducted from her house in the city limits. We don't really know where she was killed."

The prosecutor passed around a number of photographs of Ferdnand Tipton. "This is our suspect. All we have on him is a pickup order from the Department of Mental Health, but it's enough."

Trevayne didn't look at the stack of photos. "Well, Tony, my department will do what it can, but we're understaffed at the moment—"

"All we ask, Mel, is that you snag the guy if one of your men sees him."

"Be glad to keep an eye out for him."

Sheriff Early, possessing the abrasive innocence of an amateur politician, wasn't so easily satisfied. "I bet you guys will get interested when one of your wives gets butchered."

Trevayne took the time to light his pipe before replying. "Sheriff, you know our situation. We're working short shifts. I've got three positions out of eight not filled. We'll do all we can to help."

"It wouldn't hurt if you guys would start taking a few of the traffic accidents," Early said. "Damn! We don't have time to do anything but investigate accidents."

The thick smoke rolled out from Trevayne's pipe. "Now that's an exaggeration, Ted. We're carrying our load—"

Early bristled. "Are you calling me a liar?"

Tony pounded the desk with his fist. "Knock it off. I don't give a damn about your squabbles. I'm sure Trevayne's guys will help."

"The issue," Whit said, "is how we find Ferdie Tipton." God, how he despised meetings!

But Early came back with an answer. "We search Tabernacle Mountain."

Trevayne laughed.

"What so fuckin' funny?" Early snapped.

Tony leaned back in his chair and ran his hand over his face. "Ted, this is some of the roughest terrain in the East. I doubt we've got enough men to mount an effective search."

Early had come prepared. "We can get dogs. Dooley Chaffins has talked to the state correction people. They'd by happy to send their dogs down."

Trevayne's pipe had gone out. He was trying to light it again.

"That doesn't change the terrain," Whit said. "You have to be able to move through the country to track.

That mountain's laced with ravines, rock faces, briar patches—''

''And snakes,'' Trevayne said.

''Yeah, snakes too. Dooley can tell you about the snakes.''

Tony stood, pacing around the table. ''One thing, gentlemen. Besides catching Tipton, we have to prove he's guilty. I'd hate to find the bastard just to send him back to the state hospital. He'd walk away again.''

''Yeah,'' Whit said. ''Elope to get married.''

''So one of my men fucked up,'' Early said. ''He's new. Besides, if we get this idiot, he'll confess. Posich was telling me about him.''

''Telling you what?'' Tony asked.

''Ferdie Tipton! He carries a card around from the state hospital. Anytime he gets arrested he shows it and says it's okay because he's crazy.''

Tony and Whit both tried not to laugh.

''Did he try that last time?'' Tony asked.

''Sure! Yeah, when he got nabbed for stealing the poultry. That's what Hank told me.''

Tony placed his knuckles on the desk and leaned across toward Early. ''Just how likely are we to get a confession into evidence from someone like Ferdie? Hell, that's reason right there to exclude it!''

''I don't get you.''

''It means,'' Whit said, ''that his 'crazy card' may just work, Sheriff.''

''Aw, shit!'' Early said. ''You guys are the crazy ones.''

''I'm the lawyer around here,'' Tony retorted.

''Still sounds like a crock of shit to me,'' Early said.

Whit itched to be gone. ''Well, it doesn't amount to a popcorn fart if we don't find him first.''

Trevayne rose. ''I gotta run. Let me know if we can do anything.'' He turned to leave.

"The pictures," Whit said.

Trevayne turned. "Huh?"

"Would you mind taking the photos?"

"Oh, sorry. I just about forgot them. We'll get them out to the guys. The A.P.B.'s posted down at the office."

"So much for the state police," Whit said once the sergeant was gone.

"We need some kind of plan of action," Tony said, his voice sounding almost desperate. "What do you think about the dogs, Whit?"

Whit shrugged. "What else have we got? If Tipton's back here, it's a cinch he's up on that mountain."

"I guess you're right." The prosecutor turned to the sheriff. "Can you get those dogs here Monday morning?"

"I'll see what I can do."

"One more thing," Tony said. "Just so we don't put all our eggs in one basket, Sheriff, get us a list of all the people your deputies have arrested in, let's say, the past six months."

"All of them?" Early asked.

"All but the traffic citations. I guess that picnic's still on for tomorrow?" Tony asked.

Whit went to the window to stare out at the blue skies. "We can always pray for rain."

In a fashion, Whit's prayer was answered. The storm blew in around midnight Saturday. Tressa had just slipped into a light sleep when the wind gusted through her open window, sending the curtain snapping into the room. An explosion of blue white light was followed by an immediate crack as the towering clouds vented their static. Tressa sat up in bed. Her eyes bulged with an irrational fear born of near sleep. *Did I really hear that? Was it just a dream?*

Another downdraft from the base of the storm clouds gusted into her room.

It's for real.

Storms, violent with wind and rain and sound and light, unnerved her. When she was very small, she could always go cuddle up to Daddy. That made it better. But for many years she hadn't had Whit to calm her. What would happen if one of those jagged streaks of power struck the house? She thought of her mother and wondered if she was in bed. The hall light didn't fill the crack below her bedroom door.

The rain came. One moment it was windy but dry. The next, torrents of rain blew into her window. Tressa bounded from the bed to pull it down, hoping the lightning didn't catch her at the window. The rain beat with frustrated fury against the glass. Another bright flash, a sharp explosion; Tressa jumped back to the relative safety of her bed.

The lightning turned incessant—one flash after another, so close together that one seemed to feed on its predecessor. The night became a kaleidoscope of electric blue and yellow and white, of rainy gray and total darkness. Such storms didn't last long. Or at least they never had in the past, she thought . . . hoped.

Tressa drew the covers up to her neck, wanting to ignore the storm but unable to take her eyes from the window—always counting, as Whit had taught her, the beats between light and sound to see if the storm was moving away.

Earlier that evening he had called to see if she wanted to go to a picnic. Not a word about his sneaky trick the night before.

But Tressa had been gleeful. "A picnic? Really?"

Whit told her he needed a date. Would Tressa be his date?

"Why don't we invite Anna?"

The long, dead pause on the other end said it all.

"It was just an idea," Tressa had said.

"Not one of your better ones. Besides, she'll probably be there."

Would the storm scuttle the picnic?

God, she hoped not. She looked forward to it. Come Monday she was to go job hunting for the summer. She wanted to work. Usually she spent the summer lounging in the sun, going to the city pool, messing around. Not this summer.

To keep her mind off the climatic fury beyond the thin pane of window glass, she tried to catalog a list of possible employers. Following each house-jarring earth strike, she prayed for it to be the last.

After thirty minutes the storm ebbed. Tressa still counted the beats, happy that the length of time between the lightning and its rumble was increasing. The rain no longer assaulted her window. It fell in a light, steady patter.

And Tressa settled back to go to sleep.

But the sandman had abandoned her to the damp night. She was no longer sleepy.

Tressa stared at the rain-wet window, thinking of her father, wishing that he could find happiness. He tried so hard not to be bitter, but down deep he was scarred. Why, she didn't truly understand. Tressa's own love life had known some faltering first steps—dates for the movies, for a hamburger. And the boys had made their fumbling attempts to get into her pants. Their hands had made it no farther than her small, pert breasts.

Not that she was a prude. It was the guys. They were all so—so inept. She caught herself thinking about Kenny Shaffer and wondered why. God knows he wasn't the best-looking boy in school. And Linda Bowman had been right. He was a little backward socially. Still, she liked him and was attracted to him.

Then she heard sharp thunder again.

"Damn it," she whispered.

It was one of those nights. The seasons were battling for dominance. One storm after another rolled over Raven

County. *Just when you thought it was safe to go to sleep again.*

The storm hurried toward her, the grumbling turned to a roar, the roaring turned to claps of thunder and striking lightning.

Tressa squinched her eyes closed. *Ignore it.*

—crack—

Something in the room popped, crackled. Tressa leaped from the bed, sniffing the air to see if something was burning.

The wind again buffeted her window. Back into bed she climbed, puzzled that God would ever create anything as ugly as a storm. She called herself "silly" and propped the pillows up on the headboard. She fixed her eyes on the window, on the blackness outside, preparing herself for the next dazzling explosion of evil power.

It came. Tressa gasped. There, in the frame of her window, loomed the dark silhouette of a man.

Then darkness filled the window.

Tressa jammed the sheet to her mouth, choking off her scream. She waited for another flash—just to be sure. He was still here, displayed momentarily in the flash of the lightning. "Oh, Jesus," she cried.

Her feet went cold. Quaking with fear, she eased herself from her bed, praying that her legs didn't fold when they touched the floor.

Another flash.

He was closer, trying to look inside.

She whined as she inched backward toward the closed bedroom door.

Was the window locked?

No, dammit.

All he had to do was lift it.

Her hand found the knob. She turned it, then fled screaming from the room.

* * *

Whit stood at his patio door, watching the storm, thankful for the rain. His rhododendrons had started to droop. And maybe they would call off the picnic if it kept raining. When the phone rang, it was as if a bolt of lightning had struck him. He covered his hands with his face. "Please, not again. Not again."

But the voice on the other end belonged to Julia Pynchon. "Whitley"—always she called him that—"we have a prowler over here."

"What?"

"A prowler! Tressa saw him outside the window."

"In this storm?"

"Our daughter doesn't have a hysterical imagination."

That was true.

"On my way."

"I saw him, Daddy!"

Tressa verged on shock. Her body trembled, and her color was gone.

Whit wrapped his arms around her. "Okay, baby. I know you did. Can you describe him?"

"All I saw was the shape. He was trying to peek inside."

"Easy, Tressa."

Julia Pynchon loomed behind them. "What's this city coming to? People prowling. Whitley, you do realize this might have been the killer?"

Whit glared at his former wife. Even in her robe, her hair mussed, she remained a striking woman. The years had consumed her once-fiery beauty, though, transforming it into a stately severity. Julia was only thirty-nine; she looked and behaved as if she were fifty-nine.

"Julia, I know that."

"What do you intend to do?"

He dropped his head. "Julia, if I knew where this bastard was right now I'd—"

"There's no need for gutter language."

"Pardon me," he snapped. He turned back to his frightened daughter. "School's almost over. Why don't you go visit your grandmother?"

Then he spoke to Julia. "You could take a few days off too." Julia Pynchon worked at the library of the college.

"No, I could not. The summer session is under way already. My life isn't going to be disrupted, but I have no objections if Tressa wishes to go."

"It's your mother. I hope not."

"But I'm not going," Tressa said. "I'm going job hunting Monday."

"It might just have been a harmless prowler," Whit said.

Julia's laugh was full of sarcasm. "Somehow I don't think a harmless prowler would have braved this storm."

"Will you stay with us tonight?" Tressa asked.

"That's not a good idea."

Julia was quick to agree. "I have a weapon I'm not afraid to use."

"Just be careful with it," Whit said.

"So there's nothing more you can do?" Given the tone of Julia's voice, her words became more an accusation of parental negligence than a question.

The rain still fell outside. "There's no hope of finding tracks out there. I'll make a round or two around the house. And I'll make certain all the windows are locked. I'll also have the city police patrol the house."

Julia rolled her hard eyes at his offers, then said to Tressa, "If you're uncomfortable here, you can spend the night with your father."

For a moment Tressa's eyes brightened, but the moment's excitement vanished. "I couldn't leave you alone."

"I told you. I can protect myself."

Truly Whit didn't know what to do. The idea of leaving either of them, or both of them, alone put him in a quandary. On the other hand, he wasn't welcome in the house. Julia wasn't a tolerant woman.

"Leave the outside lights on," he said.

"Is that supposed to make us feel better?"

"Julia, what would you have me do?"

She stared at him. "Your job! Catch this killer." She wheeled and left the living room.

Whit turned to Tressa. "Tell me, hon, do you go to school with a Kenny Shaffer?"

Tressa didn't answer at once. When she did, there was a strange edge to her voice. "Yes, I do. Why?"

"What kind of kid is he?"

"He's a nice boy." Her eyes were defiant. "In fact, he might be taking me to the prom."

Whit clenched his jaws. "When did he ask you?"

"He doesn't know he's taking me yet."

"Is Kenny Shaffer the boy you're interested in?" The shock in his voice was obvious.

"What is this, Daddy? Why are you asking me about Kenny?"

"No reason, hon."

"Oh, sure. I know better."

"Really, hon, no reason. I met him the other day and he said he knew you."

"Where did you meet him?" Tressa's intensity was mounting.

Whit put a finger under Tressa's chin and lifted her face to his. "Why don't you go visit your grandma?"

She didn't answer. And in her eyes he recognized the same hardheaded determination he saw each morning in the mirror. Of that he was proud.

FOURTEEN

ELK RUN STATE Park, small as state parks go, occupied a plateau a third of the way up the eastern slope of Tabernacle Mountain. It offered nature trails, two ill-kept ball fields, a picnic area, and a minor waterfall. The state's guide to its parks reserved a single line for Elk Run: "A nice place to spend a day." The courthouse picnic was the biggest annual event held at Elk Run. Scheduled each year for the first weekend in June (with a standing rain date for the next weekend), it attracted courthouse employees, their families, lawyers, local law officers, and, in election years, a host of glad-handing politicians.

The photocopied handout circulated at the courthouse called it a "covered-dish" affair, meaning that everyone who attended was expected to bring something. And most everyone did. Bowls of baked beans, each individually flavored according to the distinctive recipe of its maker, filled one entire picnic table. Macaroni and potato salads filled another. Other bowls, each carefully labeled with the name of its owner, contained various Jell-o salads, vegetable casseroles, and cold cuts.

The culinary highlight of the picnic was the barbecuing of a side of beef, compliments of the Raven County Commission. It slowly turned over a bed of hickory-flavored coals. Juices bubbled and oozed from its charred surface, and its aroma drifted over the plateau. The two men who stood guard over the beef sipped at cans of beer. At the entrance to the park, a sign prohibited alcohol in the park, but the rule was unofficially waived for the picnic. After all, who was going to enforce it, anyway? The county's magistrates, judges, and police officers enjoyed a cool beer on a hot day as much as anyone. And more than one person's breath was scented with the odor of stronger spirits, sipped from bottles concealed in vehicles.

At one of the ball fields, the lawyers tackled the cops in a game of softball. Even without the arm of grieving Gil Dickerson, the barristers were no match for the younger police officers. Within a few innings the score had reached 21 to 2, advantage to the cops. It gave the police a chance to even a few scores. At the picnic area a group of women organized the late-afternoon feast. They kept wary eyes to the skies. The ground remained damp from the soaking of the night storm; forecasters predicted a forty percent chance of thunderstorms. The skies, though, remained cloudless.

Tim Franklin begged off his position at shortstop midway through the game—right after he'd knocked a fly ball to center field where a young lawyer, more athletic than his compatriots, made a spectacular dive to steal Franklin's hit. Franklin, who had something on his mind other than base running, appreciated his effort. Out of the corner of his eye he had noticed Missie Posich moving toward the rest rooms.

Franklin tossed his glove to Linnerman. "Take over for me, Lieutenant. I gotta make a trip to the john."

Linnerman threw the glove back. "Like hell! I'm not getting all hot and sweaty. Go piss over in the bushes."

"Gotta do more than piss. I wouldn't wanna get snake bit or anything, especially on the ass."

He dropped the glove to the ground, not caring who moved to his position, and headed for the toilets. Hank

Posich, unofficial coach of the team, sidled over to Linnerman. "Where's he going?"

"To take a crap."

"Lazy bastard," Hank muttered.

Missie was bored. She had Kenny Shaffer on her mind. He was so young, so inexperienced—an uncut diamond, totally uncut until she had come along. One day, if some woman didn't ruin him, he'd be a hell of a stud. She finished up in the hot bathroom and stepped out into the forest shade.

"Hi, Missie."

She yelped, startled.

"God, Tim! You scared me."

"Sorry. I saw you wander over here. Thought you might like to take a hike in the woods."

Missie quickly glanced around. "Jesus, Tim, Hank's here."

"Shit, he's back there playing coach."

"I have to get back and help with the food."

Tim tried to slip an arm around her. "Hell, Missie, they got enough cooks already. Come on."

She danced away from him. "No, Tim!" She started to walk away.

Tim reached out and snagged her arm. "Hey, what's up your ass? I was good enough for you last week."

The perspiration dampened her thin blouse. "Just leave me alone!" His grip hurt her arm.

"Are you dumping me?" The anger flashed in his dark brown eyes.

"You're hurting me," she said.

"I oughta break your neck, you two-timin'—"

They both heard voices. Tim released her arm.

Whit Pynchon and Tony Danton came around the corner

of the building. They nodded to Missie, who used the opportunity to hurry back toward the picnic area.

"Hi, Mr. Danton . . . , Whit." Franklin smiled broadly at both men.

"Figured you'd be playing ball, Tim." Whit said.

"Nature called. You understand?"

Whit looked over his shoulder at the departing Missie Posich. "I sure do."

Franklin clapped his hands. "Better get back to the game. Linnerman's too old to handle shortstop for too long." The young officer trotted off.

"You get the feeling we interrupted something?" Tony asked as they both stood at the urinals in the men's room.

"One of these days, Hank is going to find out about his wife."

Tony went to the single washbasin first. "When he does, we may have several more killings on our hands. Somehow I can't see Posich as the forgive-and-forget kind."

The wind shifted, and an upslope breeze transported the odor of the cooking beef to Ferdie Tipton. He sat at the mouth of his mine shaft home, his nose twitching at the scent. It reeked of the cooked food of the hospital, but his belly ached with hunger. He hadn't eaten since the previous day, then just a chipmunk and a handful of grub worms.

He got to his feet and traced the odor down the mountain toward Elk Run State Park.

When Whit and Tony got back to the picnic area, they found Tressa seated on a huge rock with Anna Tyree. "I was telling Anna about last night," she said as they approached.

"What about last night?" Tony asked.

"I had a prowler."

"A prowler?" Tony turned harsh eyes on Whit. "I haven't heard about this. Did you see him?"

"Just his shadow," Tressa said.

Anna wrapped her arms around herself. "It gives me the heebie-jeebies."

"I hope this isn't going to end up on page one tomorrow," Whit said.

Anna thought about it, then shook her head. "No way. Page two maybe, but never page one."

"Dammit, that's why—"

"Easy, Dad. She's kidding."

Tony slapped his friend on the back. "God, you're touchy." He looked to Anna. "He overreacts."

"Overreacts?" Anna stood. "He detonates."

Tony whistled. Anna wore a pair of shorts that barely concealed her shapely buttocks. A halter top tied beneath her breasts displayed a tanned and smooth stomach. "Pardon me," he said, "but it's a matter of sheer admiration."

Anna grinned. "It's a hot day. I dressed for it."

Whit motioned for Tressa. "Let's get something cold to drink."

As they walked away, Tressa peered back over her shoulder at Anna and winked. Her father, she suspected, was jealous.

The softball game petered out. The lawyers conceded their loss and vowed to get even in court. The cops didn't doubt that for a moment, so they took the opportunity to gloat in their victory.

"Next time we oughta make it football," Hank said to one of the attorneys.

"Yeah. Touch football," the lawyer said.

"Hell, no," Hank countered. "Real football . . . tackle football."

''Dinner's ready!'' came a loud female cry.

Missie manned the coffeepot. The first person to her station was Bill Curtis. She looked up at the tall, bulky man and was at once pleased. ''Who are you?'' she asked.

''Deputy Bill Curtis. I just joined the—''

''Oh, Hank's mentioned you. I'm Missie. Hank's wife.''

Curtis beamed. ''Hey, nice to meet you.''

They traded approving smiles and would have talked longer, but the coffee line began to back up.

Tressa was ahead of her father in line. Once her plate was loaded, she went to sit with Anna, who balanced a full plate herself.

Tony nudged Whit from behind. ''Your daughter is rather taken with Annie Tyson-Tyree.''

''Next thing I know she's going to want to be a reporter. I'll disown her.''

''Right now, I think she's more interested in being a matchmaker. I'll say this for Miss Tyree. I've never seen better legs or a more perfect ass.''

''You're a degenerate, Tony.''

''Uh-huh. I bet you go right over and sit with your daughter.''

Whit was loading Mary Linnerman's famed baked beans on his plate. It was chocked full of ham. ''Can't let you beat my time, Tony. By the way, where's your wife?''

''She never comes to these things.''

''Does she even know about them?''

Both Tony and Whit did join Tressa and Anna. Tony set his plate down and announced that he was going to try to find some beer for the three of them.

''Why not me?'' Tressa asked.

Tony looked to Whit for permission.

''No way. I might need a sober chauffeur this evening.''

Tony shrugged his apologies and headed off. Anna

waited until Tony was out of earshot. "I wanted to warn you, Whit. The newspaper's running an editorial tomorrow asking why this killer hasn't been caught."

"Jesus, what do you folks expect?"

"Hey, I don't write the editorials. I tried my best to talk them out of it."

Whit ate in silence for a moment, the joy gone from the brown beans. When he spoke, he said, "Tony will have apoplexy. He hates bad press."

"But not you?" Anna asked.

"I don't care, Anna. You can't seem to believe that."

"You're convincing me."

"We might never get him," Hank was saying to the two lawyers eating across the table from him. He swatted at a pesky fly that seemed interested in only his plate. "I think it's an out-of-towner—someone doing it just for the kicks."

One of the lawyers shook his head as he ate. "My wife's terrified, and I'm not even a cop. She took the kids to her mother's. I almost went too."

The others at the table chuckled. Missie ate in silence, glancing every chance she got at Bill Curtis, who sat with his frumpy wife at the other end of the table. She heard little of what was being said.

"Missie!"

The harshness of her husband's voice jarred her from her thoughts. "I'm sorry. I guess I was daydreaming."

Hank pointed a fork at the lawyer. "I was telling him that you had no intention of leaving town because of the killings."

"Uhhh . . . No. Of course not."

One of the young lawyers said, "It'll be my luck to get appointed to the case if and when he gets nailed."

"No way," another lawyer said. "The judge will give

the guy to one of us more experienced lawyers, just to be safe."

Hank narrowed his eyes. "I never understood how you guys can represent such sleazebags. I mean, you know they're guilty as sin."

"Not until a jury says so," the young lawyer countered.

His more experienced buddy patted him on the shoulder. "Oh, to once again have the virgin flush of innocence. You'll have to overlook him, Hank. He's fresh outa school."

"But it's true," the young man protested.

"It's bullshit," snapped Hank.

The younger attorney waited on his veteran friend to come to his assistance. The older lawyer chewed silently on his beef, then said, "Hank's right. It's bullshit . . . mumbo jumbo."

"You represent them too," Hank accused.

The lawyer nodded, his mouth full of food. "Only when the court makes me," he mumbled. "I hate handling criminal cases."

"Your heart's in the right place," Hank said.

The lawyer grinned. "My heart is in my hip pocket. There's no money in criminal cases. For the right fee I'd have represented Attila the Hun."

Ferdie lay sprawled on the edge of a high cliff overlooking Elk Run State Park. He saw the crowd below, all of them concentrated around the tables. His nose reacted to the odor of the food. His eyes reacted to the women, many of them wearing shorts, and T-shirts that accentuated the swells and hard nipples of their breasts.

Tony basked in the glow of a good meal. He smoked a long and thick cigar, its heavy smoke rising in a vertical cloud in the stagnant air of the late afternoon. Whit smoked a cigarette.

"That thing reeks," Tressa said of the cigar. "And you told me you weren't smoking, Daddy."

"It keeps the gnats away," Tony said.

"There aren't any gnats," Tressa countered.

"See . . . it works."

Anna and Whit laughed.

Tressa couldn't sit still. "I wanna go for a walk, maybe to the waterfalls."

Whit frowned. "That's not a good idea."

"You can come along. You have your gun."

"Christ, Dad," Tony quipped. "It's broad daylight. Your anxiety is overworked."

Anna got up. "I'll walk with you."

Whit relented. "Okay, but keep an eye on the sky. Be back in an hour or so. If you aren't, you're in big trouble."

"Does that go for me too?" Anna asked.

Tony grinned. "Are you kidding? Whit would love to turn you over his knee."

Tressa, Anna, and Tony were each shocked to see Whit Pynchon blush.

FIFTEEN

MARY LINNERMAN HIKED toward Elk Run Falls, too, but she had chosen a more difficult trail, one that led over a spiny rib on the mountain's slope. She walked alone. She had tried to find company, but the other wives had begged off. Not a one said she was frightened, but it was obvious. They stuck close to the protection of their men. So Mary went by herself. And she hadn't told Dan, who would have forbidden it.

Mary loved the woods. She'd been raised in Virginia near the Blue Ridge where she had spent many a summer day walking the mountains. The sensations revived vague memories. She inhaled the pungent, rich odor of the mountain. A springtime forest, it smelled of new life.

The trail made a determined climb up the slope. Huge rocks, pushed here by glaciers if she remembered her science, flanked the narrow path. Channels, their floors padded with a carpet of dead leaves and brown pine needles, ran between the rocks. Each begged to be explored. If God existed, then, in Mary's mind, he inhabited just such places.

Blankets of kelly green moss draped some of the boulders. Lacy ferns, planted in symmetry by a divine hand, fronted the boulders. The filtered sunlight and buffered silence lent the place an ethereal quality. God's Chapel, Mary thought.

She rested on a small rock, anxious not to disturb the place's peace. After she'd been still for several minutes, a small lizard peeked out its head, then dashed across the trail. A crow, cawing and graceful, settled in the branch of a tall birch. And a granddaddy longlegs stepped herky-jerky across the cushion of pine needles.

The light within the forest had already started to dim. Dusk came much earlier on the northeastern slope of the densely forested mountain. Mary rose, sorry to leave. The path peaked on the spine, then started a gentle descent toward the falls. Mary heard the soft murmur of an unseen brook, one of many that converged in the ravine below to form Elk Run.

Wood snapped somewhere.

Mary halted, listened.

The rushing whisper of the brook, she heard. Nothing else. It became louder; perhaps she was just listening harder. Mary resumed her descent.

But she stopped again to listen, certain she had heard the sound again, the sharp crack of a twig and the rustling of bushes or dried leaves—the sound of an indiscreet foot in a tender place. *A small animal.*

More likely a larger animal, she decided—a bear or even a coyote. The bear had never left the rugged mountains, and the coyote was said to be making a comeback.

The piney glade through which she had passed gave way to a stand of deciduous trees, their trunks surrounded by low dense brush—second growth, the environmentalists called it. The forest had suddenly turned ugly.

Mary Linnerman hastened her descent toward the falls.

Ferdie watched the woman scamper down. Her weight pushed her down the incline, but she moved like a person used to the forest. Ferdie wore only a leather guard over his genitals. He had fashioned it from a vest that he had found in the rubble of his house. His bare feet, now toughened, carried him from one rock to another. He moved parallel to the woman, high above her.

Ferdie got occasional glimpses of her face. Once she looked straight at him. He hunkered down, crouching as he danced to keep up. Had she seen him?

Anna and Tressa swatted at the moving clouds of gnats in their faces. "They're terrible," Anna cried. "We should have borrowed one of those cigars."

"I'd rather have the gnats," Tressa said. "You wanna turn back?"

"I hear the falls. I'd love to see them."

"It's not like Niagara Falls or anything."

Anna dug one of the small creatures from the hollow of her ear. "They ought to spray or something. I remember reading about these gnats. The sportsmen and campers want them sprayed; the naturalists don't. I just changed sides. I figured the environmentalists knew what they were talking about. Now I'm not so sure."

"I bet it's fun being a reporter," Tressa said.

Anna chuckled. "Boy, what would Whit Pynchon say?"

"Something obscene, I'm sure," Tressa said, adding, "Seriously, he isn't as mean as he seems."

Anna was becoming winded. "You keep . . . saying . . . that, but I don't know." Her words came between deep breaths. "I get the impression . . . Whit . . . can be . . . pretty rough."

"With a heart of gold. You want to stop for a breather?"

"I'm afraid . . . if we stop . . . the gnats will carry . . . carry us to their nest or something."

"The falls aren't too far."

The logging trail widened. The trees seemed to shrink. High cliffs became visible to their left.

"I have to stop . . . a minute. Whew!" Under the sun's

assault, Anna's face glistened with perspiration. "I thought I was in better shape," she said, slowly getting her breath.

The gnats swarmed her. "Damn, this is bad." She waved her hands in front of her face.

Tressa wasn't listening. Her attention was riveted to the top of a shale cliff. "I saw something up there."

"Up where?" Anna shaded her eyes as she looked up.

"There." Tressa pointed.

A dark shape hurdled over the rim. Arms and legs flopped against the air.

"Oh, my God," cried Anna.

The body crashed into heavy brush fifty yards off the trail.

Tressa's shoulders started to quake. Her hands went to cover her face. She froze. Anna started for the base of the cliff, but the wall of dense, menacing vegetation intimidated her.

She returned to Tressa. "Come on. Get yourself together. Let's get help."

The young girl's face reflected her emotional discomfort. Tears pooled in her eyes, the pupils wide with fright and shock. "It was . . . was a woman."

"Let's go, hon." Anna put an arm around Tressa.

But the young girl's gaze was locked on the high cliff. Anna grasped her arm and pulled. "We've got to hurry!"

Tressa nodded without any sense of understanding.

Anna couldn't leave her. She got behind her and pushed. Tressa moved only as far as Anna pushed. Her pupils were fixed, her face chalky. In one quick move, Anna's hand struck with moderate force across Tressa's cheek.

Whit's daughter broke down, crying but running, and running the right way. Anna ran too. They both forgot the gnats as they fled down the trail toward the picnic area.

The women moved among the dishes. Some bowls were

scraped clean; others almost full. "Boy, my casserole was a flop," one said, staring with disgust at the untouched dish of crumbs and broccoli.

Dan Linnerman mingled among them. "Have you seen Mary?" he asked.

"Let me think. Yes, right after supper."

Missie Posich shoveled potato chips back into a waxed bag. "She asked me if I wanted to go for a walk to the falls. Maybe she went up there?"

"A walk? In the woods?"

"Yes," Missie said.

"She said she loved hiking," another woman said.

"And no one tried to stop her? No one came and told me?" He was at first incredulous, then angry.

Whit put a hand on his back. "Easy, Dan. My daughter and Anna Tyree went up there too. I'm sure they're all right."

"I gotta stop!" Anna said.

Tressa stopped too, her own breath coming in deep, rasping gulps. They both were bent at the waist, their legs ready to give out at any minute.

"It's not far," Tressa said.

"Thank God."

The shadows were lengthening, darkening. The sun dipped ever lower toward the mountain ridge.

"Ok, let's go," Anna said.

"Who was it?" Tressa asked.

"Hon, I have no idea. Let's get out of here. Come on."

Anna glanced into the forest. She cried out as her eyes fell upon the man, standing near the thick base of a tree. He leered at her, a half smile showing on his dark, bestial face. Anna couldn't help it. She screamed.

Tressa hadn't seen anything yet, but the sheer terror contained in Anna's scream sent Tressa into hysterics. Her head whirled as she sought the source of the horror. She saw him too.

They forgot their fatigue.

Linnerman heard it first. He stood with Tony Danton, discussing the search planned for the next morning. "What was that?"

Tony listened. A chill tightened his neck. He looked around for Whit. The investigator now heard it. "That's Tressa!"

The screams were for "Daddy!"

Whit broke into a run up the logging trail. The other men, cops and lawyers, followed, but Whit reached the two women first. Both of them crashed into him.

"I saw him," Tressa gasped. "Back there. He was ugly and almost naked. And this woman, she came over the cliff . . . back there."

"What?" Whit tried to make sense of what she was saying.

Linnerman rushed up. "Mary? Where's Mary? Did you see her?"

Tressa stared at him.

"My wife, dammit! Was she up there?"

Anna's face twisted into a look of pity. "There was a woman. We saw her. She fell—"

Linnerman's face went slack. "Where?"

Anna didn't want to tell him. She knew the woman was dead—absolutely, positively knew it.

"Let's slow down," Whit was saying. "We need a clear idea—"

But Linnerman was frantic. "Where? God, where did you see her?" His hands shook Anna's shoulders.

"She fell—from a cliff."

"Oh, Jesus! Where?"

Whit managed to loosen Linnerman's grasp on Anna.

"Back there," Tressa said. "Almost to the falls."

It became chaos. The crowd of policemen, imbued with the sense of the hunt, surrounded the two women, demanding details. Whit tried to command order.

Finally, he bellowed, "Stop it!"

The power of his voice overcame the pandemonium. "Let's sort this out." He turned to Anna. "Tell us what you saw."

"I'm trying to think. Tressa said we were almost to the falls and—"

"Was Mary there, dammit?" Linnerman demanded.

Whit shoved him away. "Give her a chance, man!"

"My wife's up there!"

Anna clenched her fist. "Give me time!"

"She was thrown from a cliff," Tressa managed to say. For the moment her composure was greater than that of the older woman. "We were coming back to get help when we saw this man in the woods."

"Can you tell us where?" Whit asked.

Tressa nodded that she could. "We were maybe a quarter of a mile from the falls. Those cliffs there."

Dooley Chaffins was there too. "You mean the area that was timbered?"

"Yeah!" Tressa said.

Chaffins nodded. "I know where she means, at least the general vicinity."

"Now, Tressa," Whit said, "where did you see the man?"

"Not too far back."

"Was that when you screamed?" Tony asked.

"Uh-huh."

Tony began to organize the officers. "We'll divide up. Half of us will go up and try to find that cliff. The other half can search for the man they saw."

"Can you show us?" Whit asked. "Either of you?"

"I think so," Anna said, once again finding a semblance of calm. "But we could use something to drink."

Missie Posich went after it.

Whit eyed the setting sun. "We have to hurry."

Linnerman, though, was already headed up the trail. Tony shouted at him to wait.

"Let him be, Tony. He's entitled."

The women and the men who were not officers hung back, trying to stay out of the way. One of the attorneys came forward. "We'll go help in the search for the woman."

"Don't get trigger-happy," Tony said.

"Why not?" Tim Franklin asked, pushing his way to the front. "I just heard what happened."

Within a few minutes, the large group started up the trail. A few of the older men, lawyers and courthouse employees, remained with the women. Anna and Tressa walked with Whit. Many of the officers carried shotguns that they had in the trunks of their vehicles.

"Just tell us where you saw the man," Whit said once they were under way.

Dusk was upon them.

"It looks so different now," Anna said.

"Right now the important thing is locating Linnerman's wife," Tony said from behind them. "She may be alive."

"I couldn't reach her. She fell in heavy brush," Anna said, the emotion cracking her voice.

"It was there!" Tressa exclaimed.

"Where you saw the man?" the sheriff asked.

Whit looked to Anna.

"I think she's right," Anna said.

Early eyed the darkening woods. "Not much light left. That terrain is rough, too."

Tony agreed. "Perhaps we'd better put the search off for

the suspect until tomorrow. We have dogs being brought here. At least it'll give us a starting place."

"We don't even know that the person they saw was Tipton," Whit said. "I didn't bring the photo of him."

Tressa shivered. "He looked like an animal."

Hank Posich materialized from the crowd. "I'm going after him tonight."

"Y'all can do what you want," Whit said. "Our group's going on up to the falls."

Half the group left the other half debating whether to postpone the search for the man that Tressa and Anna had encountered.

The dusk had deepened when they heard the voice of Dan Linnerman. He was calling his wife's name.

"We're close," Anna said.

They could hear the soft rush of Elk Run Falls.

Some of the men carried flashlights that they flipped on as they neared the falls. The procession offered a strange sight as it wound its way along the logging road.

Anna's eye scanned the darkening road ahead. "Look there," she said.

Dan Linnerman sat on a fallen tree up ahead of them, his hands in his head.

"Why did you leave her?" he said as they neared.

Anna wanted to comfort him, but Whit held her back. "There's nothing you can say."

Anna glanced over her shoulder. "There's the cliff!"

Hank, Early, Franklin, and two state troopers fumbled their way through the shadowy woods. The forest obstructed them with every step. Vines whipped their faces. Rock crevices snapped at their feet. The flashlights they carried did little to push back the coming night.

A trooper stopped first. "This is senseless. One of us is going to end up snakebit."

"Or with a broken ankle," the other said.

Early sighed. "You guys are right. Besides, it'll be much easier with the dogs."

"And the daylight," a trooper said. "This here mountain's treacherous enough in daylight."

Hank shook his head. "I never seen such a bunch of pansies. That cocksucker might be right in our hands if we keep lookin'."

"Or we might be walkin' into his," Franklin said.

Early decided. "We turn back."

"Well, goddamn," Hank growled. "Y'all go on. I'll be there in a while. I'm going to keep searching."

One of the attorneys found Mary Linnerman. She lay face up, her back arched over a blood-splattered rock. Her face stared up at him, her eyes unflinching against the glare of the flashlight.

"She's here," he cried, his manly voice cracking.

Whit reached him first. His flashlight surveyed her body. "Nothing anybody could have done for her." It had worried Whit, the idea that the woman might have been lying in the dark woods suffering. She hadn't suffered.

Linnerman came bursting through the brush. Whit grabbed him, pushing him back. "You don't want to see."

"Is she—"

Whit held him back. "She's gone, Dan. She fell on a rock. It was quick."

Anna and Tressa waited with Tony Danton down on the trail. They heard Dan Linnerman's cry of grief. Now he knew what they both had already known.

SIXTEEN

WHIT DROVE TRESSA and Anna back to Milbrook in Anna's car. Tony followed in Whit's. They passed an ambulance about halfway to Milbrook.

"Is it going after her?" Tressa asked.

Whit said that it was. Sheriff Early's vehicle traveled just ahead of them. He had Dan Linnerman in his car. The other deputies had stayed with his wife's body.

Whit slammed his fist against the console of Anna's car. "If we could just get some evidence—"

"But we saw him," Anna said.

"Saw him do what?" Whit asked. "From what you've told me, Mary Linnerman might just have fallen from that cliff."

"But she soared, just like she was thrown," Anna protested.

Tressa sat in the back seat, saying nothing.

"Well, at least we can arrest him for running off from the state hospital."

The reporter within Anna resurfaced. "From where? You know who he is?"

Whit realized he had slipped. "Maybe."

"Is that what you meant back there when you were talking about pictures?"

What the hell! It's done now. "I think the man you saw

is Ferdnand Tipton. He escaped from the state mental hospital last Saturday.''

''They let a killer escape?''

''He wasn't a killer. He was a chicken thief.''

''A chicken thief?''

''Yeah, he went to the state hospital a thief. He came out a killer.''

''Would you kindly explain?''

Whit told her the story of Ferdnand Tipton and his brother. Tressa kept silent in the back seat, her eyes staring out at the maturing night.

''You okay, Tressa?'' he asked when he had finished with the story.

''Yes.''

''I'm sorry you had to see what you saw,'' he said, glancing in the rearview, seeing her tortured face in the headlights of an oncoming car.

''Was that the man outside our window?'' she asked.

''I doubt it,'' Whit said. ''It was probably just a prowler, maybe a peeping tom.''

But Whit too wondered.

''In other words,'' Anna said, ''you don't really know for sure that the killer is this Tipton man?''

''Huh?'' She'd caught Whit thinking, still wondering.

''You can't prove that this Tipton fellow is the killer?''

''No, we can't. He's just a suspect. And I trust that you won't print any of what I told you.''

''I'm going to say that you have a suspect.''

''But nothing more?''

They were coming into Milbrook. Closed service stations and produce markets lined the road into town. Their lights illuminated the interior of the car. Anna stared at the tense face of Whit Pynchon. ''Just that,'' she said. ''Nothing more.''

* * *

Missie Posich wanted to make love that night. She spent a long time in the bathroom, carefully and very lightly dabbing the scent of perfume in various places on her body.

Beyond the bathroom door, she heard Hank prowling the house. He had come home much later than she had, and he was a mess. The tragedy at the picnic had unnerved him. She could tell, even if he wouldn't admit it. Down deep, beneath that tough sandpaper exterior, Hank Posich was a kind man. That's what she kept telling herself.

He pounded on the bathroom. "For Christ's sake, woman, get a move on. I wanna wash off this sweat."

She smiled and opened the door, standing stark naked before him.

"Where's your robe?"

"It's so hot," she purred. She slipped her arms around his neck. The aroma of his sweat aroused her. She liked the smell of sweaty men.

He backed away from her. "I need a shower."

"You smell sexy." She pursued him.

Hank made a face. "Sexy? Jesus, woman, you're crazy. I stink. I'm taking a shower."

He pushed by her and went into the bathroom.

Missie threw up her hands and went to their bedroom to wait on him, ejecting Tear Gas from the bed. At least Hank was aroused. She had felt his erect penis as she pressed against him. Why had God been so cruel? Why had he mismatched the sexual peaks of men and women?

Back when they had first married, she couldn't keep him out of her pants. Now, when she so often felt the urge, she practically had to rape him. Visions of Bill Curtis filled her mind. Someday, she wanted to try two men at once. Sometimes, as she lay alone doing things to herself, she fantasized about a harem—her harem. She imagined a huge room, full of satin pillows, brightly colored, and a stable of young men, each of them anxious and ready to service her.

"What are you doing?"

Hank's voice startled her. She jerked her hand from between her legs. "Warming it up for you," she said.

He stood over her, wearing nothing but his pajama bottoms. His arms were streaked by scratches.

"My God, Hank!" A profusion of fine, freshly clotted lacerations laced his arms.

"I got into a bunch of thorns while we was looking for that scumbag."

She sat up and started to lick his hairy, thick arms. "I'll make them better."

He tried to pull away, but she held him.

"I gotta get up early tomorrow. We're gonna take dogs after that guy."

Her tongue drifted from his arm to his chest, down his belly. Her hand pressed into the opening on his pajamas. The snaps popped open, and the bottoms dropped down around his ankles. She kissed his belly, then the shaft of his penis. Hank grabbed her head, forcing her mouth onto him. It choked and gagged her.

She at first resisted, then gave in as he started to move violently in her mouth.

Just as she was beginning to find her rhythm, he pushed her back on the bed. "You always did know how to get me going."

Dan Linnerman returned to his house just before midnight. Earlier the sheriff had called the woman keeping their kids. Usually the kids went to the picnic, but both of them had summer colds. Mary had thought it best if they stayed in. *Mary, dear Mary, had been too right.*

"I'm so sorry, Dan." The woman who always kept the Linnerman children was like a grandmother to them all.

Dan had known her since he was a child. He went to her, allowed her arms to envelop him, and he cried, just as he had so many years before when this same woman had told him that his father had died.

"Why?" he said, her face pressed against his chest.

"God has his ways, son."

He pulled away. "God? Would a God leave those two children to grow up without a mother?"

She held his hand. "Now, don't say things you don't mean. There's a time to be born and a time to die. The Bible says so."

"He threw her off a cliff! I saw her, lying there on a rock, broken and—her blood all over it."

Dan Linnerman sunk to his knees. "I tried to get her to leave. I tried. Damn, I should have made her go. I should have made her go."

The older woman put a hand on his head. "She was willful, Dan."

The boy child came into the room, his eyes bleary with sleep. "Hi, Daddy. Where's Mommy?"

Linnerman bit his lip against his tears. "Hi, Son. Is your sister asleep?"

The young boy nodded.

"Go wake her up," he said. "Bring her in here."

"It'll keep until morning," the woman said once the child was gone.

"I've got to do it now. In the morning I may not be able to. What do I say?"

"The truth, Dan. You remember when I told you. You weren't much older than Billie."

Dan remembered.

The little boy brought his sister back into the room. They stood there, almost eye level with their father, who was still on his knees.

He smiled through his tears. "I just realized how much you both look like your mother."

"Where is Mommy?" the boy asked again.

Dan looked up to the woman. She waited.

He took both of them in his arms. "Mommy's gone to heaven. She won't be coming back."

"Did she want to go?" the girl child asked.

"Well, no—"

The woman leaned down. "Hon, sometimes we all have to do things we don't want to do. Your mother didn't want to go, but she had to. God called her to heaven to be with him."

"But what about us?" the girl asked. "We want to go too."

The woman grinned. "When it's your time, you will."

"But I thought just old people went to heaven," the boy said.

"Did God come after her?" the girl asked.

The woman nodded.

"Did you see him, Daddy?"

Linnerman's lips quivered. He fought back the emotion that wanted to burst forth as he looked into the two faces of his children. "No . . . hon, I didn't."

"I wish she had come home first." With that, the little girl turned back to her bedroom.

The boy remained. "Did the man kill her?" he asked.

"Child," said the woman, "how do you know about that?"

"I'm five. I know about things like that."

Linnerman grabbed his son into his arms and cried. The small child patted his father on the back. For the first time the woman too cried, not so much for Mary Linnerman, though God knows she mourned her, but more for Dan and the trials that he faced.

* * *

The rain came down from low, gunmetal clouds. Monday's dawn had come late and weak, the June sun shrouded by the low overcast.

"I didn't think it was supposed to rain like this," Tony said, staring out the window of his office.

Whit nodded. "It wasn't. It seems an upper-level low-pressure system slipped up from the south. Or so the weatherman said. I'm beginning to wonder if this killer can conjure weather to suit his liking. It's supposed to do this all frigging day."

"Typical June weather," Tony said. "Unpredictably wet."

Dooley Chaffins was there too, along with Sheriff Early. "The guys from the pen were willing to take the dogs into the mountains, but it wouldn't do no good. No dog could do much tracking in this kind of weather, especially on that mountain."

Tony turned from the window. "Are they going to stay?"

Chaffins shook his head. "No, they said they'd come back day after tomorrow."

Tony kicked the leg of his desk. "Dammit to hell. Why today of all days?"

Already that morning the phone calls had started. Last week it had just been ABC News. So far this morning he'd taken calls from CBS and a couple of independent television and radio stations. A reporter for a Charleston newspaper had insisted upon an interview. Tony had told him to "go to hell." The Milbrook paper's editorial had soured him on the press in general.

"So what do we do?" he asked. "Sit around and wait for him to kill again?"

Sheriff Early had been quiet, unusually so. He was in something of a state of shock. Three of his men had lost wives in less than a week. "I think I'm going to make the men send their wives out of town, every one of them. If we can't catch this son of a bitch, at least we can deprive him of his targets."

"I doubt you can do that," Tony said.

Chaffins rubbed his squared jaw. "My old lady ain't going nowhere. She told me that last night. I doubt if you fired me it would change her mind."

Whit was thinking of Tressa, thinking of what he was going to say to convince her to visit her grandmother for a while.

Tony pursed his lips. "I'm thinking about asking the FBI to come in and check out Gil Dickerson's house with a fine-tooth comb. Maybe we can come up with some trace evidence. You know what they say. No one goes into a room without leaving something—or leaves one without taking something with him or on him."

"What?" Early said, his brow furrowed.

"It's a principle in forensic investigation," Whit explained. "You remember those child killings in Atlanta? Most of their evidence was based upon fiber analysis."

"Why the FBI?" Early asked.

"Because I don't think the state lab can handle it," Tony said.

But Whit shook his head. "Hell, Tony, the crime scene's contaminated. Think how many people have been at that house since the murder."

"We should have done it at the time," Tony snapped. "You slipped up, Whit."

Tony Danton was showing his frustration. Whit understood that. Still he wasn't about to be made a scapegoat. "Look, Tony, anytime you don't think I can handle this job, just say so. I'd like to get the hell out of this town anyway."

Tony blinked. "I don't know why I said what I said, Whit. I apologize."

The phone sounded.

"Jesus Christ, more trouble." Tony answered it. "Tell them I'm tied up."

He slammed down the phone. "That makes it unanimous. That was NBC News. Jesus, they're sending film crews down here."

"We have our own serial killer," Whit said. "That's news."

Early rose to leave. "Well, I got other things to do. Are we going to plan the search again for Wednesday?"

Tony shrugged. "If that's the best we can do."

Chaffins followed the sheriff out.

Tony began fiddling with the papers on his desk. "I want to apologize again, Whit. I didn't mean it."

"We're all getting edgy."

"I feel so fuckin' helpless. And we got all these damned news people crawling around."

"Tell them to take a hike. Refuse to talk to them."

Tony gazed out at the falling rain. "Maybe I'll name you as liaison to the press during this investigation."

"You know how I'll handle them."

"From what I saw Sunday you're handling at least one of them a little different nowadays."

Whit blushed. "Tressa likes her."

"Just Tressa?"

"Okay, asshole, lay off." Whit got up to leave.

Tony followed him. "What is it with you? I think she's a pretty good-looking woman. She seems nice—for a reporter."

"Drop it, okay?"

But Tony wasn't about to drop it. Not often was he able to needle Whit Pynchon. "It's about time you showed some interest in females. People were beginning to wonder about you, Whit."

By that time Whit had reached his office. He wheeled on his employer. "Meaning?"

Tony backed away. "Meaning nothing."

"One of these days," Whit said, slamming his door.

He went to his desk and picked up the paper. Anna's story was bannered across the front page.

"WOMANSLAYER STRIKES AT PICNIC."

The byline read "Annie Tyson-Tyree."

"Damn you," he said to the byline. Tony Danton was right. As much as Whit wanted to deny it, Annie Tyson-Tyree was getting into his bloodstream—just like a goddamned disease.

Seventeen

Emma Foley's graveside service was a media event. Reporters mingled with mourners. Camera crews, their high-powered equipment protected from the rain by plastic, checked lighting and adjusted settings. They preferred the gradually thinning overcast. It eliminated the glare of a bright sun and the sharp shadows. And it created the proper ambience for a funeral. Producers and reporters hustled various public officials before the cameras for interviews.

Poor Emma—the end of her life lost to the insanity of the tale—waited in the hearse. In the past the dead were hurried into their graves. Formaldehyde, however, temporarily vanquished the Conqueror Worm and allowed grieving families the opportunity to gather. Emma's family had driven up from Florida. The autopsy too had delayed the ceremony. And gravediggers didn't work on Sundays, so the funeral had been scheduled for Monday. It was just as well. Otherwise many of those who were attending would have been at the courthouse picnic instead.

Whit, trying to stay dry under an umbrella, edged his way through the crowd.

"That's him," he heard someone say. He looked and saw Deputy Franklin pointing him out to a group of news reporters.

"Damn," he grumbled.

They charged, more than he could count. Microphones

assaulted his face. For a moment, the crush startled him. When he got his balance, he started swinging slowly with his hands, knocking the mikes aside.

"Have you a comment?" a bushy-haired reporter asked.

A young woman pushed right into his face. He recognized her from a network evening newscast. "Do you have a suspect as the local paper reports?"

Whit leaned forward on his feet, plowing through them.

"Is this case too much for the local police?" she asked, backing in front of him.

"Fuck," he said.

She pulled the mike down. "I gather you have no comment."

"No comment," Whit said, loud enough for them all to hear.

The woman stepped aside for him, but the bushy-haired young man, his mike bearing call letters that Whit didn't even recognize, continued the assault. "The people want to—"

Whit grabbed the mike from his hand and let it fall into a small mud puddle. "You jam that fucking thing in my face again and I'm gonna shove it up your ass."

The crowd parted for him.

The man patted his bushy hair and reached down to recover his muddied equipment. "Talk about an asshole," he said to the young woman.

"Yeah, but I bet he catches the killer," she said, her eyes following Whit.

Several other officials, including Tony Danton, stood behind a section roped off for the family and public officials. Whit joined them.

"I see you made it through the gauntlet," Tony said.

"Just barely. I assume you gave them a statement?"

"Yeah," Tony said, "I told them the investigation was continuing."

* * *

Bill Curtis's wife held the hand mirror for Missie Posich as she checked her hair, her makeup. "I've never been on television before," Missie said, using her little finger to blend her blush into her cheek.

Another deputy's wife held the umbrella over her head. A middle-aged, rotund cameraman stood waiting. "Jesus, lady, will you hurry before the services start? This isn't the Miss America Pageant."

"Keep your pants on!" Missie snapped.

She studied her face in the mirror. "How do I look?"

"Peachy fine," Veronica Curtis said, her arm growing weary from holding the mirror.

Missie took the umbrella and walked to the young, good-looking reporter. "I've seen you on TV before," she said.

He smiled patiently. "Yes, ma'am. I spend a lot of time there."

Missie tittered.

"Give the umbrella to the producer there."

"But it's still sprinkling!"

The reporter sighed. "Please, before the services start."

Missie slowly lowered the umbrella, dreading the effects the rain might have on her makeup. The producer snatched it from her hand. "Hey!" she cried.

"You're on!" shouted the man behind the camera.

Missie turned back. "Already?" Her mouth bumped into the microphone. "Oh, God. Did I smear my lipstick?"

"Tell me," the reporter said, his voice suddenly becoming much deeper, "as a deputy's wife, are you afraid?"

Missie showed teeth when she smiled. "Well, we're all being a lot more careful."

"Have any of you thought about just packing up and leaving until the killer is apprehended?"

Missie nodded. "We've probably all thought about it, but our place is here with our men."

The reporter repressed a smile. "Tell me, does your husband indicate that there are any suspects?"

"Oh, you'll have to ask him. He never talks much about his work at home."

"Dippy," mumbled the producer. He held the woman's umbrella over his head.

One of the officers stopped Tressa and Anna before they reached Whit. "But I'm Tressa Pynchon," the young girl protested. "My father's—"

"You can go on," the deputy said.

"I'm with her," Anna said.

"Sorry," the deputy said. "No press beyond this rope."

She saw Whit coming up behind him.

"It's okay," Whit told the officer. "Let her through."

The officer shrugged and lifted the rope for the two women.

"You should be proud," Whit said as they moved back to the group.

"Me?" Anna asked.

"Yes, I see the national media adopted the name you gave our killer."

"Can you believe all these people?" Tressa said.

"It's like car races," Anna said. "People like the blood and guts."

"And you people are more than willing to spoon-feed it to them," Whit said.

Anna pouted. "I've kept my stories very responsible, and I kept my promise and didn't name your suspect."

Tony broke into the conversation. "After we catch this guy, you and Whit here oughta collaborate on a book. You could make big money."

The idea had already occurred to Anna. "Not a bad idea, counselor. Only I don't need a collaborator."

"Nor do I," Whit said.

* * *

The woman TV reporter stood with the bushy-haired young man. He was using a key to clean the mud from the mike. "Isn't that the woman reporter from here in Milbrook?" he asked, staring over at Anna.

The woman studied her. "I think so. She came up with the name for this guy."

"How in the hell did she get such preferential treatment?"

The newswoman smiled. "She's probably fucking that middle-aged hunk of a cop."

"Not my type," the man said.

Once the crowd had gathered, the door to the first limousine opened. Even the jaded news crews were watching with interest. People were always curious about how the survivors acted, wondering how they themselves would behave in a similar circumstance.

"Look at that," Tony said.

The first person to emerge from the car was Gil Dickerson and then Dan Linnerman. They turned to help Miller Foley from the vehicle. An elderly couple also got out . . . Emma's parents, they all assumed. Other family members exited a second large Cadillac.

"That's nice," Anna said.

Linnerman and Dickerson helped Foley to an area beneath a canvas tent that covered the grave site. Other uniformed officers were unloading the dark wooden casket from the hearse. The three cops, each of them a widower, walked in front of the coffin. The other family members followed it. News cameras rolled and still cameras clicked off shots.

"You people are like jackals," Whit said.

Anna held her breath, hoping no one shoved a mike into the grieving husband's face. Anna silently agreed with him.

It did seem a blasphemy. When it was over, everyone waited for the family to move back to the cars before they moved—everyone, that is, but the TV crews, who began to scurry for new positions.

Tony turned his eyes to the sky. "It's going to clear off tonight."

"I'm heading for the car," Whit said.

Tony sighed. "I dread this." The reporters were lean and hungry, desperate for a story.

But the reporters charged Annie Tyson-Tyree. The press obeyed a herding instinct. The woman, who had tried to interview Whit, and the bushy-haired young man had been talking about her and decided it might be interesting to interview the woman who had dubbed the killer The Womanslayer. The word spread. Afraid that someone knew something they didn't, the others followed suit.

"Tell us, Miss Tyree, how does it feel to have the name you invented broadcast all over the world?"

It caught Anna off guard. She felt trapped as the people crowded around her. Whit and Tressa were separated from her. "We oughta go back and help her," Tressa said.

But Whit was chuckling. "Let her get a good taste of her own medicine."

He went to the long, dark limo. Gil Dickerson rolled down the window. "Hi, Whit. Any news?"

Whit peered inside. Gil's face showed that he was on the emotional mend, but Foley and Linnerman looked as if neither would live until the next dawn. Their faces were gray, drawn, their eyes red from tears.

"I suppose you all know that we have a positive identification on our suspect?"

They all nodded.

"We had planned to use dogs to search this morning, but the rain and all—"

"We understand," Gil said.

"It's been rescheduled for Wednesday. I'd like to go tomorrow, but we can't get the dogs back until Wednesday."

"I want to go," Gil told Whit.

"You're sure you're up to it?"

"Oh, I'm up to it."

Whit nodded. "Well, for what it's worth to each of you, we're going to nail this bastard. I don't know how soon, but I sure as hell hope it's before he—"

What word to use?

"We have confidence," Gil said.

Whit looked to the other two. From what he saw in their questioning eyes, Whit wasn't so sure.

Anna was wrapping up her story on Emma's services when the deputy entered the newsroom. She remembered seeing him at the scene of Emma Foley's services. The sports editor sat at a far desk, but the rest of the news staff hadn't come in yet.

"Can I help you?" Anna asked.

"I hope so." He sat on the edge of her desk.

"So?" Anna said, bristling at his presumption.

"I'm Tim Franklin."

"So?"

"Well, I thought I'd stop by and introduce myself. I thought maybe we could go grab a burger or something."

Anna's mouth dropped. "You're here to ask me out?"

"That's what men and women do, isn't it? They go out together. I've been meaning to introduce myself to you. I was going to at the picnic. I saw you there. I just never got a chance."

What a cocky bastard! Anna shook her head. "No, thanks, Deputy."

"You ever gone out with a weightlifter?" he asked, the smile still on his face.

"What's that got to do with anything?"

"I was just wondering. You might like me if you gave me half a chance."

She glanced over at the sports editor. He was lost to the words on his terminal—or maybe just pretending to be.

"Deputy Franklin, it sounds to me like you're asking me to go to bed with you."

Franklin leered. "Well, I wouldn't kick you out."

"It's been my experience," Anna said, "that a lot of weightlifters are either gay or want to be."

The camera was pulled in tight on Missie's face. The newsman's question was dubbed over the shot. "Have any of you thought about just packing up and leaving until the killer is apprehended?"

Missie nodded into the camera. "We've probably all thought about it, but our place is here with our men."

" 'Men'—the plural—is the right word for *that* woman to use," Whit said, sitting beside Tressa in the living room of his home.

"Daddy!"

"I'm sorry. I sounded like your mother right then, didn't I?"

"DADDY!"

He threw an arm around her and wrestled her down. "Come on, kid, let me say a few nasty things."

"Everything you say is nasty. Anna's mad as a hornet because you didn't rescue her this afternoon."

Whit laughed. "Can you imagine the reaction if I had pulled her to safety?"

"She likes you, Daddy."

He tickled her sides. "Little Miss Matchmaker."

"Stop it, Daddy."

The phone rang. Whit's mood turned black. "Dammit to hell," he bellowed, releasing his daughter.

"Whit Pynchon," he said as he answered.

It was Julia. "Is Tressa there?" There was a pronounced edge to her voice.

"Julia! Yes, she's here."

"I figured as much. Will you kindly send her on home? My sister's here, and she'd like to see her for a minute before she heads back to Charleston."

Whit rolled his eyes at his daughter. "I'm sure that will just thrill her."

"None of your sarcasm, Whitley. Just trot her on home."

"Okay, I'll throw her out the door. She—"

The phone clicked. "Damn her! She hung up on me."

Tressa giggled. "There are some people you don't intimidate. I bet she wants me home."

"Yeah, Aunt Elsi-whatever is there."

"Elsinore? Shit!"

Whit grabbed for her. "I'm gonna wash your mouth—"

But she hopped from the couch. "Gotta catch me first."

Whit didn't try. "I guess you'd better do as she says, just to keep peace in the family."

Tressa plopped down in a chair. "In a little while."

"What is it, hon? Something's eating at you."

"No, it's not!"

Whit went to the chair and sat down on the arm. He patted her blond hair. "Come on, kid. I know better."

She took his hand. "I'm scared, Daddy. I couldn't sleep at all last night. I just lay there, watching the window."

What could he say? That she was being silly? She wasn't. "I'm as close as the phone," Whit said.

"And that's probably not close enough, Daddy."

"I know. You know you're welcome to stay here."

Tressa dipped her head. "I'd feel guilty leaving Mother alone."

"Your mother's safe as can be. She's tough as a cement nail."

She looked up at the face of her father. "You know better than that."

"What can I say, Tress? Everyone's afraid. That's what happens when—well, we all get used to living in a very safe world. But it really isn't safe anywhere."

"Do you get tired of being alone? Do you get lonely?"

Whit got up. "Oh, no. I'm not going to let you get me involved in that conversation. Come on, out the door with you."

Tressa crossed her arms. "Not until you answer me."

Whit dropped his head and chuckled. "You're too damned old for your age. Yeah, sure, I get lonely, but that's no reason to . . . to . . ."

"To what? To be with someone you like? You're missing all your happiness, Daddy."

"Jesus, kid, ease up."

She stood up. "You think about what I said."

"Yes, dear. I will, dear."

"And stop trying so hard to be—" She paused to think of the right word. "—to be so damned independent."

Then she was gone. The house was silent. He thought for a few moments about the prowler outside her house, but it was just an attempt to divert his mind from her question. *Am I lonely?* He ambled onto the deck. The sun was dropping down toward Tabernacle Mountain.

Yeah. If you'd really admit it, you're so lonely it aches. But that's life . . . the way things are meant to be.

EIGHTEEN

ANNA IGNORED THE ringing phone until she finished typing a sentence on the screen of the terminal. Only then, once her thought was complete, did she answer it.

"This is Whit."

"Whit! Hi! This is a surprise."

"Yeah. For me too."

"Has something developed on the case?"

"Yeah, we got the autopsy results this afternoon on Mary Linnerman. She was probably dead when she was thrown over the cliff."

"Is that all you have for me?"

"Well, if you don't want—"

"Of course I do. Hold a sec." Anna dumped the story she was writing into the machine's memory, then began a new file of notes. "I gather this is for publication."

"You can use it. Just say you called me."

Anna smiled. "To protect your reputation, I guess."

"Something like that."

"Could they tell if she was assaulted?"

"Strangled. The M.E. found finger bruises on her neck. There were other technical indications. She wasn't raped."

"Spare me," Anna said. "Tell me, is this Tipton person strong enough to commit these crimes?"

"With a nut, who knows? One more thing. I'd like to

show you a photo lineup, just to see if you can pick out the man you saw in the woods Sunday."

"I'll know him again if I see him. Want me to come over to the courthouse now?"

"Uh, no. I've got to go over to magistrate court on a preliminary hearing in a few minutes. Why don't I bring them by your place this evening?"

"This evening?" Anna perked up.

"Yeah, then we can grab a bite or something?"

Anna's eyes twinkled. "Let me get this straight, Whit Pynchon. Are you asking me to dinner?"

"Well, I just . . . because of the photo lineup and all—but if you're busy, then we can wait—"

"No! I'm not busy. I'm just . . . just stunned."

"It's no big deal."

Now, Anna. Don't scare him off. "Yeah, sure. I didn't mean to make it sound like anything important." She realized what she had said, then started to chuckle.

"Damn! Thanks!"

"I didn't mean it like that," she said.

"Where do you live?"

She told him. "Don't forget those photos."

"I won't."

When she hung up the phone, she found her editor standing over her.

"What photos?" he asked.

"Just some shots I made at the funeral," she said, lying. Anna hadn't told her editor that she had seen the suspect. She hadn't told him that there was a name for the suspect. And she hoped to God he didn't find out otherwise. It wasn't like her to shortchange a story—to conceal news—but this case was special.

"We need you to cover the board of health tonight."

"I can't! I mean, I have another appointment."

"Business?" he asked.

"No. Well . . . yes, in a way."

He leaned down to her. "So, what is it?"

"I'm trying to get a story out of Whit Pynchon on these murders."

The editor grinned. "I hear through the grapevine that you and Pynchon have been getting chummy."

"I wouldn't say that. It certainly won't affect my job." How could she say that? It had already.

The editor waved off her worry. "Hey, I'm glad. You're a sharp lady. Maybe that's what it takes to get to first base with Whit. God knows no one else has been able to do it."

"But—" Anna stopped. If she said that she wasn't just doing it for a story, she might end up at the board of health. "Forget it."

The editor moved away, casting a knowing glance over his shoulder.

"Lecherous bastard," she mumbled.

Whit wilfully had withheld one piece of information from Anna. When Mary Linnerman's clothes had been stripped by the M.E., he'd found the number 3 carved in the flesh of her stomach.

Missie didn't need groceries. She just needed an excuse to see Kenny Shaffer. Not that she had forgotten Bill Curtis. Kenny was just more convenient. Hank would be going to work that afternoon at three. He was working a double shift. With Linnerman, Foley, and Dickerson still off, and summer vacations just starting, the second shift was two men short. Hank figured he more than made up for both.

She saw Kenny as soon as she entered the store. He nodded to her, then went back to jamming cans into a bag. "Hey!" cried the woman whose bag he was filling. "You're crushing my potato chips."

Missie wore tight blue jeans and a plaid blouse open to

her cleavage. She had paid a lot of attention to her looks that morning. She wanted to impress Kenny, but, since her appearance on television, she had also become something of a personality. Everyone must have been watching TV that night. She wallowed in her notoriety. Hank had said she looked fat. *The bastard! What the hell did he know?* Missie would be certain to bury the bags from the off-limits market deep in the trash.

In the store she spent a long time filling the basket. Then as she neared the checkout line she slowed down, trying to gauge it so that she ended up with Kenny bagging her groceries. Usually he timed it, but she could tell that he was trying to avoid her. For what reason, she didn't know.

Finally she caught him going to a car with groceries, then quickly got in the line where he was bagging. When he returned, he was trapped.

"Hi, Kenny."

"Hello, Mrs. Posich."

She waited until they were out of the store and on the way to her car. The sky had cleared, but the air was cool for June.

"Is there something wrong, Kenny?"

He opened the rear door of her car and began putting the bags inside. "No, ma'am. There's nothing wrong."

"I'd like for you to come and see me again. I enjoyed the first time. The second time, well, obviously your mind was somewhere else."

"Yes, ma'am."

He finished with the groceries. She put a hand on his arm. "Please, Kenny, what is it?"

Tears welled up in his eyes. "I can't tell you."

"Kenny, it can't be that bad."

"It is—in a way."

"So tell me."

Kenny kept glancing toward the front doors to the market. "I'd better be getting back."

"Is it me?" she demanded.

"Oh, no. I like you. I enjoyed it." His face turned red with embarrassment. "I really did."

Missie fished into her pocketbook and withdrew a deposit ticket. She stuffed it in his hand. "My phone number's not listed, but it's on this deposit ticket. Hank's working a double shift tonight and Thursday night. Give me a call. We'll talk about it on the phone. Will you do that?"

Kenny jammed the piece of white paper in his pocket. "Okay, I'll call, but it will be Thursday night."

She herself glanced around, saw no one watching, and patted his crotch. She felt his excitement. "Be sure and call me."

Anna Tyson Tyree lived in a recently completed townhouse on Milbrook's south side. Whit found it easily. "Welcome to my parlor," she said as she opened the door.

He noted the odor of new construction as he stepped into the spacious living room. "These are nice. I've been by them before, but I never paid them much mind."

"There's a pool here and tennis courts," she said. "Do you play tennis?"

Whit laughed. "Never tried it."

"You should. It's good for the bod."

"I like to swim."

Anna nodded. "I forgot. You're the beach bum."

"That's what I want to be when I grow up."

Her laugh was musical. Whit had been admiring her appearance. She dressed well without being gaudy. On that night, she wore a pale green blouse with pants that were striped white and green. They fitted her well without being whorishly tight. The aroma of her perfume—always the same—filled the living room.

"How about a glass of wine?" she asked.

"Okay. While you get the wine, I'll get the photos ready."

"Yuck. Do I really have to look at those things?"

"Damn right you do. We don't really have a positive identification of Ferdie Tipton."

She cocked her head. "Ferdie? Is that what he's called?"

"That's his nickname."

"Ferdie. It certainly doesn't sound like a killer's name."

"Neither did Albert De Salvo or Theodore Bundy."

"Ted Bundy, I know. Who's Albert whatever?"

"The Boston Strangler."

"God, I should have known that. I'll get the wine. Red or white?"

"Dry white if you have it."

"Chablis—on special at the convenience mart." She went to get it.

He sat down on a couch and opened his book of mug shots. Earlier he had arranged a page of photos, all Caucasian males who generally fit the description of the man Anna and Tressa saw. Whit knew that he should also expose Tressa to the photo lineup, but he put it off.

Ferdie glared at him from the center of the page. There were five photos. Ferdie was number three. He pulled the sheet from the notebook and placed it on the coffee table.

She came back with the wine. "Is that it?" she asked, half looking down at the page of Polaroids.

"That's it."

She sat beside him and picked it up.

"Look at it carefully. Take your time. If you see one you recognize, identify it by number."

Anna tossed it back on the table. "No problem. It's

number three. Not nearly as much beard or hair, but it's him."

"You're positive?"

"Of course. That's the man that was in the park."

Whit pulled the photo out from beneath the plastic covering and showed Anna the reverse side.

"Ferdnand Tipton," she said, reading the name. "He looks like an animal."

"They also call him Mountain Man."

"That's an insult to mountain men," Anna quipped. "So now you can arrest him?"

Whit laughed. "Hell, we could have done that all along for escaping from the state hospital. The problem is finding him. At least we know for sure that it's Ferdie."

Anna shook her head. "Ferdie . . . what a name for a mad killer."

"The Womanslayer," Whit intoned.

"Okay. Don't rub it in."

"But that must be some kind of compliment to a newsperson—to have your creation become a national whatever."

She continued to stare at the photos. "Would you mind putting those up?"

It surprised Whit. "That bothers you? You looked at Emma Foley and didn't bat an eye."

"I just controlled it well."

Whit put the page back in the book. "I hope you're good and hungry tonight."

"Famished."

"Well, let's go, unless you want to watch the news—"

"Hell, no!"

Tressa pulled the Toyota into the dark driveway beside her house. Her mother wasn't home yet from a meeting of the Milbrook Garden Council and had forgotten to turn on the spotlight that illuminated the driveway. A single grocery bag occupied the seat beside Tressa. She usually went grocery shopping for her mother. Julia Pynchon detested grocery stores. She never told Tressa that she didn't like them, but, when it came down to buying groceries, Julia Pynchon always had something else to do—just like tonight. The list had been small, just enough for a single grocery bag. Tressa's mind had been on Kenny Shaffer. Her father hadn't volunteered any more information on why he'd asked about Kenny, and Tressa knew better than to pursue it. So when her mother had given her the grocery list, she had decided to visit the market where Kenny worked.

The experience left her depressed. Kenny had been at the front of the store as she walked in. Their eyes had met. No doubt about it. And he had practically trotted toward the back of the store. Tressa had spent almost thirty minutes shopping for the short list of items and had finally given up as the store's closing time neared. Kenny Shaffer wasn't coming out of the back of the store.

The bag was too heavy to hoist across the seat, so Tressa went to the passenger side of the car to get it. As she was lifting the bag from the seat, she noticed the movement in the darkened rear of the yard, nothing more than a shift in the intensity of the darkness but enough to attract her attention—the kind of thing that makes a person look twice.

On her second look, she saw nothing. She lifted the bag and closed the door.

The sound came from behind her, from behind a waist-high hedge along the property line. The fear clumped in her throat. She backed toward the house, clutching the heavy bag to her chest. Tressa still saw nothing until the passenger-side window imploded. The bag dropped to the ground, its contents spilling out into the yard.

Her heart raced. The blood roared through her head. She

took a quick look back toward the house and knew that the door would be locked, that she would have to spend several minutes fumbling through her purse to find the key.

"Who's there?" she asked, softly.

Silence answered her.

She darted around the rear of the car toward the well-lit house of the closest neighbor. The prospect of death came to her mind just as a huge dark shape exploded from behind the hedge. She was by it, but a hand latched on to her shoulder. She whirled away from its grasp, screaming, as if the death that she so feared had just touched her. She ran by the neighbor's house. Her tennis shoes slapped one after another on the sidewalk. She could hear nothing but the sounds of her feet, the beating of her heart.

She ran and ran—straight into the massive chest of a man.

Whit was driving Anna home when the police car pulled him over.

"Let's see you talk your way out of this," she joked.

"I wasn't doing anything wrong."

The blue light flashed behind him as he brought the car to a stop along the city street. Whit rolled down his window. The city officer came up with his flashlight. He aimed it in Whit's face.

"Jesus," Whit said. "Gimme a break."

"Sorry, Mr. Pynchon. Just wanted to make sure it was you. We've been looking all over for you."

"Why?" Whit held his breath.

"It's your daughter—"

Images of horror played through his mind, visions of the body of each one of the dead women. "What is it?"

"She's down at the station. Someone vandalized her car, then gave her a pretty bad fright. One of her neighbors was out walking and gave her a hand."

"But she's all right?"

"Yeah, she's fine, just shaken up, but she wants you."

"Oh, sweet Jesus. Thank God." His head collapsed on the steering wheel.

"Where were you?" Tressa cried when she saw her father.

Whit gathered her into his arms. "I took Anna out to dinner."

Anna stood behind them, out of the way, her own face ashen and tense.

"You shoulda been home," Tressa said, clinging to him as if she were drowning in deep water.

"What happened?"

"He grabbed at me. He tried to—"

She broke down.

Anna came up and put a hand on Tressa's head while the young girl cried.

"Take care of her for a minute," Whit said.

Tressa didn't want to turn loose of her father.

"Come on, Tressa," Anna said. "Let me help you."

The young girl released her grip on Whit, then transferred it to Anna. Whit went to the desk officer. "What the hell happened?"

"Apparently someone was prowling around her house. He broke her car window, then tried to assault her. She managed to get away from the bastard and ran."

"Did she see him?"

The desk officer shrugged. "Don't know. We can't get much out of her. The neighbor didn't see anything, but somebody sure tossed a rock through her window. You probably oughta take her over to the emergency room, get her a sedative or something."

Whit turned to leave, but the officer stopped him. "When

she tells you what happened, how about having her make out a statement for us?''

''Sure thing.''

They took her to the emergency room.

Whit and Anna sat in the waiting area while a doctor examined her.

''I don't know what I'd do if something happened to her,'' Whit said.

''I think someone is toying with her, maybe with you,'' Anna suggested. ''Anyone else he's gone after he's got, assuming it's the killer, which it might not be.''

Whit looked down at the white tile floor. ''I was thinking the same thing. He probably could have killed her both times if he wanted. It makes me sick to think that.''

''What did you ever to do Ferdie Tipton?''

''Nothing,'' Whit said. ''I've never laid eyes on the crazy bastard.''

The doctor came out. ''She's fine, but you need to take her home and put her to bed. I gave her a sedative, and before long she's going to fall asleep.''

''Otherwise she's okay?'' Whit asked.

The doctor patted Whit on the shoulder. ''Just scared senseless. We've had a great increase in cases of anxiety since the killings. I hope you catch the guy pretty soon.''

''Me too,'' Whit said.

Anna was surprised to see Whit at Mary Linnerman's services Wednesday afternoon. The other newspeople were crowding around Tony Danton as he exited from the driver's side of Whit's vehicle. Anna slipped away from them and went to the passenger side to greet Whit.

''I figured you'd still be on the mountain.''

Whit shrugged in frustration. ''We never made it up to the mountain. The goddamn dog handlers couldn't make it.''

Anna was stunned. All day she had waited to hear some word on the search. "Why not?"

"An inmate escaped from the state prison. They needed the dogs up there."

"Did you have to have the dogs?"

Whit waved his hand at the hulking mass of Tabernacle Mountain. "Would you want to try to find a needle in that goddamn haystack?"

"Hey, it's not my fault, Whit."

Whit made a face. "Jesus, I forgot. None of that's for the damned paper."

Anna laughed.

"What's so funny?"

"For a second, I thought you were going to apologize for being so rude."

Tim Franklin ambled by them. "Afternoon, Anna." He tipped his hat, giving her an obvious once-over with his leering eyes.

"What the hell was that all about?" Whit asked.

Anna started to express her true feelings about Tim Franklin, but she caught herself. "Tim? He asked me out the other night."

"Did you go?"

"I was tied up. He's kinda cute though."

Whit's face swelled. "That hunk of mindless muscle?"

"I've always found weightlifters sexy," Anna said.

Nineteen

A man carries his own worst enemy between his legs. Even the most mature males have followed its turgid, indiscriminatory lust to perdition itself. A boy, not quite yet a man, exhibits even less temperance over the small demon that, at that age, provides the sole reason to be.

Kenny Shaffer battled his demon as courageously as any young male. He succumbed to its tenacious nature late Wednesday night. There came no relief with the submission. Was he possessed of some dark, deep psychotic sickness that kept his penis in so anxious a state? Sex remained something sinister to him, something to be done in the night's darkness and not to be talked about at all—anytime.

What if he caught something? AIDS maybe? It was spreading to women too. Kenny remembered the wasted faces of the men whom he had seen on the television screen—young men they were, too, not much older than he.

On top of that fear piled others.

Hank Posich.

Several places on his body still ached, still bore the marks of the man's ungentle touch. And Hank had done that simply because Kenny was walking in front of his house. What if he caught him in bed with his wife? It caused Kenny to shake.

A final fear hounded him, the worst of them all. Would

the demon, which so tormented him, humiliate him when the time came?

Every night Kenny performed the same ritual. He latched the door to his bedroom. Before he had been with Missie, he'd retrieved three worn, stolen pornographic magazines from a dark corner of his closet and studied the grainy but explicit photos as he masturbated.

Since that first night with Missie, he hadn't touched the magazines. He didn't need them. He lay in his shadowy bedroom, his hand busy beneath the covers. Once it was ended, the temptation to call Missie evaporated. His weakness then disgusted him. What he did was wrong. Everyone said so. What if people knew? What if his grandmother knew? The thought deepened the night's blackness. And he vowed that the next night he wouldn't do it at all, that he would climb in bed and go to sleep. But each night, as it came time for bed, his demon arose, like some gloomy monster from a corrupt abyss.

It happened on Wednesday night. Kenny fought it. He tossed and turned, ended up on his stomach, pressing his rigid penis into the mattress. Before he knew it, his hips were moving, grinding the demon against the pressure of the bed.

Why not? The voice spoke to him from a realm of his mind that he wished did not exist. *Do it. Do it now.*

"Nooo," he moaned, softly so his grandmother would not hear.

But he did. This night, when it was done, the thoughts did not end. Missie, her soft and electric touch, stayed in his mind. He tried again to sleep, but before sleep came he was erect again.

God help me. I want her again.

He wanted to feel her mouth on him again, hot and wet, wanting him. All he had to do was call her. It wasn't that late. His eyes looked to the blue light of the digital alarm. *It's just 11:38. Go on, call her.*

The phone in the hall had a long cord that Kenny himself had installed—so that he could take it into his room for private conversations with his girlfriend, when he got one.

Other than Missie of course.

He crept into the hall and brought the phone into his room, then stared at it for what seemed an eternity. His stomach did funny things. What if Hank Posich answered? What would he do then? Hang up of course, but was there any way for the call to be traced? Surely not. According to the TV, it took a long time to trace a call. Even then the arrangements had to be made ahead of time. Of course, you couldn't believe everything you saw on TV.

But he wanted Missie.

His hand quivered as he lifted the handset. A nervous cramp knotted his gut.

The dial tone buzzed at him, urging him to do something—*shit or get off the pot.*

He keyed in the number slowly, knowing that at any time he could hang up the phone, that he didn't have to finish it. But he pushed all seven digits, then inhaled deeply, as if the act he was about to commit was to be the climax of his life.

Whit brushed his fingers up and down the hollow of Anna's spine. She shivered. Goose bumps erupted on her skin. "I love that," she whispered. "Do it forever."

"You're sexy," Whit whispered.

"I'm a slut," she said, giggling.

"I wouldn't go that far."

He stroked her back, down to her full and soft buttocks.

"Ummmmm, I love it."

As he caressed her, his mind returned to the events of

the past few days. Could this killer, fresh from a nuthouse, be so damned cunning? They would search again.

"You're slowing down," she said.

"Huh? Oh! Sorry, I was thinking."

She rolled in his arms to face him. "About this killer, I guess."

"About The Womanslayer," he said, smiling at her.

"Where do you go from here?"

Whit sighed. "I don't know."

She eased back from him. "Is that a nice way of saying 'no comment'?"

"I'm serious. I really don't know. Tony and I are going to get together tomorrow morning. I think he's planning a press conference tomorrow afternoon."

She rose up in bed. "A press conference? You knew this all along tonight?"

Whit was taken aback. "Yes, I did. What's—"

"I'll be damned!"

"What's wrong?"

"You could have at least told me that. Hell, it would have made a great sidebar to the story tomorrow, especially if I could have scooped all these hotshots."

Whit couldn't help himself. He laughed.

"What's so damned funny?"

Whit was laughing so hard he couldn't answer.

"I mean it," she snapped. "What's so funny?"

"We can't even screw without getting into an official debate."

She flopped back onto his bed and pulled the covers up around her neck. "You mighta told me about the news conference."

Whit pressed closer to her. She inched away. "You wouldn't want me to show favoritism, would you?"

"Fucking right, I would."

Whit's hand searched out her breast. He cupped it, his

finger massaging the stiffening nipple. "Come to Carolina with me."

Anna started to giggle.

"What is it?" he said, offended by her reaction.

"That sounds like a song title. 'Come to Carolina with Me.' "

"I mean it."

She turned her face to him. "When do we leave?"

"A year from now. June one of next year."

"A year? My God, Whit!"

"It's not so far off."

"If you stay in your job, and I stay in mine—which I intend to do—we might kill each other before a year passes."

"Will you think about it?"

"Think about what? Killing you? I do—often."

He squeezed her hardening nipple. "You know what I mean."

"Owwwww! Police brutality!" And her hand went down to grasp testicles.

Whit rolled away from her. "Just like a goddamned reporter."

Missie Posich fumbled for the telephone. "Hello," she mumbled.

"Missie?"

She'd gone to bed early that night. And she had fallen asleep quickly.

"Who is this?" she asked.

"Kenny."

Missie sat up in bed. "Kenny? You called!"

"Can you talk?"

"Of course I can talk."

"I woke you up. I can tell."

Missie used her free hand to rub at her eyes. "That's all

right. I was just bored so I turned in early. I had a little headache, too.''

''Oh.'' Kenny was disappointed.

''I gave up on you calling,'' she said.

''I . . . uh, what I mean is—''

''I still want to see you, Kenny.''

''Really? I'm sorry I acted like such a jerk the other night, but I was having some problems with my grandmother.''

''I can hardly hear you,'' she said.

''I gotta be careful. She's not too far away. I mean, her room's not too far away.''

''Oh, okay.''

''Can I come over?''

Missie made a face into the phone. ''Oh, Kenny. It's not a good night.''

''I thought you said—''

''I know, but Hank said he might come home early tonight. I want to see you, but it would be risky tonight.''

''I see.''

Missie's hand slipped beneath the covers of her bed. ''Maybe tomorrow night, Kenny?''

''I guess.''

''I tell you what, Kenny. You call me tomorrow night at eleven P.M.''

There was a moment of silence on the other end, then Kenny said, ''Well, okay. Sure.''

Missie's fingers pressed into the moist warmth between her legs. ''Are you horny tonight?'' she asked, her voice soft and sensual.

She heard the sharp intake of breath from his end. ''Come on, Kenny. You can tell me if you are.''

''Kinda.''

''Want me to tell you what I'm going to do to you tomorrow night? Maybe that will help. Do you ever jack off, Kenny?''

''No!''

''Now, Kenny,'' she purred. ''I do, and I bet you do.''

''Well, yeah . . . sometimes. Not very often.''

''Let's do it together tonight—over the phone.''

The rhythmic sound of his breathing deepened.

''Do you know what I'm doing to myself, Kenny?''

''Uh-huh.''

Missie smiled. ''Come on, honey. Talk to me. Talk dirty to me.''

''Gawddamn!'' Hank slammed the receiver into the cradle.

''Still busy?'' Curtis asked.

''Yeah.''

''Who would your old lady be talking to this time of night?''

Hank snapped up his evening's report from the desk. ''She wasn't feeling too good. I guess she took the fuckin' phone off the hook.''

Tony Danton faced an aggressive, fact-starved press corps Thursday afternoon. The news conference was held in the large courtroom. Tony stood up behind the massive bench, his eyes locked on his notes. The bright glare of the lights blinded him. He knew there was a herd of newspeople out there, but he couldn't see them—a strange sight in a Raven County courtroom.

Whit Pynchon sat in the clerk of the court's box, not at all happy to be a part of Tony's circus. Somewhere out there among the herd of newshounds was Anna, on this day playing the part of Annie Tyson-Tyree. He liked Anna Tyree much better, maybe too much.

''I have a statement to make,'' Tony said, his voice

booming from the speakers that provided quadraphonic sound to the courtroom. ''Then I'll take a few questions.''

He cleared his throat. ''First of all, the citizens of Raven County can rest assured that the total law enforcement attention of this county is being directed toward the apprehension of this monster who is cowardly preying upon the families of law enforcement officials.

''Because of the nature of these crimes, we have managed to accumulate very little physical evidence to aid us either in the capture of this maniac or in his subsequent conviction. For that reason we are turning to our fellow citizens for assistance.

''We do have a suspect. We have a name, and we are going to release that name along with photos in the hope that we might secure information on his whereabouts.''

Whit could hear the sound of shuffling paper. He could hear the soft whir of cameras. Perhaps he was wrong, but he thought he could hear the sound of pencils and pens on paper.

The prosecutor of Raven County paused for effect, then moved on. ''Two weeks ago, a man escaped from the state mental hospital, a local man who was committed to that institution by the courts of this county some six months ago. This individual has a history of mental illness. I'm not going to get into any specific details as to the evidence we've gathered. However, I am going to provide you with that person's identity and a photo.''

Again a pause. The press corps grew agitated. They wanted a name.

''I emphasize that at this point this individual is merely a suspect. We have not yet secured warrants for his arrest on any of the murders. At present we do hold a warrant charging him with eloping from the state mental hospital.''

''Come on, man. The name!'' a male voice shouted.

''In good time,'' Tony retorted.

The crowd seemed to be inching forward toward the bar. Whit felt their pressure.

Tony looked down at him. "Whit, would you begin passing out the photos."

A stack of them, all blown up from the jail's mug shot, rested on the clerk's desk. He obeyed Tony's directive.

"The man's name is Ferdnand Tipton, a.k.a. Ferdie Tipton." Tony went on to explain Tipton's history, his criminal record, the circumstances surrounding the death of his brother, and concluded with a detailed description of Ferdie Tipton.

"At present," he concluded, "we are asking that all residents of Raven County be on the lookout for this individual and report any sightings to the sheriff's department. I emphasize again; at this time he is wanted for questioning and on an escape charge. He should be considered armed and dangerous. Also we have been in contact with the Federal Bureau of Investigation. They have kindly offered the services of their technical people. We have also taken steps to bring in a group of specialists in serial murders to organize a task force. Details on that will be forthcoming. Any questions?"

The first one came from the young woman with ABC News. "Do you have the evidence to charge him at this time?"

"Not enough."

The photos were snatched quickly from Whit's hands. The scene was chaotic, so much so that when Anna reached out for her copy Whit didn't even realize it was she.

"I figured you already had one," the bushy-haired reporter said to Anna.

Whit looked up.

He saw Anna and then understood the meaning of the man's remark. Whit remembered him from the funeral.

"You want me to shove that photo up your ass instead of the microphone?"

Anna shook her head. "Ease up, Whit."

The questioning continued.

The young woman from ABC again. "Mr. Prosecutor, I understand that there has been tension among the various police agencies in the county. Is that true?"

"Hogwash," Tony responded.

An older man from CBS, the network that had displayed the least interest in the story, asked, "Since only deputies' families have been the victims, is it your theory that this Tipton guy is getting even for the death of his brother?"

"That's a possible motive," Tony said.

"A follow-up," the CBS man said loudly. "What were the names of the officers who shot Tipton's brother?"

"No comment."

"Ah, come on!" cried the man from CBS. "People have a right to know."

"Next question."

This one came from the bushy-haired reporter. "I have a question for Investigator Pynchon."

By that time Whit had returned to the clerk's box. The prosecutor was grinning at him. "I'm sure Whit wouldn't mind answering a question."

The reporter moved his head to where he could see Whit. "Investigator Pynchon, some of us with the national press feel that you have shown favoritism to members of the local press. Do you have a response?"

Whit heard the silence.

The smile was gone from Tony's face, but he wasn't about to come to Whit's aid.

"Well," Whit drawled, "I don't think I've made any secret of the fact that as a profession I consider reporters irresponsible and rude pests . . ."

He too paused, enjoying the dismayed reaction from

those who did not know him. ". . . but as people I like you all, some more than others. The national corps, as you call them, are the worst of a bad lot."

A few of them laughed. The reporter who had asked the question, however, wasn't satisfied. "That's not responsive to the question, Mr. Pynchon."

Whit smiled at him. "So say something nasty about me. I don't give a fuck."

When Whit looked up at his boss, he saw a man stricken with disbelief. Even the newspeople were momentarily stunned, but they quickly recovered.

"Prosecutor Danton," the reporter cried, "does he speak for you?"

"Uhhh . . . no, but he's entitled to his opinion of the press. I can assure you that this office has been fair and unbiased in its dealings with the press."

Whit left the clerk's box and exited through a door that was used by the circuit judge. Once in the hallway, he smiled, very pleased with himself. So what if Tony fired him? He was getting to the point where he really didn't care.

Anna found him getting a drink from a water fountain. "That wasn't very smart," she said.

"But it was a load of fun. Can they put what I said on television, the word 'fuck' I mean?"

Anna just shook her head, amazed at this man. "No, they probably won't, but even if they bleep it out there won't be any doubt about what you said."

Whit shrugged it off. "You know, Anna, I have this overwhelming desire to spend this summer at the beach. I might not be alive next summer."

They ambled toward the steps leading down to the first floor. "Just what does that mean? Do you have some terminal disease?"

"Oh, no. I'm just tired of putting things off. You're missing the rest of the news conference."

They started down the steps. "You ever heard of a sugar daddy?" she asked.

"Of course."

"Well, I guess you're my news daddy. That's what a lot of those folks think in there."

"Fuck them, Anna. I mean that. Why the hell should I care about them? Why should I even give them the time of day? I have nothing to lose. I don't want anything from any of them or from anybody here."

Anna stopped, amusement on her face. "Even from me?"

But Whit was serious. "Even from you if it costs my soul."

"Your soul?"

"My self-respect."

She took his arm, starting him down the steps again. "I love you as you are. I must admit, Whit Pynchon, I've never met anyone like you before."

TWENTY

PLEASE LET IT be tonight. Kenny's urge had become a consuming passion. He lifted the phone to dial Missie, to be certain that it was safe for him to visit. Already he was aroused. He thought of her voice from the night before. His mind went back to the time that he was with her. The softness of her skin, the sensuous and warm touch of her body which seemed to unite with his, her mouth, her woman smell; God, he wanted her.

The phone started to ring. Kenny closed his eyes. *Please, say it's okay.*

"Hello."

"Missie. It's Kenny."

"Hi, Kenny."

"I'm getting ready to leave the house."

Silence. No answer.

"Is it okay?" He knew the answer. He could tell. She wasn't talking sexy. She sounded bothered by his call.

"Maybe another night, Kenny."

"Why?" he demanded.

The voice turned softer. "I just don't feel too good tonight, Kenny."

"You didn't feel like it last night," Kenny countered.

When she spoke again, the softness in her voice was gone, replaced by a sharp edge. "I don't have to give you any reasons, Kenny. It's not a good night."

"Is Hank there?"

"I have to go, Kenny."

Try for something. "Maybe we could talk like we did last night?"

"Not tonight, kid."

Kid. It brought tears to Kenny's eyes.

"You there?" Missie asked.

"Yeah."

"Look, I'll stop by the market sometime this weekend. Maybe we can get together next week. Okay?"

Next week! No, it's not okay. "I'm sorry about the last time," he said, thinking maybe that was the problem.

"I have to go," she said. The phone clicked.

Kenny stared at it. The rain drummed softly on his bedroom window, his passion withered. He came to know, in those few moments, the second greatest of love feelings. The jealousy was born in the ruins of his ego and reared up like some evil cinematic gargantuan from the depths of a black swamp.

Someone else is with her.

The suspicion made him clench his jaws, his fist. Kenny Shaffer pondered the matter for only a few seconds, then made his decision.

Missie felt sorry for the young boy, but, if she was going to take risks, it might as well be with a man. Not that she had planned to burn Kenny Shaffer. It just sort of happened when the phone rang the first time. She had expected to hear the hesitant, immature voice of Kenny Shaffer. Instead a deep masculine voice had said, "Hope I didn't wake you."

"Who is this?" she had asked. It wasn't anyone she had been with before, not unless he was disguising his voice. For a moment Missie thought she was getting an obscene phone call. It thrilled her, the thought of some unknown man talking dirt to her on the phone.

"This is Bill Curtis."

"Oh, Bill. How are you?" Then came the instant of fear. "Is it Hank? Is he okay?"

"Oh, he's fine," Curtis said. "He just headed out on patrol."

Missie sighed her relief. "I thought maybe something had happened to him."

"I just thought I'd call and yap a few minutes."

"Good!" Missie sat up in bed, her mind thinking about Curtis, big and thick, not quite fat but nowhere near slender. He reminded her of a big bear. And in her mind she imagined that he possessed a very hairy body. "Where are you?"

She knew Curtis was married, that it was unlikely he was calling her from his home.

"I'm still at the station. Back in the deputies' room. I got off duty at eleven."

"Oh, really?" Her mind had started to race. Kenny was supposed to call her. *Wonder if this grown, mature man has the courage of young Kenny Shaffer?*

"Well," Missie said, "I'm lonely tonight."

That had been enough. After a few more minutes of suggestive banter, she had invited Bill Curtis to her house—to their house, hers and Hank's.

He had considered her invitation. "Does Hank ever come home during his shift?"

Missie smiled. "Never. There's always a first time though."

"I'll be there."

She had told him to come around to the back of the house and just walk in. She promised to leave the back door open.

Missie padded barefoot from the bathroom to the bedroom, her body freshly showered, smelling of Chanel, which was a gift from her sister. Hank called perfume "toilet water"—an apt description for the cheap stuff he bought. The bedroom window was open so that Missie could hear the noise of the rain. Usually, when it rained, she had to close the window. It faced the west; almost always the rain blew into it. Not this night though. The steady, persistent drizzle came straight down, its descent true because of the lack of wind.

Missie adored the sound of rain, finding it sensual, relaxing. For years she had nagged Hank to buy her one of those machines that created the sound of falling rain. The machine she wanted reproduced other sounds, a rushing mountain brook, pounding surf, even thunder, but it was the rhythm of a light rain that both turned her on and lulled her to sleep, depending on her mood. Hank called it "bullshit" so many times that she had surrendered. Instead, during the hot summer months, she slept to the sound of a room fan.

White noise, it was called.

The fan helped her sleep; it did nothing for her passion. On this night she needed no fan. The rain peppered the shrubs just beyond her window. She peered out, sensitive to the urgent heat in her loins.

The yellow light from the window glittered in the eyes of the hunter. As the woman filled the window, he eased back into the cool, misty shadows. The rain did not bother him. In fact it aided his mission. The wet, soft earth muffled his steps.

The window framed the woman's lush figure.

Her turn had come.

Tressa stayed late at Whit's house. School was out for the year, and they celebrated. She tried to drag out the celebration as long as possible. Her mother had been especially sardonic that night. For an instant, just as Tressa was preparing to leave, her mother had threatened to make her stay home.

Make me stay home.

Tressa might have stayed, out of respect, but no way could Julia have *made* her stay home. Her mother, though, had not gone that far. Instead she had assumed the posture of a martyr.

Tressa had told Whit about her mother.

"She's afraid of losing you," Whit had said.

"Losing me?"

"Yeah, another school year's gone. You're growing up. To a parent, that's like losing you. I'm losing you too."

Tressa pondered what he'd said. "Okay, I think it's silly, but I guess I can see that. But why should she blame you for any of it?"

Whit swirled the ice cubes around in his near-empty glass. "She blames everything on me. You should know that."

"What about Anna?" Tressa was smiling. She had noticed a change in her father in the past few days.

"What about her?"

"Well, she's had an effect on you."

Whit chuckled. "Really? Not according to the nightly news." They had watched it together.

"My dad said a nasty word on national television. It's a good thing you don't embarrass me."

"I didn't say a nasty word. I said 'bleep.' I imagine Tony is beside himself."

"It was him you embarrassed. I'm surprised you keep your job."

"He'll get over it. So, are you going to try to find a summer job?"

Tressa sipped the last few drops of wine from her glass,

a wine cooler actually. She'd been allowed one bottle that night as part of the celebration. "You've changed the subject, Daddy."

"I did? What subject?"

"We were talking about Anna."

Whit shook his head. "No, I wasn't. You were talking about Anna."

"I like her a lot, Daddy."

"Okay, Cupid, I like her too."

Tressa smiled. "She's good for you. You know that, don't you?"

Whit leaned forward, his face becoming serious. "Hon, don't get your hopes up. As I said, I like her, but our jobs are always at odds. It's a bigger problem than it seems."

"But you're retiring! Why can't you lower that wall you keep around yourself? Did Mother hurt you that much?"

Whit slumped back in his chair and finished his drink. "Funny you should put it that way. She hurt me by taking you away from me."

"My golly, Daddy, you get to see me all the time."

Whit nodded. "That's true, but there's still a difference, a distance that can't be narrowed. At the time of the divorce, I had no way of knowing what was going to happen—how things were going to work out. I could imagine Julia, in her petty vindictiveness, packing up after the divorce and taking you to some—to God knows where!"

"But she didn't."

Whit nodded. "True, she didn't, but the apprehension took its toll. Then something happens like the other night when that bastard was outside your window. And here I was blocks away when you needed me. It doesn't make me feel good."

He rubbed his eyes. "Whew, I'm exhausted. This case is about to grind me down. Do you want to stay the night?"

Tressa glanced at the clock. It was nearing midnight. "I told Mother I'd be home."

He rose from his chair. "I'll follow you."

"You don't—"

Whit closed off her protest. "No way, kid. I'm not taking any chances. Let me fetch an umbrella. How's the plastic on the window doing?" It had been a temporary repair until the window on her car could be replaced.

"It's okay. Before I go, I want to ask you a question. And I want you to be honest with me." She blocked his way to the door.

"Is this about Anna?"

"Nope. The other day you asked me about Kenny Shaffer. I saw him after that and he practically ran from me. Why did you ask me about Kenny?"

Whit didn't know how to answer. "He was picked up late the other night and—"

"Picked up? Kenny Shaffer?"

"He was on the streets awfully late. With all that's been going on, the police decided to check him out."

"And?" Tressa asked.

"And nothing. I talked with him."

"You thought he was the killer?" Tressa was on the verge of laughter.

"Everyone's a suspect, hon."

"But Kenny Shaffer?" She left Whit's house giggling.

The pungent sweet odor of blooming lilac surrounded him. In a way it was stifling, mingling with the rich odor of earth rot. The woman in the bedroom moved about, primping, unconcerned that outside eyes might be watching her through the window. When she turned, the hunter scurried crablike toward the foundation of the house, to the cover of the shrubs that were planted alongside the house.

He rose to his feet. The scent of perfume drifted out the window. Dark eyes peered in.

He crouched, ready to spring through the window.

—footsteps—

The hunter scampered back to the cover of the lilac as the soft rhythmic thumping of feet approached. He waited for the sounds to pass.

But they didn't pass.

The shuffling figure of a man stepped off the sidewalk and came through the yard. He walked straight toward the hunter's hiding place. The hunter's muscles tensed. He sensed fear preceding the form of the man.

The light from the bedroom window spilled out into the wet yard. Bill Curtis, after making sure it was the right house, used it to guide his path toward the rear of the building. He had left his car a block away.

"Hi, handsome."

The feminine voice startled him. Missie smiled down at him from the window.

"Jesus, you scared the pee outa me."

She grinned. "You wanna crawl through the window?"

"My feet are muddy."

"Ah, come on," she urged.

Curtis glanced around, concentrating his attention on the dark street. "You're sure he isn't going to be home?"

"Not a hundred percent." She leaned forward so that Curtis could see her breasts, hanging like plump balloons beneath her thin robe.

"Ummmm . . . nice."

Curtis put his hands on the sill and hoisted his gut onto the ledge. She backed away from the window, opening the robe for him to see. He hung there, enchanted by her sensuality, his feet flopping against the aluminum siding. Rain dripped from his face onto the hardwood floor.

"I'm wet," he said.

"I like it wet."

The man's momentary pause gave the hunter just enough time. He lurched forward.

"You like?" she asked.

A shrug of her shoulders, and the robe fell from her body. She wore nothing beneath but small white bikini panties. A smile swept over Curtis's red, straining face.

It froze there.

Missie smiled back—just for a moment—then frowned. "What on earth is wrong with you?"

The smile on the man's face degenerated into a twisted grimace of confused pain.

"Get yourself in here," she said, thinking that he was somehow pinching himself on the window.

He answered her with a shrill hysterical cry that drove her back against her cluttered vanity. The mirror cracked as it slammed against the wall. Perfume and makeup and hair spray clattered to the floor. Tear Gas, who had been lounging on the bottom of the bed, hissed and darted into a closet.

"Jesus! What is it?"

The man bleated in his agony, his cries rocking the walls of the house itself. Missie covered her ears. Her eyes remained glued to the man. His upper torso flopped and jerked. Blood poured from his lips as his teeth champed into flesh. He writhed and flung his hands in the air, trying to escape the spasms of gut-wrenching pain.

Missie babbled. Something god-awful was wrong, but she didn't know what. She didn't want to know.

Outside, the hunter's powerful hands dug into the man's groin. The steely fingers crushed testicles underneath the blood-soaked pants. The fluid warmed the hunter's hand. He inserted the other hand into the back of the pants and pulled down. The pants snap popped loose. The hunter released the grip on Curtis's genitals only long enough to strip down the pants. Quickly the hand returned to the gory crotch. With his free hand the hunter leaned down to lift a long crooked stick from the ground.

TWENTY-ONE

THE LIGHT, CHILLY shower was uncommon to the late Appalachian spring. June rains usually came in orgasmic deluges, accompanied by wind and lightning and ponderous thunder. Milbrook's streets twinkled with the slow-falling moisture. Glistening drops dripped from the new green foliage. The farmers called it a soaking rain, the kind that fell so gradually it seeped deep into the soil. And the ground was already warm, so warm that some of the moisture rose from it in wispy threads of night mist that hugged the summer-warmed earth.

Kenny hunkered into the rain slicker he wore. In spite of the chill, he sweated beneath it. He marched with head down toward Missie's house. The sticky moisture of his sweat gathered in his armpits. Perspiration trickled from the back of his neck. He walked briskly, his gait full of determined purpose, his tennis shoes thumping on the rain-shiny sidewalk.

What if Posich—or some other cop—saw him? How many times was he going to get away with the long hike across town?

Fear threatened to turn him around, but his anger overcame it. He remembered her voice, her empty promises made to him the night before. She had talked love to him . . . lust to him. Never before had he been so aroused, not even the other times with her. She had encouraged him to stroke his penis—"your sweet cock," she'd said, saying the word sharply. She told him what she was doing to herself, whispering dirty words to him, describing sexy things that he'd only read about. He had almost come at once, would have for sure if he hadn't had the orgasm earlier.

A cock-teaser. Now he really knew what the word meant.

Headlights found him. A car turned onto the street, coming toward him. His balls tightened. What would he say? How would he explain this time? Would he even get a chance to explain? He wanted to leap for cover, but too late for that—surely whoever was in the car had already noticed him in his bright yellow reflective rain gear. Kenny tucked his head deeper in the slicker. The car passed, a small compact looking nothing at all like a police cruiser.

Kenny's shoulders slumped in relief. His pace quickened.

It was as if he stood outside of his body watching it do things he'd never dreamed of doing. Why did he feel so vile? All the guys talked about sex like it was nothing . . . as if they had it—did it—every day. They joked about "blowjobs" and "pussy eating"—all sorts of things, even the glory of older women. A part of Kenny wanted to believe that it was true, just so his behavior—and his feelings—wouldn't be unique, maybe even abnormal. Another part of him wanted to believe that the talk of the other guys was just that, hot air . . . nothing else; that he had something special—or had had something special—that set him apart. Maybe this obsession with unnatural sex was a disease afflicting his generation? The product maybe of nuclear testing? Or too much TV?

In a way, he wanted it over, done with. In another way, a more powerful way, he never wanted it to stop, and he wanted to tell Missie that. Maybe she'd change her mind?

* * *

Bill Curtis's eyes threatened to explode. The pupils were fixed on Missie, begging her to do something. She collapsed to the floor, her fingers inside her mouth clamped between her teeth. Terror gripped her as she watched the man's useless panic.

The final cry that came from Curtis ended in a gurgling expiration of air and blood. His face went slack; his body came flying through the window, skidding across the floor, stopping at Missie's knees. She saw the red slash of blood across the hardwood floor, the crooked stick protruding from—

"Oh, God. Help me!" she wailed.

—the window—close the fucking window!

She crawled around his body, avoiding the glistening track of blood. When she reached it, she paused, her ears tuned and her eyes squinched closed. At first she heard nothing but the sound of the rain, but, as she started to rise from the floor, she heard the sound of raspy, labored breathing—the sound of her death.

She reached up for the window.

The hand snagged her wrist.

Kenny approached the house with the stealth of a wrongdoer. He held to the darkest shadows, trying to keep the slicker out of the light. The glare from a nearby streetlamp illuminated the front porch of the Posich house. Instead of walking into the yard of the house, he stayed in the shadows of a line of shrubs that led to the backyard of a neighbor's house, then to Missie's backyard. All the neighbors' houses were dark, but as an added precaution he slipped off the slicker before he headed for the small back porch. He wadded it into a small ball and carried it in his hand.

Just as he was prepared to knock, he heard the first sounds. Something shattered, something made of glass. Kenny froze, his heart in his throat.

Then came the soft feminine cry. Kenny inched away from the door. Posich was there. He was beating her. Or maybe it wasn't Posich. She'd talked of such things the night before, of being tied and softly spanked or even whipped. Maybe that was what was going on.

He stopped to listen.

The cry that reached his ears sent a bone-rattling chill down his body, a sound ripe with terror . . . with death. There was no pleasure in it. Kenny's bladder emptied. The banshee cry came, it seemed, from the far side of the house, the side next to the woods.

As he eased down the steps, he noticed the warm dampness in his jeans. Quickly it turned cold, and his trembling became worse. At the edge of the house, he peeked around. Inside light spilled out of a window. Kenny wanted to run away as fast as he could, but something stopped him. The night had grown still. Cautiously, he crept alongside the house. The intensity of the rain, as if flogged by the sounds of violence, had worsened. His hair washed down in his face. Rivers of water ran down his neck.

As he neared the window, he saw the splotch of dark red on the side of the house. With the mounting strength of the rain came a cool wind that drove the cascading sheets of water into the side of the house. Red ran down the white siding, staining the block foundation.

The window was open. Kenny stopped beneath it, repulsed by the sight of the drooling blood. Blood it was, too. No doubt about it. He stood on tiptoes to lift his eyes to the windowsill.

At that instant Kenny Shaffer lost control. The scene that greeted him pulled a scream from the depths of his guts. A figure loomed over the two bloody bodies. Its eyes met Kenny's.

The boy dropped to the ground and crashed through the

undergrowth into the drenched forest. The form of the hunter came flying through the window in pursuit.

Gil Dickerson received the disturbance call and at once recognized the address of Hank Posich.

"Where's Posich?" he asked of the dispatcher.

"At the hospital doing a follow-up on an accident."

"An accident?" Gil didn't remember any radio traffic about an accident.

"It happened last night. He's trying to get the results on a blood-alcohol test."

"I'll handle it by myself for now." Gil's mind raced over the possibilities. He'd heard tales about Missie Posich. Maybe she got ahold of a man this time that liked it rough? Or maybe something worse had happened? Either way, he didn't want Hank notified.

"So you don't want me to notify him?"

"Damn it to hell," Gill said, not keying the mike. When he did open the radio mike, he said, "Affirmative. I will give you a public service shortly."

That was the bad thing about radios. No security to a conversation.

He arrived at the Posich residence a few minutes later. Porch lights burned on several houses, but he saw no one. Lights also burned in Hank's house. He pulled to a stop in front of the house and got out of the car, his hand on the butt of his revolver.

"Officer!"

He looked behind him. Across the street a man stood on a porch in his bathrobe. He was motioning. Gil crossed the street.

"We heard the awfullest screams from over there," he said before Gil could ask. "I thought I saw some movement in the bushes on the left side there."

"Has anyone gone over there?"

The man, short and pudgy, his face full of fear, shook his head. "No, sir. You know Officer Posich lives there, don't you?"

"Yes."

"From the sounds I heard I wouldn't dare go over there. You be careful."

Gil turned back toward the Posich home. He drew his revolver. No matter what he found, it couldn't be any worse than what he had found that night at the high school. No way could it ever be that bad again.

He wished he had some backup, just like the night at the high school. The call should have been forwarded to the city police. The dispatcher probably chose not to because the suspect address was Hank Posich's house. Good police practice dictated that he call and request city backup if his other unit was tied up. Gil ignored that policy. Hank might overhear the call. Certainly he would recognize his address. No reason to put Hank through what he had gone through—if it came to that.

The front door was locked.

He pounded on it.

No answer.

Gil tested its strength, then put a foot to it. The wood around the lock splintered. The door swung open. A small lamp burned in the living room.

He inched his way in, his gun ready.

No sounds at all—just his own labored breathing.

As he searched the front rooms, his anxiety mounted. If Missie Posich was here . . . was alive, he'd know it by now. Gil postponed the bedroom for last.

The scene took his breath. The incongruity of it only added to the horror. The uniformed figure of Bill Curtis lay in a thickening pool of blood in the middle of the hardwood floor. His pants were gathered down around his ankles. His face bore the look of an agonizing death. The jagged branch stuck up in the air. A trail of blood led from an open window to the body.

Missie Posich lay flat on her back, clothed in blood, most of it hers. At least he assumed it was Missie. Her face was so badly disfigured that Gil couldn't be sure. Gil's breathing became rapid, just as it had at the high school. The battered remains of the face of Missie Posich turned into the grinning, mocking face of DeeDee. Gil couldn't help himself. Yet another cry floated that night from the open window of the Posich house.

A phone ringing . . .

Whit looked at the clock.

Twelve forty-five . . . he hadn't been in bed more than twenty minutes, but he'd fallen right to sleep.

The phone still ringing . . .

"No more," he said, his belly knotting at the sound. It had become a standard response, even when the phone rang during the hours of daylight.

He forced himself to answer it.

A sheriff's department dispatcher was on the other end. "We've got two more killings, sir."

"Oh, shit. Two?" He dreaded to ask who it was.

"This one's strange."

"So tell me about it."

"Well, it happened at the residence of Hank Posich. We got a call about a disturbance. Gil Dickerson answered it. He found Bill Curtis and Hank's wife dead at the scene of the crime."

"Who's Bill Curtis?" The dispatcher had spoken the name as if Whit should have known.

"The new deputy we just hired. He's been dispatching."

Whit remembered then—the officer who had thought that Ferdie Tipton had run off to get married.

"Give me the address. Oh, and tell Dickerson not to disturb a thing. Also get me a photographer at the scene pronto . . . and give the M.E. a call." From sheer instinct he barked a series of directives to the dispatcher. "Tell the M.E. we would appreciate it if he would come out for this one."

"Yes, sir."

Whit got out of bed. He ached for rest. The murders were taking their toll both physically and emotionally. Never did he go to bed so early, but on this night he'd practically fallen asleep behind the wheel of his car after he'd followed Tressa home. He tried to blame it on the drinks, but he knew better.

The medical examiner gave both bodies a quick once-over, his eyes pausing momentarily on the woody protrusion from the man's rectum. The ambulance attendants waited for instructions.

"You can roll him over now," he said.

"What about that?" one of the attendants said, nodding at the stick.

"Good point." The local M.E. performed only a gross examination of the body. His preliminary opinion was subject to the detailed findings of the state medical examiner's office. "Just turn him on his side."

Only then, when Bill Curtis was turned on his side, did the full extent of his injuries become apparent.

"My God," intoned the M.E.

Whit stood over the body. His face paled.

The deputy's genitals were a mass of bloodied pulp.

"What a way to die," the doctor said.

When he could speak, Whit said, "How did he die?"

"Hard to say what actually caused death. Internal bleeding . . . maybe shock."

"And her?" Whit asked.

"Hard to say too. I'd say she was beaten to death."

Whit looked around to Gil Dickerson. "What about Posich? Has he been told?"

"He's at the station. Dooley Chaffins came in to tell him."

"Where did you say he was at the time of the killing?"

Gil paused. He knew what Whit Pynchon was thinking. He'd thought the very same thing. "According to the dispatcher, he was at the hospital."

Whit made a note of it, not wanting to pursue it in the presence of so many people.

The M.E. was finished. "They can move the bodies."

The photographer too had finished up.

Whit spoke to Gil. "I want this scene secured. All these people have probably fucked it up already."

"What's to find that we haven't found?" Gil asked.

Whit hiked his brows in surprise. "A hell of a lot!" He explained about trace evidence.

"Makes sense, I guess. If you can find someone smart enough to study it all." Gil's voice trembled.

And Whit noted the lack of color on his face. "Are you okay?" Gil nodded that he was.

Whit was leaving the room when he noticed the cloth bag hanging on a closet door. He studied it for a moment, perplexed by the strange bulk. "What's that?"

Gil hadn't noticed it. "Got me."

Whit walked over and lifted the bag off the clothes hanger. "It's heavy, lumpy."

He opened it. "I'll be damned."

"What is it?"

Whit held the bag so Gil could look inside. At first Gil couldn't decide what he was seeing. "Hank's cat?"

"It's a cat," Whit said.

The black furry body retained much of its warmth.

"He killed Hank's cat?"

The M.E. came over. Whit showed him. "Do you do cats, too?"

The doctor curled his lip. "Dead animals nauseate me."

TWENTY-TWO

"THE RADIO LOG says he was at the hospital from eleven twenty-five P.M. until twelve-forty A.M.," Gil said as they emerged from the sheriff's department. "That would clear him."

The clouds were gone. A moon, its glory concealed most of the night by the low rain clouds, hung low on the southwestern horizon. Stars sparkled brightly.

'So, let's go make sure," Whit said.

"He wouldn't pull something like this. And he was crazy about that old tomcat. Hell, he'll grieve more for it than for Missie."

They had reached Gil's cruiser. Whit, still determined, went to the passenger side and climbed inside. Gil hesitated. He didn't like this, checking up on another officer. Hank Posich was many things, and in the right circumstance Gil had no doubt that he could kill. But not Missie. He loved her too much. Gil sighed and climbed behind the wheel.

"This is—"

"Absurd," Whit said for him. "I know that's how you feel, but you know the tales about Missie Posich. She fucked around. Hank caught her this time. Maybe the cat got killed in the struggle. And Bill Curtis was with her. I don't think this killing is even related to the others."

"Why do you say that?"

''First, only women have been killed up to now. Second, in case you didn't notice, there was no 'Number 4' anywhere at the scene.''

''Okay,'' Gil said, ''let's go check him out.''

In the hospital emergency room, the first nurse they approached went after the nursing supervisor. In strode a severe-looking woman, glowering at both Whit and Gil as if they carried a deadly infection. ''Can I help you?''

''Do you know Deputy Hank Posich?'' Whit asked.

''Yes, I know him.''

''Can you tell me if he was here earlier tonight?''

The supervisor eyed him with open hostility. Clearly she didn't like answering questions. ''I'll have to call our assistant administrator before I talk with you.''

Whit cast Gil a disbelieving look. ''Ma'am, I don't think you understand—''

''We have a policy,'' she said. ''Before we talk to police authorities we must get permission from the administration.''

Whit's face turned beet red. ''Lady, this still happens to be the state of West Virginia. To my knowledge, this hospital has not seceded from the Union.''

''Rules are rules,'' she said as if remonstrating a student nurse.

''And the law is the law!'' Whit countered.

The personnel in the emergency room went about their business, but, every chance they had, they snatched glances at the three of them.

Whit showed her his badge. ''Look, lady, we can do this the easy and quick way, or we can make it hard and slow. If you answer my questions now, and I mean right now, then it'll be easy and quick. If this deputy and I have to take you down to the courthouse, it'll take much longer. You make the choice.''

The supervisor glared at him over the top of her glasses. "We are very busy right now."

She's a tough one, Whit thought. "Suit yourself. Let's go."

The cool veneer slipped. "You're surely kidding!"

Whit checked his watch. "Ma'am, at three A.M. I don't kid. Now let's go."

"But I can't leave."

"I think you're a material witness in this case. I can place you in custody if I have to."

Whit's bluff amazed Gil Dickerson. If he tried the same thing, Ted Early would have him up on charges jiffy quick. He gloried in Whit's bravado even if he did think the suspicion behind it was nonsense.

She reached for the phone. "Just let me call the assistant—"

Whit reached over the counter and caught her hand. "I don't have time for that."

"He was here," she said, exasperated.

"Hank Posich was here?"

"That's what I just said."

Gil gave Whit a look of "I told you so."

"What time was that?"

The supervisor reached for a chart and studied it for a moment. "He was here around eleven-thirty P.M."

Whit tried to peek down at the chart, but she placed a hand over it. "How can you be so precise about the time?" he then asked.

"We had a man brought in who was suffering cardiac arrest. That was at eleven twenty-five P.M. If I remember, Hank was kind enough to assist us."

"Is that the man's chart?" Whit asked.

"It is, and you will need a release to see it." She gloried in that small victory. No doubt about that, by God. He'd have to have a medical release for the records.

Whit waved it off. "No, I just wanted to be sure. What time did he leave?"

"Right after that, maybe eleven thirty-five or so." It was Whit's turn to glance at Gil. The neighbor had heard the commotion around midnight. That gave Hank Posich plenty of time to reach his house.

"He went to the snack bar," she then added.

"How do you know that?"

The supervisor rolled her steely blue eyes. "He told me that's where he was going."

"But you don't have any personal knowledge that he went there?"

"I was too busy to go myself," she said, the sarcasm heavy in her voice.

"I appreciate your information," Whit said. He turned to leave.

"Don't you want to know when he left?"

Whit stopped. "If you know."

"He left just before they phoned here for him. I'd say it was about twelve-forty. Like I told the gentleman on the phone, he'd just walked out."

"Again I thank you."

But Whit didn't head toward the outer doors. Instead he turned toward the interior of the hospital. "I guess you're going to the snack bar," Gil said.

"Damn right."

Whit again showed his badge, this time to a thin young woman behind the cash register on the snack bar.

"I have a question or two," Whit said.

"I gotta call somebody if I'm gonna talk to you," she said.

Gil snickered.

"Young lady, I don't have time for this," Whit said, raising his voice so loud that it attracted the attention of two orderlies, the only other people in the snack bar.

"But I don't wanna lose my job," she whined.

"All I want to know is if Hank Posich, a deputy sheriff, was in here tonight."

"Oh, yes! He was."

"What time?"

The girl's face went blank. "Gosh, I don't even know for sure what time he was here. He got a grilled cheese though, and he sat over there." She pointed to the table.

"How long did he stay?"

"I don't know. We had a few customers, and when I wasn't here I was in the back cleaning up. I guess he stayed long enough to eat."

"You have no idea on times?"

The question puzzled the young woman. "Huh?"

"You don't know what times he was here and he left?"

"It was after I came to work, which was ten. I'd say he was here around eleven-thirty. You'll have to ask him how long he stayed."

"Does that satisfy you?" Gil said as they left the snack bar.

"Posich doesn't live that far from here," Whit countered.

"It sounds to me like you wanna force the facts to fit the case, Whit."

Whit nodded. "Maybe, but let's talk to Posich."

Gil used his radio to track down Posich. According to the dispatcher, Dooley Chaffins had taken Posich home so that he could collect some of his belongings since the house was being sealed.

"Step on it," Whit told Gil.

"What's wrong?"

"Maybe there's evidence there he's wanting to destroy."

Gil looked over at the investigator. "You want it to be Hank."

Whit rubbed his weary eyes. "Just go, Gil."

Two police cars were still at the house when they arrived. Whit sent Dickerson in to watch Hank—"just in case," Whit said.

Then Whit made a circle around the house, stopping at the open window. He pulled a small flashlight from his coat pocket. With it he studied the smear of gore on the side of the house. He moved the circle of light around on the ground until it illuminated footprints in the soft ground. Bending down, he studied the outline of the footprint. He then turned to the dripping foliage that flanked the Posich property. A sudden reflection caught his attention. The investigator found a small stick and used it to lift up the yellow item.

A yellow rain slicker. Not much chance of getting anything from the jacket, but, if there was something there, he didn't want to compromise it.

"Whatcha got?" It was Gil.

"Watch your step!"

Gil halted.

"What about Posich?" Whit cautiously stepped from the woods.

"He's just sitting in the living room. He hasn't even gone into the bedroom yet. Dooley's with him. He's takin' it hard. I know how he feels. What's that?"

"You have any evidence bags in your cruiser?"

"I got some plastic zip bags—"

Whit shook his head. "I need something bigger. Go inside and see if you can get a large trash bag."

Whit continued to examine the perimeter of the house. The neighbor from across the street had ambled over. Whit started to send him home, then thought better of it. "What's beyond these trees?" he asked of the man.

The man, tickled pink that he'd been asked something, hurried toward Whit. "Uh, about a hundred yards straight over there's another street. Willow Road, I think it's called. Bear to the right and it's just woods and a cliff."

"A hundred yards?"

"Well, maybe not that far. It turns off our street up there and angles away from us."

Gil reappeared with a black bag.

The neighbor eyeballed the yellow slicker as Whit dropped it into the bag.

"What went on in there?" he asked.

"Can't say for sure." Whit wouldn't have told the man if he could. "You're sure you saw no one?"

"I just saw movement. Mighta been a person. Mighta been a dog. We got dogs all over the neighborhood, a lot of them strays. While I'm thinking about it, I wish you folks would enforce that leash law. Them dogs are ruining my garden. You'd think people would keep their dogs tied or penned."

"That's not our department," Gil said.

"You're the cops!"

"That's a city law. You should call the city police."

"I have! They tell me to call the county humane officer."

"Oh," Gil said.

The tone of the deputy's answer made Whit ask, "Why?"

"Dooley Chaffins is the humane officer," Gil said, eyeing Whit sheepishly.

"Isn't he one of your deputies?" the neighbor asked.

Gil nodded. "Yes, sir. He is. I don't think though that he operates inside the city. I'll check on it."

"Let's get this over with," Whit said. He'd lost some of his inquisitional interest.

"He's in pretty rough shape," Gil said.

"But what about the dogs?" The neighbor fell in step behind the two law officers.

"Fuck the dogs," Whit said over his shoulder.

Dooley Chaffins leaned on the door facing, staring into the Posich's living room. Whit laid a hand on the deputy's shoulder. "How is he?"

Chaffins shrugged. "He took one look in that bedroom, then came in here and sat down."

Whit clenched his lips. "Well, brace yourself."

Chaffins gave Whit a puzzled look as the prosecutor's investigator eased by him.

"How are you doing, Hank?" Whit asked the question as he approached the sullen officer.

Hank Posich looked up with red-rimmed, empty eyes. "I'll manage."

"Are you up to answering a few questions?"

Posich massaged his forehead with both of his hands. "What kinda questions?"

"You know the routine as well as I do, Hank."

Hank's eyes turned cold and settled hard on Whit. "You wanna know if I knew she was fuckin' around on me? You wanna know where I was tonight?"

Whit looked over his shoulder at Dooley Chaffins. The veteran deputy's face displayed no sympathy for Whit's position.

"That's the way of it, Hank," Whit said.

Hank buried his hands in his face. "Well, I didn't know diddly shit. If I had, I would have . . ." His voice trailed off as he heaved a deep breath.

"According to the dispatcher, you were at the hospital tonight?" It wasn't the way Whit should have asked the question, but he felt sorry for Hank Posich.

"You've checked already. You know where I was."

Whit dropped his head. "Yeah. Okay. Look, Hank, neither of us cares much for the other, but I'm sorry. I really am. And we'll do our damnedest to catch whoever did this.''

Hank Posich's eyes had turned cruel. ''You better find that bastard before I do. Find out where that damned kid was tonight.''

''Kid?'' For the moment Whit Pynchon had totally forgotten about Kenny Shaffer.

''The one you let walk.''

Whit remembered. ''No way that kid could have done this, Hank.''

''Oh,'' Hank snapped, jumping to his feet. ''I'm a suspect, but he's not. The little bastard was casing my house a week ago. The least you can do is check him out like you checked me out.''

Whit nodded. ''You're right, Hank. We'll check him out.''

TWENTY-THREE

MRS. BODINE SMITH dreaded getting out of bed in the mornings. Her arthritic joints screamed in protest as she lifted her legs to the floor. After an hour or so, they'd loosen up—not hurt quite so bad, but never stop hurting, even with all her pills. What would she do without Kenny? A dozen times a day she thought about the prospect, knowing someday it would come. It was a selfish thought, so she kept it to herself. At least he was going to go to college here in Milbrook, but then what? A nursing home for her when she got to the point she could no longer care for herself, when her joints just wouldn't move anymore.

With a grimace of pain she pushed herself up. *Keep moving, old lady. Don't let it get you.*

Before she limped into the kitchen, she glanced at the alarm clock. Seven A.M. On her way through the hall, she pecked on Kenny's door. "Time to get up, boy."

She listened for an answer.

"Kenny?"

She inched her ear close to the door.

"Come on, sleepyhead."

Bodie didn't want to barge into his room. Privacy was one thing she respected. She pecked on the door. That simple act alone sent shooting bolts of pain up her arm, filling her shoulder with it.

"Kenny!"

Privacy or not, Kenny's grandmother opened the door to his bedroom. The bed was a little rumpled, but it was made. Kenny never made his bed until later in the day.

And it was so early, too early for him not to be there. She hobbled into the kitchen, by the bathroom on the way, then into the living room, her panic mounting with each empty room. She went to the back door and opened it. The cool morning air braced her.

"Kenny? Kenny Shaffer?"

She headed straight to the phone in the kitchen.

Corporal Sanchez was just getting into the station of the Milbrook Police Department when Bodie Smith called. Usually he didn't answer the phone, but the third-shift dispatcher had asked him to man the desk while he went to the bathroom.

The woman was elderly, her thin, reedy voice ripe with worry. "My grandson's missing," she said.

Sanchez fumbled through a form rack for a missing person's report. They weren't used too often in Milbrook. "Hold a sec."

"I know something's happened," she was saying.

Sanchez cursed the dispatcher for having to go to the john right at that moment. The proper form continued to elude him. He settled for a yellow legal pad and tried to remember all the information that was needed. His stomach rumbled with hunger, and an infant headache was just beginning to make its presence known. It had been a long night, what with the mess at Hank's house.

"Your name?" he asked.

"Smith. Mrs. Bodine Smith. People call me Bodie. Please, I know he's in some kind of trouble."

"Your address?" Sanchez asked.

She provided it. Something clicked in Sanchez's head. What, he just didn't know.

"What's your grandson's age?"

"He's seventeen."

"His name?" Hell, yes, Sanchez told himself. *Don't forget that.*

"Kenneth Graham Shaffer."

The click turned into a mental clap of thunder. "Kenny Shaffer?"

"You know him?" Mrs. Smith asked.

"Uh, yes." Sanchez forgot his notes. "What makes you think he's missing?"

"He was here at ten last night. This morning he's not here, and his bed hasn't been slept in."

"Maybe he left early?"

"Officer, I know my grandson. He didn't sleep here last night. It's too early for him not to be here."

Unless he committed a double murder last night, Sanchez thought to himself.

"Do you know what he was wearing last night, Mrs. Smith?"

"His robe when I saw him, just before I went to bed. He was going to take a shower."

"So you don't know what he might be wearing now?"

Bodie clicked her false teeth. "Officer, I just told you—"

"Okay. Okay. Now, Mrs. Smith, does he have any friends that he might have spent the night with? Maybe a girlfriend?"

"He wouldn't have left me alone here in the house. Not all night. He's a good boy . . ."

Sure he is, Sanchez was thinking.

A phone call caught Anna Tyree just as she was heading out the door of her condo. She started to walk on out, but she thought better of it. Maybe it was Whit.

It was the young Milbrook city cop with another of his "hot tips" for her. "Have you heard about it yet?"

"What?" Anna asked.

"We had a double homicide last night."

"You're kidding me. The Womanslayer?"

"Some think so. Some think not."

"Let's not be coy this morning."

"Okay, but one of these days I'm gonna call in all of these due bills."

Anna smiled. "I'll buy you dinner sometime."

"Really?"

"Sure, dinner for two."

"When?"

"I don't know—when you find someone else to go with you, I guess."

"Smartass."

"Do I detect some anger?"

"Abso-fucking-lutely."

"Do I still get the details on the murders?"

A long silence, then, "I guess. It was Hank Posich's wife—"

"Oh, my God."

"Yeah. Wait till you hear the rest. Bill Curtis, that new deputy, was killed at her house too."

Anna's mind cataloged the information. "Were he and she—"

"You know it. Hank's wife was a whore. Pardon my language, ma'am, but she was. She'd been screwing around on him for years."

"I didn't know," Anna said.

"I expect half his buddies at the department got in on the action."

"Who says it wasn't The Womanslayer?"

"From what I hear," the officer said, "it just didn't fit the other killings. Needless to say, I hear they questioned Hank himself last night."

"Who's 'they'?"

"Whit Pynchon. Say, I hear you've been seeing him. I thought you had better taste than that."

Anna's face flushed. "You hear a lot, don't you?"

"It's a small town."

"If you hear so much, who was Mrs. Posich's latest conquest?"

It was as if he'd been waiting for the question. "I don't know about her latest, but I hear she dumped Tim Franklin not long ago. You met Franklin?"

"I've met him."

"He's a strange one."

Anna silently agreed. Still, she asked, "How do you mean?"

"Well, a bunch of us were going to a pistol match up in the mid part of the state last year. Tim was gonna ride with me, so I stopped by his place to pick him up. He wasn't quite ready, so I went inside. He's got all this weightlifting stuff in his living room. He opened this drawer, and it was full of goddamned pills. I mean, full of them, Anna! And he took a crappin' handful."

"What were they?"

"I don't know. They all were in prescription bottles. He said a lot of them were vitamins, but I know he takes stuff to build up his muscles. He's kooky."

"Is he a suspect?"

"I don't know. He is as far as I'm concerned. Can you believe it? All these cops for suspects? Whit Pynchon's in hog heaven."

Whit Pynchon didn't receive the call from Corporal Sanchez. The city cop had decided instead to phone the prosecutor himself. Like most of Raven County's police officers, Sanchez didn't have much use for Whit. Tony was waiting for Whit when he got to work.

"Guess who's missing this morning." Tony said as Whit was pouring himself a Styrofoam cup of coffee.

"Is this twenty questions, Tony?"

"You remember a kid by the name of Kenny Shaffer?"

Whit was reaching for the sugar. He stopped. "Of course I do. Why?"

"His grandmother reported him missing this morning."

The doubts exploded. Had Whit been wrong all along? Could a scrawny, bashful kid be the killer? A kid who knew his daughter?

"Kind of a strange coincidence, wouldn't you say, Whit?"

Whit loaded his coffee with sugar. "You don't think he's the killer, do you, Tony?"

The prosecutor made a face. "Hell, I still think Ferdie Tipton's our man. At least in the first three killings. I don't know about this one. I know one thing. I got newspeople up to my ass. If this keeps up we're gonna replace Detroit or Atlanta or whichever as the murder capital of the world, at least on a per capita basis."

"I agree with you on one thing. I don't think our killer last night is the same one as in the other cases, but I don't think Ferdie Tipton is the killer in any case."

"On what facts do you base that opinion?" Tony's mood reflected his frustration.

"We're dealing with a psychopath, not a mental retard."

Tony shook his head. "For the time being, let's keep looking for him, Whit, in spite of your opinion."

The prosecutor went on to update Whit on the missing person's report on Kenny Shaffer.

"I found a raincoat outside Hank's house last night," Whit said. "I'm going to run it over to Shaffer's house, see if his grandmother can identify it."

"Not a bad idea," Tony said, "but you don't think the kid's guilty. I can tell."

"He's guilty of a juvenile sex drive, probably was being entertained by Missie Posich. I don't think he could mess those people up like that."

"And you don't think it's Tipton?"

Whit slowly shook his head.

"I hear you questioned Hank last night."

"I tried."

"And you think it's him. Is that it?"

Whit shrugged. "I honest to God don't know, Tony. A couple of days ago, we didn't have one damned suspect. Now I've got three. And, as far as last night is concerned, I've got as many as Missie Posich had affairs."

Tony rose to leave. "You solve the case. I'll keep the press off your back, all except Anna Tyree, whom you probably want on your back or front or whatever position you prefer."

"Not funny," Whit said.

Whit reached Anna at the newspaper.

"I hear you had a long night," she said.

"News travels fast."

She told him most of what she knew. "Will you confirm it?" she then asked.

"I didn't know that I was calling officially."

"Wanna know who Melissa Posich was banging last . . . or next to last?"

Kenny Shaffer. How had she found that out?

"Sure, if you think you know."

"Tim Franklin."

Whit catapulted forward in his desk chair. "The deputy?"

"So I hear. And I'm told he's a real flake."

Whit was writing Franklin's name on a yellow pad just below that of Kenny Shaffer, Ferdie Tipton, and Hank Posich. After she was done, Whit thanked her. "That's one bit of information I didn't know."

"If you weren't such an asshole, maybe your cop buddies would share some info with you."

"Not unless I had legs like yours."

Bodie Smith weeped when she saw the yellow rain slicker. "It's Kenny's."

Whit suspected as much.

"Is he . . . is the boy dead?"

"We don't know, Mrs. Smith. He's missing. That's all we know."

Huge tears rolled down her withered, discolored cheeks. "He was always a good boy. Why would anyone want to hurt him?"

Whit had planned on telling the old woman where he'd found the raincoat, just to shock her into being honest with him. There wasn't any need. He could tell she was being straight.

"Can you tell me the names of any friends he had?"

"He knows your daughter."

It caught Whit unprepared. "Uh . . . yeah. They're the same age. They go to school together."

"You were on TV one night, last night maybe. That's when he told me. Is it this crazy man—this killer? Has he got anything to do with it?"

"Honest, Mrs. Smith. We really don't know. Any other close friends?"

She shook her head. "No, he worked, you know. Down at the market. And he took care of me. He never talked about any close friends. I told him he didn't have to stay with me so much, but he's a good boy."

"Would you object if I looked around his room?"

"Of course not. Not if it'll help you find him."

"I appreciate it. Do you have anyone you can call to stay with you?"

The woman offered Whit a weak, sad smile. "No one but Kenny."

TWENTY-FOUR

WHIT CARRIED THE magazines folded under his arm as he came back into the office. He'd found them stuffed far back in a corner of Kenny Shaffer's closet. An old *Playboy* and a worn, ragged copy of *Hustler*. The third one was a crude porno magazine. When he was a boy, Whit had had a stash of magazines. He couldn't remember their names, but in those days the display of mere breasts was considered "obscene." His prize possession was a magazine that showed Sophia Loren, naked from the waist up.

Trouble was, in Kenny Shaffer's case they were incriminating. He had found nothing else out of the ordinary. And he had tried to reassure Mrs. Smith, which was a mistake. The old woman had an edge on him when it came to experience.

"I'm obliged for what you're trying to do," she had said, "but you know he's not okay. I can read it in your eyes, mister."

And she had been right, damn her.

Tony practically pounced on him. "Whit! Come in here!"

"What's going on?"

"They found the boy."

"Kenny Shaffer?"

"Yeah. He was lying at the bottom of Cooper's Cliff."

Whit felt the bile rise in his throat. "Dead?"

"Almost, but not quite. A farmer found him. He's at the hospital. The preliminary examination says he has a few broken ribs, a broken leg, and a broken ankle on the other leg. He suffered a serious head injury and is unconscious.

"Jesus Christ."

"What's that?" Tony asked.

Whit tossed the girlie magazines on the desk. "I found them in the boy's room."

"Bingo! That just about cinches it."

Whit threw up his hands. "Hellfire, Tony. You talk about me jumping to conclusions! Didn't you have some nudie mags when you were a kid?"

"Okay, but those cliffs are right near Posich's house. I mean it all fits."

"And the slicker does belong to him. I have another name for you. Tim Franklin. He was balling Missie Posich. She dumped him. You remember? We saw them together at the picnic, and she was clearly uncomfortable."

Tony stood up, running his hands through his dark Italian hair. "I'd rather have no suspects than too many."

Whit stared at the window, at the bright sunshine. "And none of it really fits, not with The Womanslayer case. Somewhere we're missing something."

"Maybe it's none of these people," Danton said. "You ever think of that?"

"Yeah. Scary prospect, isn't it? In the meantime, I'd like to see both Posich and Franklin suspended pending the outcome of the investigation."

Tony's dark swarthy face reddened. "We can't do that!"

"With pay, I mean."

"I'm sure the county commission would love that, not to mention Ted Early."

But Whit persisted. "They're too close to the investigation."

"I hear Hank's taking a few days off. You'll just have to work around Franklin. Now get over to the hospital. If that kid comes around, he might confess and solve all our problems."

"Wanna bet?"

Anna's attention homed in on Tim Franklin. He'd given her unpleasant goose bumps the day he had appeared in the *Journal* newsroom. Maybe it was because he was the killer? She called the jail and found that it was his day off. The dispatcher refused to give her his home phone number. She lowered her voice to a conspiratorial whisper. "He gave me his number a few days ago, but I lost it. I have his permission to call, if you get my drift."

The dispatcher chuckled. "That sounds like Timmy, but I can't. It's policy. If you weren't a reporter, well, then maybe, Miss Tyree, but under the circumstances—"

"Tell you what," Anna said. "Why don't you call him, see if it's all right, then call me back? That would be okay, wouldn't it?"

"Yeah, I guess. Ah, what the hell. I don't have time for all that. I'll just give you the number, but I hope you're not jerking me around."

'I'm not," Anna said.

Anna thanked the dispatcher, then placed the call. No one answered.

In a small town one person's secret is another person's gossip. Tressa found out that Kenny Shaffer was in the hospital from a friend who had heard it from her mother who worked at the hospital. She went straight to Whit's office. She had also heard that Kenny Shaffer was in some kind of trouble. She caught Whit just as he was leaving for the hospital.

"Hi, hon. You caught me on the way out."

"What's going on with Kenny Shaffer?"

Whit took a few steps back. "How do you know anything's going on?"

"He's in the hospital. And he's in some kind of trouble."

Tony Danton had heard her voice. He stuck his head out of his office. "Does she know him?"

"I go to school with him," Tressa snapped.

Tony arched his eyebrows. "Yeah, I guess you do. I'd never put that together. What kind of kid is he?"

"Just a minute," Whit said. The one thing he never wanted to happen was for Tressa to be exposed to the seamy side of his job. That was one reason he never talked much about it.

"I wanna answer, Daddy. He's quiet, shy—I guess some people would call him a loner."

Tony gave Whit a knowing look. It fit the mold of the typical psychopath.

"Go on out in the hall," Whit told Tressa. "I'll tell you what's going on. I was just on my way to the hospital."

She hesitated as if she didn't believe him.

"Honest, hon. Just give me a sec with Tony."

"You promise to tell me?"

"Cross my heart."

Tony was baffled. "What's the big deal, Whit?"

"She has a crush on that kid, goddammit. I don't like it, but I want to tell her easy."

"A crush? On Kenny Shaffer?"

"Just fuck off, Tony."

Whit marched from the office. Tressa waited for him. "So tell me," she said as they both walked out of the courthouse.

"Have you heard about the murders last night?"

"Uh-huh."

Whit spoke to two attorneys who were headed up to the

courts on the third floor. He waited until they were in his car to finish. "Kenny may—notice I use the word 'may'—have been involved."

"Kenny?"

"Yes, Kenny. I think he was having an affair . . . well, maybe not the right word—a liaison with Mrs. Posich."

"Kenny? Kenny Shaffer?" Her voice lifted a full octave.

"She's an attractive woman with the morals of a she cat," Whit said.

"But Kenny?"

Whit pulled the car into the heavy afternoon traffic and headed for the hospital.

"Anyway, he wasn't home all night. His coat was found at the scene. Last week, he was caught prowling—again not the right word; let's say 'lurking'—about her house. He was arrested and I got him out. He as much as told me he had been seeing her."

"Kenny!" This time it came out like a sigh.

"Will you stop that?" Whit said.

"I just can't believe it. I was beginning to think he was—" She used her hand in a fashion that symbolized swishiness.

"Tressa, he is a suspect in the killings—in all the killings."

"Kenny?"

"Tressa!"

"It's impossible," she said.

Whit weaved through traffic waiting to pull into the bank. "Now how do you know? You don't know him that well. At least if you do, you've never let on. You haven't dated him, have you?"

"No. They say he's hurt pretty bad."

"Well, we'll find out." Whit pulled into the hospital parking lot. The sky had turned milky.

"Can I go in with you to see him?"

"No reason to," Whit said. "He is—or was—unconscious."

A Milbrook city police officer stood outside the door to the intensive care unit. As soon as Whit had learned that Kenny Shaffer was there, he had asked Tony to arrange for city security. The case was just too close to the sheriff's department.

"Any change?" Whit asked of the officer.

"I thought you would know," the officer said, eyeing Tressa with curiosity.

"My daughter," Whit explained. "What do you mean? What should I know?"

"He came to. I figured that's why you were here."

"No shit," Whit said.

"Can I go in with you?" Tressa asked.

"No," Whit snapped.

Tressa caught the city officer grinning. "Your old man's a peach," he said.

"Up yours," Tressa countered.

Anna had tried to call Whit and was told he was out. The secretary wouldn't tell her where he'd gone. She tried Tim Franklin's number again. A male voice answered.

"Deputy Franklin?"

"Yes." The voice wasn't friendly.

"This is Anna Tyree with the *Journal*."

"Oh, Anna. Yeah. How are you?"

"Fine. I managed to wheedle your number from the sheriff's department. I hope you don't mind. It was like trying to pull chickens' teeth."

Franklin laughed. It was a strange sound, somewhere between a chuckle and a high feminine giggle. "Well, they aren't s'posed to do that, but for you it's okay,—that is, unless you wanna ask me embarrassing questions."

I'd love to, she thought. She said, "Well, not exactly. What I'd like to do is—" She fumbled for her words. It was an intentional act.

"I mean, would it be possible sometime to ride with you while you're on duty? You've seen those kinds of feature stories before, haven't you?"

Franklin sounded surprised by the request, honored by it. "Oh, yeah. I sure have."

"It might help me familiarize myself with the area. I usually try to do it when I arrive in a new town."

"I'd have to check with the bigwigs, make sure it's okay."

"Could you please? To be honest, I need some kind of feature story."

Franklin again laughed. The sound was just as repulsive. "What with all this stuff over The Womanslayer I'd have thought you had plenty to write."

"Oh, I do on that, but newspaper editors are funny. They also want you to do a feature a week in addition to the regular assignments."

Franklin said nothing for a few seconds. "Uhh . . . Miss Tyree, Anna, would you like to have dinner with me tonight? Nothing fancy. Maybe a steak and a drink; maybe even a movie?"

"Tonight?"

"If you're not busy."

He'd taken the bait. "Well, I guess," Anna said, trying not to sound too anxious. The pace of her heart quickened as she thought of her suspicions.

Kenny Shaffer looked hog-tied in the hospital bed. Bulky casts encased his uplifted legs. The upper half of his body was also surrounded by plaster, and a bandage covered the wound high on his forehead. Both eyes had been blackened by the force of the blow to his head. Whit started into the small cubicle.

"Hold it there!" cried a female voice.

He turned to see a nurse charging toward him. "He's only allowed family visitors. Are you family?" she demanded to know.

Whit brandished his badge. "Lady, I don't have time for your crap. I'm gonna talk to that boy, and that's the end of it."

She started to protest. Whit held up his hand to silence her. "I won't take long."

She looked over her shoulder at the other members of the ICU staff. "Just for a short time," she said.

The boy had his head turned, staring out the window at the vanishing blue sky.

Whit moved beside his bed. "How are you, Kenny?"

The boy slowly turned his head, grimacing in pain. "I wondered when ya'll would get here."

"It's just me," Whit said.

Tears filled the boy's gray eyes. "I can't remember anything."

Whit rolled his eyes. "Come on, kid. That's been tried by the best of criminals. It won't wash."

"It's true," Kenny said, his voice soft, submissive. "I went to her house. I remember that. I heard her screaming. I remember that too. And I can remember blood, deep red blood on a white wall, the wall of her house. That's it. That's all. I've been lying here trying to remember more."

Whit massaged the bridge of his nose. "Right now, you're the only suspect we have. Do you wanna be convicted of two counts of murder, maybe even more? That's what will happen if you stick to this amnesia crap, selective amnesia yet."

"Is she dead?"

The question, the tone in which the boy asked it, produced a frown on Whit's face. "Of course she is. And Bill Curtis too."

"Who's he?"

"He was the man who was with her."

Kenny lifted both hands to his face. Whit saw the angry red welts, caused by slashing briars. The boy smeared the tears on his face. "I knew there was someone with her. I was supposed to see her, but she changed her mind. I knew she wasn't alone."

"So you killed them both." It wasn't a question. It was a statement.

"I did not!"

"How do you know, if you can't remember?"

"I just didn't!"

"Jesus, Kenny. Do you know what kinda hole you're digging for yourself? Shit, kid. Even if you manage to convince a jury of that bullshit, Hank Posich will still skin your ass and hang you up on a streetlight on Main Street. You'd better wise up in a—"

"You'll have to go." The nurse appeared at his shoulder. "You're upsetting him."

Whit glared at her. "Lady, I don't have time for you. And I don't think you have anyone here who would dare try to put me out."

"It's okay," Kenny said. "I want to talk to him."

The nurse whirled and pranced away. Whit waited until she was out of earshot.

"Let's talk turkey, Kenny. I don't think you killed Mrs. Posich or Deputy Curtis, but I also don't buy this crap that you don't remember what happened. I think you saw the killer. Now, it's real simple. It's you or him. If we don't nail the real killer, then you're gonna take the rap. Bank on it. And you're gonna have most of the cops in Raven County on your ass, too."

"I can't remember," he cried.

"Suit yourself." Whit turned to leave. "By the way, I guess you know that you're in custody. There'll be a city officer outside the door to this unit at all times."

"Mr. Pynchon?"

Whit stopped, then turned. "What is it?"

"Where's my grandmother?" he asked.

"Uhh . . . at home I guess. I don't know."

Kenny sniffed back the mucus in his nose. "She doesn't have any way to get here. Could someone bring her to see me?"

The soft politeness of the request reached deep into Whit's heart. "Yeah, kid. I'll see that it's done."

TWENTY-FIVE

"THAT BASTARD KID'S in the hospital. Unconscious, they say." Posich, his eyes weary, darkly circled, sat on a metal barrel in the office of Tiny's Wrecker Service. He sucked on a beer can.

The office of the tow truck service was something of a hang out for the local cops. Tiny, who stood six foot four and weighed almost 330 pounds, didn't mind at all. The cops kept him in business. He got just about every tow in Raven County, most of them because of arrests. So he took good care of his cop buddies, even buying them each a fifth of liquor for Christmas.

Tiny loomed tall above the deputy. "When's the service, Hank?"

"Monday," Hank said. He looked up at the gorilla of a man. "I listed you as a pallbearer, Tiny."

The businessman, his face streaked with grease, walked over and laid a hand on Hank's shoulder. "Hey, man. Sure, you know I'd do it, but what about the other guys on the force?"

"Fuck 'em, Tiny." Hank crunched the can in his hand. "Gimme another."

Tiny went to a grease-blackened refrigerator and opened it. The interior was loaded with beer, just beer—nothing else.

"That gawddamned kid," Hank said, ripping the pop

top off the beer can. "You better know one thing, Tiny. Come hell or high water, that kid's gonna pay. Yes, sir. That little fucker's got it coming to him."

Tiny knew the circumstances around Missie Posich's death. And he knew she fucked around. Hell, when Hank wasn't around, it was a favorite topic of conversation among the other cops. Not a one of them openly admitted having her, but Tiny could just about tell the ones who had. There were several. It made Tiny ache for his friend. In Tiny's book, women weren't anything but trouble. And he by God should know. He'd married four of them.

"You know, Hank, anything I can do I will. You know that, doncha, Hank?"

"Sure, Tiny. I know it."

"What about that nut what ran off from the crazy house? Don't they think he's the one?"

Hank sipped the beer. "Mighta been on the others. Not Missie though."

The phone rang. Tiny answered it, then handed it to Hank. "For you."

The voice on the other end was that of Sanchez, the city cop. "Thought you might wanna know, Hank. The kid's conscious."

Hank bolted to attention. "He say anything?"

"I don't know. Pynchon talked to him alone. He told Wilson, the officer we had there, to keep it quiet, but Wilson figured you had a right to know. He called me. I was calling around for you and figured you might be at Tiny's."

"Thanks, Sanchez."

"Any time," the city officer said. "Anything we can do for you, man, just shout."

"Sure. Thanks again."

"Good news?" Tiny asked as Hank handed him back the receiver.

"Yeah. That kid's come awake." Hank stood up.

"Watcha gonna do, Hank?"

"Think about it," he said.

Anna was just about to leave the house to meet Tim Franklin when the phone rang. It turned out to be Franklin. "Anna, I can't make it tonight. Something came up. How about tomorrow night?"

"I don't know," Anna said. The development stunned her. She hadn't expected to be stood up. "You have to work?"

"Not exactly," he said.

"Well, I don't know about tomorrow night. Look, call me tomorrow morning, say around ten. I'll let you know."

"Please try," Franklin said. "I know this sounds bad, but I just have something I have to take care of."

What if there's another murder tonight? The prospect sent chills up Anna's spine.

"You'll be at home around ten tomorrow?" he asked.

"As far as I know."

"I'll call. I promise. It's worth the wait."

Anna slammed down the phone. It didn't make sense. Just then, a sharp pounding on her front door startled her. She hurried to answer it.

Whit, looking limp from a hot day's work, stood in her doorway.

"My God, Whit. You look like hell."

"I feel like hell, too."

"Come on in. Want a drink?"

Whit went to the couch and sagged down on it. "Yeah, a double."

When she returned, he was loosening his shirt collar. He'd already removed his shoes. "What a day!" he said, snatching the strong drink from her.

"So tell me about it."

"That kid came out of his—" Whit stopped. "This is off the record, by God. I mean it."

He looked so weary, so frazzled. "Sure, Whit. Whatever you say."

He leaned forward. "That kid came out of the coma."

"What did he say?"

"Nothing. Not a goddamned thing. Says he can't remember who he saw there or what happened or anything."

Anna came over and sat beside him. "And you don't believe him?"

"Of course I don't believe him." Whit gave her a look of disgust. "I've heard that same ploy a hundred times. Juries just eat those kinda guys alive, those that can't remember. Somehow, these jerks don't think it's nearly so wrong if they can't remember what they did."

"You said you didn't think the kid was the killer."

Whit leaned forward burying his face in his hands. "I don't, goddammit. Hell, I don't know what I believe."

"So maybe he doesn't really remember."

Whit sighed. "Maybe. I managed to make Tressa madder than hell too. She goes to school with the Shaffer kid and has a crush on him. Can you believe that?"

Anna smiled. "She told me."

"My kid! She's got the teenage hots for the prime suspect in a serial murder case!"

"Why is she mad?"

"I won't let her see him."

"She'll get over it," Anna said.

"I know. It's just the idea of it."

Anna's face was pensive, distant. "What's eating you?" Whit asked, his attention snagged by her momentary silence.

"I just thought of something."

Whit cocked his head toward her. "Thought of what?"

"If the Shaffer boy really can't remember, maybe you can refresh his memory."

Whit leaned back, now not paying much attention. "Yeah, maybe so."

"I mean it," Anna shot back.

"Just what do you mean?"

Anna pressed forward. "I mean hypnotism. Forensic hypnotism."

Whit stared at her for a long moment, then smiled. "Forensic hypnotism? You're shitting me."

"I'm serious."

"Come on, Anna. I don't believe in voodoo."

Anna's tanned face reddened. "I'm not 'shitting' you, as you so crudely put it. I've seen it work."

"Oh, yeah? When?"

Anna collected her thoughts. "Let's see. It was last year. There was a terrible car accident. A car sideswiped another car it was trying to pass and forced it into the opposite lane. It was a three-lane road. Anyway, witnesses said the car that sideswiped the other vehicle was all over the road."

"A drunk driver," Whit said.

"Yes. Anyway, it didn't stop. It just went on. One whole family died in the wreck. There was a single person in the other car. He died too. It caused a big stir."

"I can imagine, but what does that have to do with hypnotism?"

Anna was warming to her subject. "There were several witnesses. Someone came up with the idea of contacting one of the nation's leading forensic hypnotechnicians. He'd read about the guy in one of the police trade journals."

"Hypnotechnician?"

"That's what they call themselves."

"Jesus Keerist! I've heard it all."

Anna sprung to her feet. "Damn you, Whit! Just hear me out!"

Whit nodded. "Okay, I'm sorry."

"He came up from Atlanta, and worked with all the witnesses. Two of them were able to recall most of the license number, all but the last digit in the case of one of the witnesses. They ran the partial number through the computer and came up with one local name. It was some guy whose license had already been revoked for driving under the influence."

"I bet he wasn't convicted on that kinda evidence."

"When they went to talk to him," Anna said, "he confessed at once. He said it had really been eating at him."

"So what are you suggesting? That we hypnotize Kenny Shaffer?"

"Sure. Why not?"

Whit laughed. "I can think of a bunch of good reasons, the first of which happens to be the kid's Miranda rights. I can hear Tony Danton now."

Anna persisted. "I'll give Tony the name of the D.A. in the case. He can vouch for the results. And he'll give us the name of the hypnotist. I know he will."

"And just what will the press say about that?"

Anna cuffed him on the shoulder. "I am the press, dammit. Besides, what do you care?"

"I don't," Whit admitted.

Tressa had been angry but not anymore. The complexity of her scheme replaced the irritation she'd felt toward her father. He'd told her that he was going to visit Anna, then go see Kenny Shaffer's grandmother—to offer the elderly woman a ride to the hospital to see Kenny. According to her father, the woman already knew about her grandson's predicament.

Tressa had no trouble finding Kenny's house. What to say once she was inside? *Why not the truth? Well, most of it, anyway.* It took a long time for Kenny's grandmother to reach the door. Her face was pale, her eyes red and weakened by tears.

"Mrs. Smith, I'm Tressa Pynchon. My father's the investigator for the prosecutor's office." The words were rushing from her mouth as she tried to get the explanation out in a hurry, before the small, bowed woman could ask any questions. "I know Kenny. I go to school with him. I thought I'd stop by and see if I could drive you to the hospital."

The woman was suspicious. "Well, I surely want to go to the hospital, but I don't know. Seems kind of out of the ordinary that you'd want to take me, girl."

Tressa felt the sweat seeping beneath her arms. "Mrs. Smith, I don't think Kenny would hurt anyone. Neither does my father, not really."

The woman still didn't offer Tressa admission to her home. "That's not the way I was told it."

"Please, Mrs. Smith, trust me."

Bodie Smith wanted someone to trust. She needed someone. "You say you go to school with Kenny?"

"Yes, ma'am."

"And you'll take me to see him?"

"Right now if you want."

"I'll need a little time to get ready."

Tressa smiled. "Can I help you?"

"Come in, child."

"So you're not even going to consider the hypnotist?"

Whit shook his head. "Look, Anna, I know you're trying to help, but that's just hogwash."

"I'm telling you it's not!"

Whit rose. "Well, maybe not, but this isn't the case to experiment with. I've got to be going."

"Experiment! Whit Pynchon, you undoubtedly are the most stubborn asshole I've ever met."

"I've got to go offer that kid's grandmother a ride to the hospital. Wanna go?"

Anna read his mind. "You just want company. You can handle that one yourself." She remained angry with him.

Whit sighed. "It's not my night. I can't seem to do anything without making somebody mad."

"Irritating people is your strong suit," she said, ushering him to the door.

Angry eyes caught sight of the familiar Toyota as it pulled to a stop in front of the hospital. They watched as the old woman painfully pulled herself from the front seat and hobbled into the hospital lobby. The car itself, operated by the young woman, made several trips up and down the clogged aisles of the parking area, then vanished into a distant corner of the lot.

The eyes sparkled in an evil smile. Things were going almost too well.

Tressa had let Mrs. Smith out in front of the hospital and then gone to find a parking place. The small parking area was nearly full, and she ended up parking in the far corner of the lot. Mrs. Smith was waiting for her in the lobby.

The cop on the second floor remembered Tressa. "Well, if it isn't the chip off the block."

"This is Kenny's grandmother. We're going in to see him."

"Kenny?" The cop eyed Tressa. "You know that little scumbag?"

Tressa cringed. Mrs. Smith, in spite of her arthritic back, stood almost straight up. "You've got nerve!" she said, pressing in on the startled officer. "Who's your boss? He's going to hear from me. My boy's a good boy—"

"Easy," the officer said, inching back. "I'm sorry. It just kinda slipped."

"What's your name?" the woman asked.

"Look, lady, you and the kid go on in. I apologize for what I said. I wasn't thinking."

But Mrs. Smith wasn't having it. "No, sir. I want your name. You got no call calling people names."

Tressa put a hand on the woman's arm. "Come on, Mrs. Smith. Let's go see Kenny."

"You better go now," the officer said. Clearly he had embarrassed himself.

Mrs. Smith went, but she continued to chatter as they entered the intensive care unit. A nurse approached, and Tressa told them who Mrs. Smith was. "I'm helping her," she added. The nurse nodded and went back to her station.

Whit rang first, then pounded on the door to Kenny Shaffer's house. He waited, giving the boy's grandmother plenty of time to come to the door. It suited him just fine when she didn't. Maybe she had taken a taxi or found a friend to take her. As he pulled away, he thought about returning to Anna's to take her up on her offer on the hypnotist. Not that he had changed his mind. He just wanted some company. Instead he decided to go home and enjoy the final few minutes of daylight on his back porch.

Tressa left the hospital alone—and with mixed emotions. Mrs. Smith had decided to spend the night with her grandson over both his protestations and those of the medical staff. Mrs. Smith insisted. Other than his protests to his grandmother, Kenny Shaffer had seemed morose, almost unfriendly.

"Why are you here?" he'd asked of Tressa as she followed Mrs. Smith into the small cramped unit.

"I just wanted to see how you are. I want you to know, too, that I don't think you did anything wrong."

He'd said nothing else to Tressa, not much else to his grandmother. Tressa felt like an intruder. The "Goodbye" to Kenny Shaffer had produced no response.

Outside, dusk was at hand, a dusk darker than normal because of a thick cloud cover. A gentle breeze had turned into a leave-rattling wind, but it didn't look like thunderstorm weather—rain maybe, but no violent storms. The parking lot had emptied, and in the murky gloom she could see all the way across the parking lot to her car. It relieved her. She had a clear path to her car. At such times, when she felt alone, she remembered the threatening silhouette at her window. As her father had said, it challenged the basic assumption she had enjoyed—that she was safe.

Her leather shoes clicked across the macadam. The earlier heat of the day had been captured by the parking lot, and it rose up around her legs. Her upper torso chilled.

The shadow of the hunter hunkered in front of the car, his view of the young woman obscured by the car itself. He heard her approach, and, as she moved toward the driver's door, he scurried silently toward the passenger side, careful to keep the bulk of the small car between them.

His hand crept up to the door handle.

Tressa's mind had settled as she neared the car, her thoughts by then upon Kenny Shaffer. His shame was so obvious. It sprung not from any criminal act but from a moral violation.

She opened her door and slipped down into the low seat. As usual her car keys had become lost in the infinity of her purse. In the dim light of near dark, she felt for them. The sound of the click to her right did not at once catch her attention, not until the door flung open.

The figure came driving in at her. She screamed as she stared at the face, concealed by a black hood, the whites of the eyes piercing her.

TWENTY-SIX

THE WIND BRACED Whit. It blew from right to left across his deck. In his hand he clutched a sweating glass of bourbon, his third. A spotlight illuminated most of his backyard. The blossoms of his plants were gone, and Whit mourned them. A little giddy, he lifted the glass to toast the vanquished beauty. Another full year before he could enjoy the deep lavender and orange of his garden. What would another year bring? The fingers of his Spanish moss floated in the arms of the gusting breeze, as if to return his toast. The dark rhododendron leaves revealed their lighter underbellies under the soft glow of the spotlight.

Sometimes, Whit questioned his basic being. Maybe he was too much of a bastard. True, years ago he had tried to be cantankerous, but now it had become his second nature . . . no, his first nature. Should he have let Tressa visit the kid?

Hell, no. A killer the boy wasn't, but neither was he without sin. So what if Missie Posich had wiggled it under his nose? Whit tried to remember back twenty some years to when he was that age. What would he have done? *Hell, nothing!* He'd have been too damned scared. That he would have wanted to was a harsh fact he chose to ignore.

The voice of the wind had become so strong that it buried for a few moments the sound of the phone. When Whit heard it, he thought at first that it was a torture inflicted by his psyche. Then he heard it again.

Whit looked at his watch and cringed. *Past eleven. And another body.*

Eleven o'clock . . . and all is not well.

Whit wanted to cry.

When he answered it, resigned to the news he was about to receive, he heard the sharp, angry voice of Julia Pynchon.

"Whit, is Tressa there?"

"Julia!" He was pleased to hear her voice. That's how bad it had become.

"Is Tressa there?"

"Uhh . . . no. She's not. Isn't she home?"

"Are you lying to me, Whit Pynchon? Is she running out the door right now, waving at you?"

"No, she's—"

"Dammit," Julia cried, "is she there?"

"Easy, Julia. Maybe she had a date or something? Maybe she forgot to tell you?"

"It's after eleven, Whit!"

"Well, she's grown up," Whit heard himself saying. Why? He didn't believe it. A sickness was mushrooming like a cloud of noxious gas in the pit of his gut. "I saw her late this afternoon. Right around supper. Hasn't she been home?"

"I haven't seen her all evening, Whit."

Anna! Maybe she's there! "Let me check a place or two, Julia. I'll call you."

"I want to know where she is, Whit. You've exposed her to—"

"So do I." He hung up the phone and dialed Anna Tyree's number. She answered on the fourth ring, the sound of sleep in her voice. The sick fermentation in his stomach escalated.

''Anna, have you—''

''Whit?''

''Yeah, have you seen Tressa?''

''Uhh . . . no. Why?''

''She hasn't been home.''

A pause. ''It's not even eleven-thirty, Whit.''

''It's not like her,'' Whit said. ''Something's wrong.''

''Oh, Whit. Maybe not. It's not that late yet. Maybe she ran into some friends.''

''I gotta go, Anna.''

''I'm coming over—''

Whit hung up the phone. *What to do? Who to call? Where to go?*

His thoughts were an unassembled jigsaw puzzle.

Jesus, man! Get it together, for God's sake.

He phoned the jail. A weary voice answered.

''Who's working tonight?'' Whit asked.

''Who is this?'' the voice on the other end was alert, put off by the demanding tone of Whit's unrecognized voice.

''Whit Pynchon. Who is—''

''Oh, Mr. Pynchon. Gil Dickerson's out in the field. Hank's on station, but he's not working.''

''Ask Gil to come by my house. Tell him it's an emergency.'' In spite of his desperation, Whit didn't want Hank Posich knowing of his panic.

''Does he know where you live?''

''Hell, yes. Now get on the horn and give him the traffic, goddammit.''

Whit could hear the dispatcher relaying his message. He heard Gil respond by saying that he was on the other side of Milbrook and was en route. Whit jammed down the receiver and then dialed the number of the Milbrook Police Department. Officer Sanchez was on station and took Whit's call.

"I wouldn't worry," Sanchez said after Whit explained the situation to him.

"Jesus, do I have to remind you what the fuck has been happening around this town?"

"Is there anywhere for us to look?" Sanchez asked. "We'll go look, Whit. You know that."

"Just make your units aware of it."

He had no more than hung up the phone when it rang back at him. He snatched it up.

"Whit, this is Hank Posich. If there's an emergency, maybe I can help. We've had our differences, but—"

Hank Posich sounded especially un-Posich-like. Whit, caught off guard, answered. "It's my daughter. She's missing."

"I'll get a an A.P.B. out. And Dickerson's on his way."

"Thanks," Whit said.

Whit then called his ex-wife back. "We've got the wheels in motion to find her."

Julia's tone was frightened but biting. "Is that supposed to make me feel better?"

"You don't feel any worse than I do." Whit hung up the phone.

Whit was dialing Tony Danton's number when Gil arrived. Whit stopped to take the time to explain the situation to Gil. The sheriff's department hadn't advertised the situation over the radio.

Whit saw the pain in Gil's eyes. "It's not that!" Whit snapped.

"Probably not," Gil said. "She's probably fine."

Jesus, how Whit wanted to believe that.

The phone rang again. Gil answered it for Whit.

"She was?" the deputy said to the unknown party. "We'll meet you there."

"What was that?" Whit asked.

"The A.P.B.'s out, and the officer at the hospital just

got relieved and said he saw your daughter there earlier this evening. She visited that Shaffer kid. In fact she took the grandmother to see him."

A look of relief swept over Whit's face. "That's it. I bet she's there, I mean at the grandmother's home. She would do that—"

But Gil was shaking his head. "I don't think so, Whit. The boy's grandmother stayed at the hospital. She's still there."

"Then where—"

"Let's go talk to her. Maybe Tressa told her something."

They met Anna on their way out. Whit explained as they hurried to Gil's waiting cruiser.

"I'll go with you," Anna said.

"No," Whit said.

It took Anna aback. "Look, Whit, I've come to care a great deal for Tressa—"

Whit stopped her. "I know, but I want you to do something else."

"What?"

"Get ahold of that specialist you were talking about earlier tonight."

Anna gaped. "The hypnotist?"

Gil heard her. "A hypnotist?"

Whit ignored him. "Get him up here. Tell him that cost is no obstacle. Do whatever you have to do to get him here."

A myriad of other obstacles danced through Anna's mind, but all she said was, "I'll try."

"A hypnotist?" Gil asked when he and Whit were under way.

"Don't even ask. Just blue-light this damned thing."

The odor!

It assailed her in rhythmic waves. The smell of rot.

It turned her stomach, made her eyes tear, her body quiver.

Water dripped, agonizingly slow, but it offered Tressa her only external sense of passing time. The other sounds, what few there were, came sporadically, and she did not recognize them. The damply chilled atmosphere shrouded her with a sense of corrupt menace.

Tressa had no idea where she was. Her hooded kidnapper had forced her to stop her small car. An oily-flavored gag had been knotted across her mouth. He had then dropped a cold silk hood, without eye slits or breathing holes, over her face. He had tightly lashed her hands, then shoved her into the back seat. And he had driven her car. To where, she had no idea.

Her shoulder still throbbed. Tressa had felt it wrench as he dragged her from the car into the newborn night. Her ankle had scraped across the frame of the car, and it burned. But those discomforts were hardly more than distractions. The worst pain came from deep within her chest where her heart thudded away, its every beat like a sledgehammer of fear. Tressa had never before known such fear, not even on the two prior occasions when she had been menaced. She had passed out as he dragged her through damp grass. When she came to, the gag remained in her mouth, which itched with greasy dryness. And the hood remained on her face, but some inner voice told her that the hood mattered little. The place in which she was a prisoner was cold and wet and musty and pitch-black. She knew the feel of the grave.

Her hands were bound behind her, her feet strapped to something that gave not at all when she exerted against it. And in truth she had not struggled very much. Her stillness came from terror. After she had been bound, the sounds of her assailant had ebbed away, but for all she knew he sat across the room, those cruel eyes fixed upon her.

She wanted to retch, but with her mouth clogged as it was surely she would drown in her own vomit. *Please, God! Don't let me die. Don't let him—*

The fear of rape terrified her more than death itself.

Sounds.

Her body went rigid. Her ears ached, she listened so intently. Furtive sounds. Something scurrying. The thunder of her heart deepened. It threatened to beat itself free of her chest.

What's that?

Something touched her arm, something soft and—

A *rat*!

The thought came like a stroke. And Tressa screamed and screamed into the saliva-soaked rag.

Jacob Reese had started his career as a cop. Once, many years ago, he had been accustomed to the shriek of a phone in the middle of the night. No more. When the phone beside his bed rang, Reese shot up in bed, his first reaction one of fear. *Who's hurt?* His daughter maybe, away at college. He reached a hand over to touch his wife. She was there.

"Hello," he said, breathless.

"Mr. Reese?" The feminine voice sounded official.

"Yes."

"My name is Anna Tyree. I'm sure you don't remember me, but—"

"What is it?" he demanded to know, interested in nothing but whatever bad news he was due to receive.

"I need to explain," the woman insisted.

"What's this about?" Momentary fear was turning to anger.

"I'm familiar with your work, and we have a situation in which we need your services almost immediately."

Jacob Reese's hand squeezed hard on the handset. "Is this a business call?"

"Yes, sir."

"I'll be in my office Monday morning at—"

"But this can't wait until Monday morning!"

"Then you'll have to call someone else." He started to hang up when he heard her cry, the word "Please," spoken with such panic and urgency that he brought the piece of plastic back to his face.

"Lady, do you have any idea of the time?"

"I apologize, but it's a matter of life—"

"Or death," he said for her. "Do you know how many times I've heard that?"

"Just hear me out. That's all I ask."

Nancy Reese was eyeing her husband with irritation. "Just hang up, Jake."

Jacob shushed her. "You've got five minutes."

Whit and Gil found Mrs. Smith napping in the ICU waiting room. Gil awoke her gently.

"What time did my daughter leave?" Whit asked.

The woman's eyes displayed her confusion. "Your daughter?"

"Tressa. The girl who brought you here."

"Oh, Uhh . . . let me think. Maybe eight-thirty."

"Did she say where she was going?"

"No, she did not. What's wrong?"

Whit collapsed in one of the worn chairs. "She never came home."

The old woman seemed truly shocked. "She's a nice girl. I hope she's okay."

"Maybe she told Kenny where she was going," Whit said.

"Kenny was kinda rude to her. Well, I mean he just didn't have much to say. He's ashamed."

Gil started for the door. "I'll talk to him just the same."

His grandmother started to protest. Whit laid a hand on the wrinkled skin of her arm. "Come on, Gil. That's okay."

Jake Reese's interest turned sincere when he heard that a cop's daughter had been kidnapped, cops' wives killed. "I've seen some news reports on it. I just can't quite grasp why a newspaper reporter is phoning me," he said.

"To be honest, Whit Pynchon—the girl's father—and I are close. We've been seeing each other. He's out looking for her. Since it was my idea to call you, he told me to do it."

Reese's voice revealed his misgivings. "Even in big cities, like Atlanta here, some cops are skeptical. Are you sure this Pynchon fella is really serious?"

"He was skeptical at first, just like I was until I saw the results in that trial where I met you."

"I'll come, but I want you to know up front that the chances of succeeding are not very good."

"Why?" Anna asked.

"In the case of a head injury, the chances are about one out of ten. Is the subject well educated?"

"He's in high school."

"High school? He's a minor?"

"Yes," Anna said. "Does it matter?"

"Well, his parents would have to sign a hold-harmless agreement for me. It's just a precaution, but I insist on it."

"His grandmother is his guardian."

Jake Reese made a sound over the phone that was anything but optimistic. "Miss Tyree, you're asking me to drive a long way on what will probably prove to be a disaster." They discussed travel plans. Reese insisted on driving.

"You'll be paid for it either way."

"That's not the point. I'll come, and given the circumstances all I'll ask is that I be reimbursed for my expenses, but I want you to tell your friend that it's likely going to be a waste of time."

When they got back into the cruiser, Gil radioed the sheriff's department. "We're ten eight. Any word for us? Or any messages?"

"Ten four, Gil. A Miss Anna Tyree needs to talk to Whit. She says it's urgent."

Gil waited for more details. None were forthcoming. He jerked the mike to his lips. "So where can Whit find her?"

"Oh," the dispatcher said. "At his house. She said she would meet him there."

"Ten four." Gil turned to Whit. "More about a hypnotist?"

"Just go."

Whit's front door was unlocked. Anna started to wait in the car, then changed her mind. She didn't want to admit it, but she was frightened. She felt a little more secure inside the house. She turned on every light she could find, even the spotlight in the backyard.

When the phone rang, she decided, at first, not to answer it. *But maybe it's Whit.*

It wasn't. A female voice asked, "Who is this?"

"Anna Tyree."

"Where's Whit?"

"He's—" Come to think of it, Anna didn't know. "I'm not sure."

"You're a liar!" screeched the woman. Anna knew it was Whit's ex-wife.

"Mrs. Pynchon, he's out searching for Tressa. I don't know where he is. I've left a message for him. When he gets in touch with me, I'll have him get in touch with you."

From the corner of her eye, Anna saw the doorknob turn. For an instant the terror flared in her stomach. When it opened, she sagged in relief as Whit and Gil entered. She handed Whit the phone. "Your ex," she said.

"Julia, we're doing the best we can."

Whatever the woman said, it made Whit slam down the receiver.

"She's got to be worried out of her mind," Anna said, trying to put herself in the other woman's shoes.

"Maybe," Whit said, "but right now all she wants to do is blame it all on me. And I don't have to put up with that bullshit right now."

Whit's eyes were red, the skin beneath them pasty and sagging. "You need to rest a few minutes," Anna said.

"What did you want?" Obviously he had no intention of resting.

"The hypnotist will leave Atlanta at dawn, which should put him here in late afternoon," Anna said.

"Is that the best he can do?"

Gil stood at the door, staying out of the conversation.

"Damn, Whit. I had to twist his arm to get him to come, and then he tells me there's only a ten percent chance of success."

"Why can't he charter a plane?" Whit persisted. "I told you cost was no—"

Anna sighed. "Maybe he's afraid to fly."

"Oh, that's just peachy," Whit countered.

Anna looked to Gil. "Would you excuse us a moment?"

"Sure," Gil said, backing out the door.

"Have you checked out Tim Franklin?" Anna asked.

"Not yet."

"He's weird, Whit."

"That's the first requirement for being a cop," Whit said.

"I'm serious."

"So am I."

She studied his face and saw that he was.

"Do you really think Franklin's our killer in all the cases?" Whit said.

Anna shrugged. "Why not? He's a bodybuilder. God knows he's got the strength."

"Let's broach it with Dickerson." Whit started after the deputy.

"Whit! Do you think that's a good idea?"

"Hell, Anna. His wife is one of the victims."

Whit called Gil back inside and told him of Anna's suspicion.

Anna could tell by the look on the deputy's face that he wasn't buying it either. "Not Franklin. Down deep, the guy's a chicken shit. No guts. Besides, he's out of town this weekend."

"Where?" Anna asked, her face incredulous.

"At some bodybuilding contest or something."

Anna didn't want to tell Whit that she'd tried to arrange a date with him, but she had no choice. Whit turned purple with rage. "You damned stupid woman! We're the cops around here. What if you turned out to be right? You wanna end up with that long, pretty neck torn away?"

"So now you think he's dangerous?" Anna countered.

"I think you're dangerous," Whit said.

Twenty-Seven

Tressa's captor returned many hours later—she had no idea how many. In the distance, she heard something that sounded like a door slamming. During the long, dark hours that had passed, her heart-throbbing fear had eased. The terror remained, but it had moved into her mind. Fatigue racked her body. The rat—if that's what it had been—had gone its way without touching her again, and she had managed to relax a little. Numb perhaps from the strain, she had dropped into a fitful, short-lived sleep. Pain had yanked her out of her sleep. Just as soon as her leg muscles had relaxed, contorted as they were, they had cramped. Tressa had struggled against the vise of the pain and in the end could do nothing but shriek her misery into the oily gag. After what seemed an eternity of hell, the cramp had released. For an instant Tressa had experienced utopia, that fraudulent emotional high that often comes when severe pain ends.

That had been hours before. The prospect of another leg cramp kept her awake. Now, as she heard the sound of movement, the pounding in her chest again intensified. She wanted to grab something, anything, and hold on to it as if it were her very life. *He's coming.*

She heard his breathing. His presence stirred the rank odor of her prison. The smell worsened, deepened, became different somehow. She tried to beg, even to scream, but all she could manage was a pitiful, muted babbling that, even to her, sounded silly.

If he would speak. . . .

A hand touched her hooded face. Her bladder turned loose. She tried to press back, escape his touch. The hand dropped to her chest, to her breasts. They were squeezed, first the right and then the left.

God! Please! It's not fair. It's not right.

I'm going to wake up in my bedroom, and the sun will be shining and . . .

The sounds of his breathing grew softer. She heard shuffling, crunching feet. He was leaving.

Tears dampened the fabric of the hood.

Anna and Whit breakfasted at a fast-food restaurant. Both of them had been awake throughout the night, waiting, hoping . . . worst of all, helpless. If Whit could have, he would have searched every house in Milbrook.

"What about Franklin?" Anna asked.

"Anna, leave the police work to the police."

"Oh, yeah," she said. "You all have done so well so far."

Whit allowed his plastic fork to drop into a plate still full of biscuits covered with thick sausage gravy.

"I'm sorry," Anna said.

Whit shrugged, his eyes moist. "Maybe you're right. We haven't exactly shined in this case—or these cases."

He had just finished visiting his ex-wife. Anna had waited in the car. He hadn't told her what had gone on inside Julia Pynchon's house. He didn't have to. When he had walked out, she had followed him, screaming and cursing and berating him. Whit's face was colored with anger and humiliation as he had gotten into the car. Anna was embarrassed for him.

"I just have this sixth sense about Tim Franklin."

"So what if you're right? I'm told he's out of town. Dickerson even went by and checked his house. It's locked tight. You want me to break into it?"

"If you thought Tressa was there, you'd break in without blinking your eyes."

"You're damn right I would, but I don't think she's there."

"Have you ruled out Hank Posich too?"

"Not completely, but I can't get over him calling me last night."

Anna picked at her food. "Everyone has some good in them. Maybe his wife's death has changed him. What's Tony saying about all this?"

"Hell, he's just as stymied as the rest of us." Whit fidgeted in the plastic molded chair. "What time did that hypnotist expect to get here?"

Anna sighed and smiled. She reached over and laid her hand on his. "This afternoon sometime. It's a long drive."

He slammed his other fist against the table. "I feel so fucking helpless."

Heads turned in the restaurant.

Anna saw the deep pain in his face. Here was a man who didn't know helplessness. It grated on him, stole from him the one thing on which he could always count—his confidence in his own ability.

She didn't want to say it, but she did anyway. "You know what the man said. It's a long shot."

"It'll work," Whit said, softly. "It has to, Anna. It just has to."

Tony Danton and Whit met just before lunch. Whit had dropped Anna at her place so she could freshen up. "What's the deal?" Tony had asked as they settled down in the prosecutor's cluttered office.

Whit's jaws rippled. "I may have acted beyond my authority last night. If so, I'll foot the bill."

Tony's brow furrowed. "What in the hell are you talking about? What bill?"

"I have a hypnotist coming here."

"A hypnotist?"

"A forensic hypnotechnician," Whit said.

The confusion on Tony's swarthy face became more intense. "Jesus, Whit, if it'll help Tressa, I don't care about the cost, but what the fuck is a forensic hypnotechnician?"

"This one's from Atlanta. He's a former cop. Anna knew about him. He was used in a case in the town where she lived before. By hypnotizing a subject, he managed to get that person to remember a license plate." Actually, it had been only five digits of a six-digit number, but Whit kept that to himself.

Whit could tell that Tony wanted to call him crazy, that he want to make a wisecrack, but the prosecutor held back. For that Whit was thankful.

"You're wanting to hypnotize the kid?"

"Yeah."

"You think he knows who the killer is?"

Whit nodded. "At least in the case of Missie Posich."

"And you think her murderer is not The Womanslayer?"

"If it is, he changed his mode of operation. Anna thinks Tim Franklin is involved."

Tony rose from his chair and went to the window. Warm June sunlight flooded the courthouse lawn. The street was Saturday-afternoon quiet. Tony could remember when downtown Milbrook bustled on Saturday afternoons. No more. Most of the stores were closed—for good.

"Whit, do you think you're able to handle this case now, I mean . . . are you too involved?"

Whit's eyes snapped up at his boss. "Are you saying I'm off the deep end? Because of the hypnotist?"

The lawyer wheeled. "Because, goddammit, you're now a victim of sorts."

"You can't stop me from being involved."

Tony gazed into Whit's intense eyes. "I guess not. So, have you checked out Franklin?"

"Supposedly he's out of town."

Tim Franklin was a cop, no matter Anna's suspicion. And there was a criminal case to consider. That meant playing it close to the chest.

"Why don't you look at his personnel file?" Tony suggested.

"If he was a psychopath, you think he'd list it on his medical history?"

The lawyer choked back his anger. "Ease up, friend. If I remember, Franklin's not a local boy. Maybe it'll help to know where he came from."

Whit dropped his head. "Sorry, Tony. I'm on edge."

"You're entitled."

Whit stood. "At least it'll give me something to keep my mind occupied."

Gil Dickerson struggled with the small filing cabinet key. "If Early ever finds out I was in here—"

"How did you get the key?"

"I conned the office secretary. Tell me, Whit, first you suspect Hank—"

"I still suspect Hank," Whit interjected.

"Okay, but now— Got it!" The key turned in the small lock. Gil slid out the drawer. "Anyway, what makes you so damned sure it's a cop?"

Gil was leaning on the drawer, waiting for an answer.

"I'm not sure," Whit said. "But all these killings have something to do with the department. Franklin was getting it on with Missie Posich. I hear she dumped him. That makes both him and Hank suspects.

''The kid was getting it on with her too,'' Gil said. He turned to the files and withdrew a thin manila folder. ''Not much here.''

There was nothing there but a single letter to the county clerk asking that Franklin be placed upon payroll. ''What the hell is this?'' Whit said. ''Is this all you put in personnel files?''

''Hell, Whit. Don't ask me. Franklin was hired by Sheriff Kelly a year before Early was elected. Kelly hired most of his people because of politics. Hell, he hired me because my old man worked for him in the campaign. I didn't fill out anything but my tax info.''

They checked other personnel files. Most of them were just as empty. Whit slammed the drawer shut. ''It's a piss-poor way to run a department.''

Anna, no longer the dispassionate observer of events, navigated the unfamiliar corridors of Milbrook Hospital in search of a woman she didn't know. Down in the lobby, a volunteer (who gave the morose impression that she had been drafted) directed her to the third floor, where Kenny Shaffer now occupied a private room. Anna couldn't find the damned room. The hospital was a confusing maze of hallways that all ended up back at the nurses' station.

To ask for help seemed an admission of weakness, but Anna eventually gave in. A line of women, some in white and others in hospital green, sat behind the long desk, each with her head buried in her work.

''Excuse me,'' Anna said.

One of them mumbled something without raising her head. The others existed in a different world, a place of charting pills and bandages and lotions, each charged on a per-piece basis.

"What did you say?" Anna's voice was sharp, angry.

Finally, the nurse—an oversized hunk of woman with orange hair—looked up. "I said, 'What do you want?' "

"Kenny Shaffer's room."

The woman perused a list. "I don't see anyone by that name."

"Look, I know he's here. There's a police officer with him—"

"Ohhhh." The nurse drawled out the exclamation. "He's in the secure room."

"And just where might that be?"

The nurse pointed straight down the hall toward a closed door, then yanked her finger back. "What's your business with him?"

Anna had followed the woman's finger to an unmarked, battered door. "I'll discuss that with the officer." Anna turned to leave.

"He's down having lunch," the nurse said, a certain satisfaction in her voice. "You'll have to clear it with me."

"Having lunch? You mean there's no one guarding him?"

"We're watching."

Anna came back toward the counter. "Lady, from what I've seen you weren't doing anything but tallying hospital dollars. I'm here at the request of the prosecuting attorney, and I'm going down that hall to that door and open it. Trust me, you can't stop me."

Anna had visions of opening the door only to find a broom closet inside. As she marched away from the station, she knew that the nurse was grabbing for a phone.

Down in the hospital lobby, Hank sat with the city officer whose job it was to guard Kenny Shaffer.

"I know how you feel," the city officer was saying, "but I can't let you in there."

Hank swirled ice around in a Styrofoam cup. "I ain't gonna hurt the kid, Ralph. I just wanna know what he saw that night. Hell, man, that fucker Pynchon isn't telling me a damned thing. I know the boy didn't do it, or at least I'm taking Pynchon's word on it."

"No can do, Hank. Besides, man, the kid doesn't remember anything."

"Like shit," Hank said.

"Really, man, he doesn't! I've chatted with him." The officer really didn't want to tell Hank that he liked the kid. After all, the boy had been banging Hank's wife. Of course, so was half the male population of Raven County.

"Officer!" The cop turned around and saw one of the clerks behind the cafeteria waving at him. She showed him the phone.

"Can't even eat in peace," he said to a sullen Hank Posich. He went to answer it. Hank waited.

When the cop came back, he gathered up the balance of his lunch. "I gotta get upstairs now."

Hank lifted his head. "Trouble?"

"Naw. Look, Hank, anything I can do, you call me. Okay? I mean it."

"I've told you what you can do," Hank said.

"Like I said, Hank, I know how you feel, but the kid's my responsibility. They'd have my ass if I let you in there. I got strict orders. No one goes in unless I get approval from Pynchon."

"By the way, have they found his girl?" Hank asked.

"Nope. Never will, either. I'd say The Womanslayer's struck again. We'll find her rottin' in some roadside ditch. You mark my words, Hank." Then the cop remembered. "Damn, Hank, I'm sorry. I didn't even think—"

Anna found Bodie Smith dozing in her chair. Kenny

Shaffer swiveled his eyes to see who was coming into the room.

"Hi," she said softly. "I'm Anna Tyree. Whit wanted me to come—"

His grandmother opened her eyes. "Who the devil are you? What do you want?"

Anna introduced herself again. She told them both that she was a reporter.

"If you want a story from me," Kenny said, his voice scratchy, "you can forget it."

"No, Whit Pynchon wanted me to come by. Mrs. Smith, could I speak with you outside a minute?"

The woman was gathering herself together. Her joints rebelled as she tried to move. "Anything you got to say to me you can say in front of Kenny here."

"Have they found Tressa?" Kenny asked.

"No, that's one reason I'm here."

Mrs. Smith massaged her swollen knees. "You folks gonna blame the poor boy for that too?"

What am I doing here? Anna's voice of professional conscience kept asking the same question over and over again. *Why am I doing this?*

Anna moved closer to Kenny Shaffer. Dark purple circles hung below his eyes. His lips appeared parched. "Can I give you a drink?"

"Just tell me what you want."

"We need your help, Kenny."

Mrs. Smith made a clicking noise with her teeth. "I don't like the sound of that."

"Just hear me out," Anna said.

The door burst open. A cop stuck his head in. "What are you doing here?" He recognized her. "Miss Tyree, I don't really think you should be here."

"Whit Pynchon told me to come by. I'm not here as a reporter." Which was true, and Anna felt like a traitor to her profession. She had always abhorred reporters who allowed themselves to become a part of the story they were covering.

The cop appeared to doubt her. "Maybe I oughta check."

"Fine. Go call Whit if you can find him."

Anna saw the roly-poly nurse lurking behind the officer, egging him on. "You know Whit's daughter is missing. He needed some information, and I offered to help."

The cop smiled at her. "I trust you, Miss Tyree." The door closed.

"I don't," Bodie Smith said. "Young lady, you get to the point. Tell us what you want. No more jaw jacking."

Anna dreaded telling them, but she strangled her doubts. "Kenny, we want to try to hypnotize you—see if we can refresh your memory."

Kenny's face, already pale save for the ugly bruises, turned alabaster white. "You what?"

"Sakes alive!" the grandmother cried. "You folks is off your rockers. I won't allow it. I won't!"

Anna sighed. "Look, we have a hypnotist—a forensic hypnotechnician—"

"Don't care at all!" the old woman proclaimed. "Them fancy words don't change it any."

"He used to be a police officer, Mrs. Smith. He's good. Just hear what he has to say before you decide."

But Bodie Smith was slowly shaking her head. "No way, miss. You folks are trying to trick that poor boy. You folks are sure he's done somethin' wrong—I mean, somethin' agin the law.

"No, we don't—" Anna couldn't get a thought out.

"I called a lawyer," Mrs. Smith was saying, "the lawyer that did my will for me. He told me to tell Kenny not to say nothing . . . not a word. He said if you folks was to come around and try to ask the boy any questions, to call him. I'm gonna do that, miss. I'm gonna call him."

"A lawyer?"

"Yes'm. Morton Lanier's his name."

Anna persisted. "Mrs. Smith, the police don't think that Kenny committed any crimes."

In her anger, Bodie Smith found the vigor of youth as she hoisted herself from the chair. "Then what's that policeman doing outside this room? It's mortifying. I have friends in this town. So does Kenny. They can't even visit. He's being held in the jail room."

"It's to keep him safe," Anna said, which in a way was true.

"Poppycock!"

"Grams!" Restrained to the bed, Kenny could do nothing but plead. "It's all right. I want to help."

The woman, still incensed, turned on her grandson. "You shush, boy. If you had any sense in the first place, you wouldn't be in this fix."

Anna looked over her shoulder as if she would find someone there to help her. It was a silly gesture. "Okay," she said to Mrs. Smith. "Call the lawyer. Have him here."

"I don't want him here!" Kenny screamed.

The cop opened the door. "Everything okay in here?"

The sharpness of Kenny's voice had startled both the old woman and Anna. "Uh, yes," Anna said.

The officer shrugged and closed the door.

Anna went over and put a hand on Kenny's arm. "Your grandmother has to sign a consent for the hypnotist to do his thing."

"That's crazy," Kenny said.

"You're underage. So if your grandmother wants the lawyer here, let her call him."

"Who says I'm gonna sign any such thing, lawyer or no lawyer?" Mrs. Smith's legs were aching. She settled back into the chair. "Hypnotists and stuff. That's magic-show tomfoolery."

"It's not," Anna said. "I've seen it work. It's not what you think."

"Grams, that young girl who is missing, she's a nice person. I like her. She's always been real nice to me, and I want to help her. I know I saw something the other night. I know I did, but it's like a television picture that's all snowy."

"But this carnival stuff—"

"Grams, I got myself in this. Let me get myself out."

Bodie Smith crossed her wrinkled, frail arms. "You're a kid. You did a kid-stupid thing. That's all."

"Grams?" Kenny pleaded.

Anna held her breath.

"The lawyer, he's gotta be here." his grandmother proclaimed. "And he's gotta say it's okay."

Kenny nodded as best he could.

Bodie Smith looked up at Anna.

Anna nodded too. "That's fine," she agreed, wondering if it was.

TWENTY-EIGHT

THE PHONE CALL from Jacob Reese came at 2:32 P.M. Five minutes earlier and Anna would have missed it. She had just returned to her apartment from the hospital. Reese was at the motel where Anna had made reservations for him. Anna began the search for Whit. She called his house and received no answer. She then phoned the sheriff's department. They transferred the call to the office of the prosecutor. Tony Danton answered the phone, then handed it to Whit.

"He's here," Anna said.

"Thank God. How did it go with the kid's grandmother?"

Anna made a face. "Awful! The boy wants to do it, but the old woman demands that her lawyer be there."

"Her lawyer?"

"Somebody by the name of Lanier."

"Well, shit," Whit said.

"I did my best." Anna had suspected that Whit wouldn't be pleased.

"So how soon can we get this thing under way?"

"I took a chance, Whit, and set it up for three-thirty in Kenny's hospital room."

"Okay."

"Any new information on Tressa?" Anna asked.

"No. You pick up this forensic whatever he is and have

him there. Tony and I will meet you there. Hold a sec."
Anna heard muffled voices in the background. When Whit came back on, he said, "Meet us in the lobby. Tony wants to talk to this character."

"He's making fun of it," Anna said.

"No, he wants to be cautious. So do I. At three-thirty sharp, Anna."

Tressa wasn't alone. The sounds came from nearby, loud noises, as if someone were moving something. Still bound, gagged, and blindfolded, Tressa's world had been reduced to the sense of smell. She wished her kidnapper had somehow taken that from her. A series of different odors had touched her olfactory senses, none of them pleasant. Occasionally, her cold skin sensed the movement of the dank air—as if something had sent waves of air to communicate with her.

Once, something—someone—came very close to her. An especially foul smell reached her, strong and yet familiar. She could mumble, but she didn't dare. She felt safer if she brought no attention to herself.

Please, Daddy. Find me. Please.

Tressa knew he would be looking. And she knew, too, that he would be hurting.

The sound came closer. Shuffling feet. A waft of air caressed her face. The familiar stench drifted into her nose, and she wanted to gag.

Rough hands wrapped around her arm, dragged her along the floor. She screamed into the gag. Her heart found its rhythm of fear, and this time Tressa thought it was going to pound itself to death.

The rank odor mutated, becoming even more foul. The smell of death. Once again Tressa choked back her vomit. This was it. She knew it.

* * *

Tony Danton spent five minutes grilling the tall, gaunt man who called himself Jacob Reese. The man from Atlanta wore a four-pocket safari shirt and faded blue jeans. Years of suntans had wrinkled his face. He looked more like a big game hunter than a hypnotist. Whit and Tony had expected a suave showman rather than this rugged-looking ex-cop with icy gray eyes and thick gray hair that he combed straight back from his high forehead.

"So you're telling us that the odds are—what? One out of ten?"

"With a head injury, yes," Reese said.

Tony stalked the man as if he were on a witness stand. "So why did you drive this far when there's so little chance of success?"

Jake Reese was accustomed to cross-examination. "The young lady there"—he nodded toward Anna—"persuaded me. I'm basically still a cop. I teach at Georgia's police academy. If you've got some psycho murdering cops and their wives, then I want to help."

"Let me fill you in," Whit said, anxious to get started.

Jake stopped him. "Not too specifically. You can stay in the room with me. If I have questions, I'll write them on a piece of paper. You write the answers back to me."

"You mean you don't need to know the details?" Whit was surprised.

"Why?" Jake asked. "The boy's hopefully going to tell me. I can't refresh his memory. He has to do that. Just give me a framework."

Whit looked to Tony, who said, "Makes pretty good sense to me."

Whit then provided Reese with a modest scenario. He also warned the former police officer about the boy's grandmother.

"I have to get the documents signed," Reese said.

"She says she'll sign," Anna added.

"But," Whit interjected, "that was two hours ago."

Jake gathered up a large tape recorder he'd brought along with him and a battered briefcase. "Well, let's go find out."

"One last question," Tony said. "Can the kid fake it?"

Jake shook his shaggy head. "Not at all likely. There are certain exercises that can't be faked. Oh, one more thing, counselor. Don't forget that this becomes a matter of identification. You know the constitutional issues and the evidentiary problems. If this young man doesn't know the person whom he saw, then that makes the odds worse than they are already."

The lawyer stood outside the security room making strained small talk with the officer. He wore baggy Bermuda shorts and a gut that proclaimed his love of beer. Morton Lanier wasn't much of a lawyer, which made him all that much more difficult. He practiced his craft through deception, bombast, and intimidation.

Tony, leading the procession, nodded to Lanier. "You look as fit as ever, counselor."

Lanier curled a fleshy upper lip. "Don't be a wiseass, Tony. I'd say you were at my mercy on this one."

There were no handshakes. "I don't know about that, Mort."

"Whadaya mean?" Mort stuffed an unlit cigar in his mouth. It surprised Whit that he didn't light up. He was the kind of fellow who would delight in choking even a sick person.

Tony grinned. "I understand the young man in there wants to talk no matter what you like or want. And, as long as he doesn't implicate himself, then Miranda doesn't apply."

"Do it!" Mort dared. "See how far you get with a statement taken from a juvenile against advice of counsel."

Tony turned to Jake Reese. ''Pardon this jerk's ignorance. Most members of the local bar aren't so wrongheaded.''

''I don't have to put up with this garbage,'' Lanier said.

''You can leave then,'' Whit said. ''We're in a hurry.''

The lawyer huffed into the room. Bodie Smith stood by her grandson's bedside. ''Mrs. Smith, I strongly urge that you not sign anything. And, young man, don't you say a word to these men.''

''What's going on?'' the elderly woman asked.

Tony was right behind his colleague. ''I made Mort here angry. Mrs. Smith, I'm the prosecutor. This gentleman is Jake Reese. He's the forensic hypnotechnician.'' Tony glanced over his shoulder at the tall, lanky man, just to be certain that he had employed the right title. Reese nodded and offered Mrs. Smith a warm, friendly hand, but his eyes were locked on the boy—on his prospective subject.

''Don't talk to them,'' Lanier squalled.

''Please,'' Anna cried, pushing her way inside. ''Kenny's still weak. Remember where you all are.''

Whit was in the small room too. ''And remember how little time we have.''

Lanier took a deep, loud breath. ''Mrs. Smith, may I see you outside?''

Bodie Smith looked to her grandson, then said, ''Well, I guess.'' He started to usher the woman outside but stopped at the door. ''And not a question, young man. Don't answer a single question.''

''What a nerd,'' Kenny said. ''Mr. Pynchon?''

Whit pushed in close to the bed. ''Yeah, Kenny?''

''I guess you haven't found Tressa.''

Whit shook his head.

''I want to help, no matter what that lawyer jerk says.''

''Anna told me, son. I appreciate it.''

Reese was shaking his head. "All this commotion may be a moot point."

"What does that mean?" Tony asked.

Reese waved a hand at Kenny. "Well, I knew he'd been injured, but no one bothered to tell me that he was trussed up like a bull about to be deballed."

Anna knew the comment was directed toward her. "What difference does that make?"

"What I do, Miss Tyree, is a matter of relaxation. I must be able to get the subject to relax. Look at him. No way can he relax."

"Yes, I can," Kenny countered.

Reese remained unimpressed. "Tell me, young man—Kenny—have they been giving you drugs for pain?"

"I don't know."

Reese's comments stopped.

Whit waited for the debate to be resolved. When it wasn't, he asked Reese, "Okay, so what? Is there something else you want to say?"

Reese gave Whit a look of warning. "Not in here."

Whit got the message.

Lanier and Mrs. Smith came back in the room. The flushed look on the lawyer's porky face left no doubt about his unhappiness. "I'm leaving it up to my grandson," the woman said. "Kenny, it's your decision."

"I want to try it, Grams."

"Over my protest," Lanier interjected. "I'm advising you, Kenny, not to say a word."

Kenny's eyes locked onto those of the lawyer. "Get out of here."

The lawyer puffed up to even greater proportions. "You'll get my bill, Mrs. Smith." He turned to leave.

"And if she pays you what you're worth," Tony said, "you might be able to buy a cup of warmed-over coffee with it."

Reese took Whit and Tony by the arm. "Let's go out for a minute."

In the quiet hallway Reese became exercised. "This is absurd. There's not much of a chance at all. The boy's flat on his back, can't move, probably is either in pain or under heavy sedation."

"You've got to try, dammit!" Desperation threatened to steal Whit's usual composure.

"Have you ever tried it with someone in his condition?" Tony asked.

"Never," Reese answered.

"So how do you know it won't work?"

"I know."

Whit's first impression of the man had been favorable, but he was beginning to wonder. "Look, I thought this whole idea was absurd to start with. I think you're just making excuses because it's all a pack of nonsense."

Reese's washed-out pallor took on a glow. "Don't bait me, mister. This is no parlor game. I don't have to prove anything. I get paid a lot of money by the state of Georgia because they know it works. I've got more credentials than that lawyer's got ass."

"Forgive him," Tony said to the visitor. "He's on edge."

Reese nodded. "Yeah. I forgot. Look—" He spoke to Whit, softly, without rancor. "I know how you feel, and I ache for you. The drive wore me out. I'll do my damnedest, but, please, don't pin your hopes on this. If you've got other avenues of action, move on them."

Whit massaged his weary eyes. "I am on edge. If you'll try, I'll be grateful. If the boy is lying and really does remember, maybe it will offer him a chance to save face—a way out."

Back in the hospital room, Reese pulled two pieces of paper from the small briefcase he carried. "Mrs. Smith, here are the papers I need signed. One is a hold-harmless agreement, which protects me. The other is a request for a hypnotic interview. I'm going to get you and Kenny each to sign one."

Mrs. Smith went to her grandson. "Are you sure about this, son?"

"I'm sure."

She turned to Tony. "What if he says he killed her?"

Tony and Whit exchanged glances. "Then we'll charge him with murder," Tony said, "but I am ninety-nine-point-nine percent certain he didn't."

She looked back to Kenny. "Are you that certain, boy?"

"Yes, ma'am."

After the legal documents were signed, Reese surveyed his workspace. "Let's see, I want whichever one of you is most familiar with the case to stay. The rest wait outside."

"No way," the grandmother said. "I'm staying."

Reese's eyes pleaded with Tony for help. "Any distractions can make it all that much harder," the hypnotist said.

"Just do your best," Tony answered. "Anna and I will wait outside."

Reese managed to lower the hospital bed to a position where he could sit in a chair, gazing directly at Kenny's eyes. He set up the recorder and turned it on. "Okay, the time is three forty-six P.M., on June eighth. My name is Jacob Reese, and I operate a forensic consulting firm known as the Reese Company. With me, incapacitated in a hospital bed at —" Reese looked back at Whit, who stood against the room's lavatory. "What's the name of the hospital?"

"Milbrook General."

"—at Milbrook General Hospital in Milbrook, Virginia, is Kenny Shaffer, a high school student seventeen years of age."

"West Virginia," Whit corrected.

Reese scowled. "Okay, West Virginia. Now, Kenny, prior to my turning on this tape, you and I had no conversation whatsoever about the incidents of the night of June sixth, did we?"

Kenny did his best to shake his head.

"Answer aloud," Reese said.

"No, sir."

"Do you have any phobias? Anything that really scares you out of reason . . . or out of proportion? Water maybe? Dark places?"

"Snakes," Kenny said.

Reese smiled. "Me too. Now, where do you feel most relaxed? What kind of place, I mean? Right now, if you could be anyplace that you wanted to be, where would that be?"

Kenny thought about it. "The beach, I guess. I like the beach."

"Good. Now all this amounts to is relaxation. I know it's going to be hard for you to relax, but I'll try to help you. You can stop this interview anytime. The first thing I want to do is explain to you what hypnotism really is so you won't be afraid of it. It's not witchcraft or anything like that. And all I want to know about is what you saw that one night when Missie Posich died . . . and then just about a few minutes of time. I'm not going to go digging into your mind or try to get you to reveal secrets about yourself. Do you understand?"

"Yes, sir."

Whit stood at the sink, wanting to scream at Reese to get a move on. Mrs. Smith was leaning forward in the chair, her attention fixed on this exercise in witchcraft.

Reese continued. "Do you know anything about hypnosis?"

"No, sir. Not really."

"I understand. And I want you to understand that you'll

always be in control. You'll be awake, and you'll know what's going on."

Mrs. Smith frowned. "That's not like I've seen it done."

Reese's eyes snapped at the woman. "Mrs. Smith, please! You must just sit there and watch. Please don't interrupt."

"Well, I—"

"Please!" Reese said.

The old woman shrugged.

"Now, Kenny," Reese said, moving a little closer to the bed, "on a scale of one to ten, assuming one to be asleep and ten fully awake, where do you think you will be on that scale when you are hypnotized?"

The boy shrugged. "Maybe three?"

"No, lad, much higher. Around seven. Now, Kenny, I want you to tell me what you remember of that night."

Whit sighed. The sound was loud enough to turn Reese around to him. The man said nothing to Whit. He didn't have to. The anger in the man's eyes was enough.

Tressa wasn't certain she was conscious—or even alive.

Had she passed out?

Really she couldn't remember. Her last thoughts were of her legs dragging over a rough, rocky edge. The pain had been scalding . . . then nothing.

She lay on her side. A new odor filled her nose. She smelled rich earth—the same odor that rose from a turned spadeful of earth. The aura of cool earth rose around her. She heard nothing but the beating of her heart and the screaming of dead silence. Fine threads caressed her face.

Spiderwebs.

Tressa began gasping against the gag. Something small crept up her jean-clad leg, inside the pants leg itself. She tried to move, but she couldn't. Scalding bile rose in her throat, threatened then to take the path of least resistance and spew from her nose, but Tressa swallowed it—again and again.

Anna paced outside the door. "Damn, I'd like to observe. It would make a hell of a story."

Tony managed a smile. "I bet! Especially if the kid names a killer. Not that I expect it."

"You're a faithless soul."

Tony checked his watch. "I don't believe in Santa Claus or the Easter Bunny or—"

Gil Dickerson turned a corner and came toward them. "No one knows where Tim Franklin went."

Anna tensed. "So you're all finally coming to your senses."

"We're just checking all angles," Tony said. "Have we checked his residence?"

Gil nodded. "It's locked tight as a drum."

"Does anyone know where he came from?" Whit asked.

"Some say the northern part of the state," Gil said. "Others say Kentucky."

"I tell you," Anna said. "He killed Missie Posich."

"What about the others?" the prosecutor asked.

"Don't forget you have an escapee from a mental hospital still on the loose."

"And Franklin used the killings as a cover for doing in Missie Posich," Tony mused.

"Sure," Anna said.

"So which one of our killers has Tressa?"

The question, when phrased in that fashion, stymied Anna. "How should I know?"

TWENTY-NINE

THE LAST THING Kenny remembered was the splash of blood on the side of the Posich home. The image of it running down the white siding, diluted by the rain shower, became a wall beyond which he could not proceed.

Bodie Smith was rapt. She hadn't heard the story before. She hadn't wanted to hear it.

''Good enough,'' Reese said when he saw the agony on Kenny's face. ''Relax a minute. Before we go on, I want you to know a little more about hypnosis. Like I told you, the trick is relaxation, and you can better relax if you know you won't lose control. I want you to think of me as a guide, a guide that's going to take you into a nice and deep relaxed state. We'll take a good, long look at that night, and, if you have any memory beyond the point you just reached, maybe you can find it.''

Whit's back ached. He changed position often, trying to be silent but still perturbed by the pace of it all. To him, it seemed as if Reese were willfully trying to prolong the procedure.

''There's a fellow at a university up north who has developed an eye technique to help you relax,'' Reese was saying. ''It's called an eye roll, and this psychiatrist says that there's a relationship between rolling your eyes and relaxation. You just roll your eyes up in your head as if you were looking right up through your scalp.''

Whit caught himself trying it.

"Watch me do it, Kenny. Can you see from the position you're in?"

The boy said that he could.

"Good. On the count of one, I roll my eyes all the way up as if I'm looking right through my scalp. On two, my eyes flutter, and on three I close my eyes, breathc deeply, and think of relaxing and floating, and allow my eyes to return to their normal position. Try it."

Whit inched forward to watch.

"Good," Reese proclaimed. "Any questions?"

"No," Kenny said.

"Now this is easy," Reese said. "I'm going to show you a pen. Follow it, then when I ask you to roll your eyes and end up with them shut, keep them closed. All right, one, all the way up. Two, three. Now close your eyes, breathe in, breathe out, think of floating."

The room was quiet except for the sound of Mrs. Smith's breathing.

"I want you to count backwards, Kenny, from one hundred. Do it to yourself in a rhythmic and easy pattern. Something like this."

Reese counted for the boy. "Now, Kenny, you begin." Reese continued to talk. Kenny began to sway just a little as he counted.

"There's something else we're going to use, Kenny, called progressive relaxation. It's been used for people in a lot of pain, and we're going to use it because of your condition. With that method we're going to get you to relax various parts of your body."

Reese moved even closer to the boy. "I want you to think of the top of your head, Kenny. Think about your hair, about the place where it goes into your scalp. Make believe you're looking into a mirror very closely at each of your hairs . . . at the place where they go into the scalp. Think of them as becoming very relaxed and loose.

"Now if you happen to notice a lot of saliva in your mouth, that's natural. Swallow anytime you want. Now stop counting and remember where you were at. Think about your relaxed hair. Think about your forehead, the muscles becoming loose and relaxed. Think about the beach. A warm day, you lying there, the hot sun enveloping your body. Feel your face relax . . . the feeling going downward further, faster.

"Further, down through the cheek, your chin, your neck. The sun warming your bare chest, bringing beads of sweat to it; feel the tension melt away. The feeling goes lower."

Whit's eyes were on the boy's grandmother. She too seemed to be responding to the voice of Jake Reese.

Reese himself studied the young man with trained concentration. "Close your eyes, Kenny."

Kenny obeyed. Reese looked around to Whit and gave a gesture of frustration. It wasn't going well.

If only he could have bound her heart. . . .

The pounding threatened to become painful again as Tressa's skin shrank from the real or imagined touch of creepy, crawly things. The silence ended in a din of crashing sound.

Voices.

Two of them.

In the clash of the two male voices she heard anger and rage, even fear.

The noise of a brawl.

Then an explosion that made her squinch her eyes shut beneath the suffocating hood.

Then a second blast. . . .

"You're a high school student, Kenny. I want you to

picture yourself in a classroom, maybe one of your classrooms at school. You're sitting in the first row.'' Reese was navigating Kenny toward a state of relaxation, and the boy was trying to get his savaged body to cooperate.

''In front of you is a door. In your mind's eyes, get up out of your seat. Go to the door. Open it. You're in a hallway. It's a dim hallway, but you feel safe, very secure. You see stairs, which you approach, and you see a sign that says 'ten.' It's the tenth floor. You put your hand on the rail and start down, floating down, spiraling down into a comfortable state of relaxation. down to the eighth floor . . .''

Tony pressed his ear to the door. The uniformed city cop didn't have the slightest idea what was going on inside the room. He'd gone for a cup of coffee when the prosecutor and his group arrived.

''What's happening?'' he asked of Anna.

She shrugged, then asked Tony,''Can you hear anything?''

Tony shook his head.

''You open a door and find yourself looking out into a dense, green, lush forest. It's cool, a crisp wind rustling the green leaves. Slowly, you walk into the woods, feeling the wind brush your face. The forest smells pine good. You come across a path that runs along a crystal-clear brook. You follow it, listening to the trees, the birds, the rushing whisper of the brook, until you see a small, cozy cabin.''

Reese's voice became a little faster and at the same time softer. And Kenny no longer seemed to be trying so hard. Whit could tell by the voice of the hypnotist that he was beginning to get somewhere. Whit's impatience turned to fascination. Something was going on before his eyes—something, if not supernatural, at least unusual.

"You're in the cabin now," Reese said, "and you see a blazing warm fire, crackling and popping, and a nice comfortable reclining chair. You sit down in the chair. In front of you, to the side of the soothing fire, is a large television. It has a VCR attached to it. You have the control in your hands. Now, Kenny, I want you to press the VCR button."

Whit saw the boy's hand move. It was as if he held the control, as if he were pushing the button. Mrs. Smith saw it too. She glanced at Whit with a look of dismay.

"This is a very special VCR, Kenny. This plays a tape of your memory. You can make the machine play louder or softer, you can make the images go slower or faster. You can do anything you want with it because the control is in your hands."

Reese held a hand back toward Whit and made a sign that Whit thought was a thumbs-up. Whit moved a little closer.

"What I want you to do is look at the screen. Today's date is on that screen. It's June eighth. I want you to push the reverse button. Come on, Kenny, push that button."

Kenny's face, marred by black eyes and long, deep scratches, twisted into a face of revulsion.

"Come on, Kenny," Reese said, the urgency in his voice buffered by its softness. "It's just a movie. Let it play back. Press that button."

The boy's hand imitated the action.

"That's good, Kenny. The film is going backwards, back to June seventh, back to June sixth."

Kenny's body twisted in bed.

Reese pressed in on the boy. Kenny's eyes were open, staring into the shadows of the ceiling. "You're standing outside the window. You're staring at the blood. When I touch your hand, Kenny, I want you to tell me what you see."

* * *

The sounds of battle ended with the gunshots. Tressa held her breath as her chest heaved.

She heard more sounds. Furtive movement, the shifting of metal, of wood. Then the air around her moved. Light again filtered ever so slightly through the hood. Rough hands latched on to her ankles.

Reese watched the agony on the boy's face. It was, he suspected, a psychological resistance rather than any physical injury that blocked the memory. Kenny Shaffer just didn't want to remember what he saw.

"Let it play, Kenny. Where are you, Kenny? Where are you right now? What are you seeing? What are you feeling?"

"Rain," Kenny said. "Soft rain beating on my coat. I hear it hitting leaves."

"What do you see?"

"Blood. Blood and rain, mixing, dribbling down."

Whit's stomach bubbled with excitement. Kenny's grandmother held her hand over her mouth.

"What do you hear?" Reese asked.

"Nothing now. I heard screaming. Missie's screaming. I want to back away, turn around, run away."

"What then, Kenny?"

"I just want something to hold on to, something to grab."

"What do you do, Kenny?"

"I put my hand over my face."

The boy didn't see the killer. The thought smashed into Whit with the force of a runaway train.

"What then?"

"The blood's still running down the side of the house."

"Go ahead," Reese said.

"The window's open. Someone's moving. I remember Missie's screaming. I try to move toward the window."

"Go on, Kenny."

"My legs are numb."

"What are you doing now, Kenny?"

"I'm crying. I know something awful's happening."

"Go ahead."

Whit grabbed a quick peek at Bodie Smith. Tears trickled down her face. In her eyes he saw the love she felt for this young man.

"I make myself go to the window. I have to help Missie. I can't be a coward."

Reese found Kenny's hand and took it in his. "Then, Kenny, what happens?"

"I don't want to touch the window. It's covered with blood."

"Do you touch it, Kenny?"

"Yes, so I can look in. It's quiet inside now."

"What happens then?"

Whit found himself using body English, trying to urge the young boy forward.

"I hear a cat cry—like it's hurt—real bad."

"Go on, Kenny."

"I lift myself up to where I can see."

"And then?"

Kenny screamed, loud and low, a sound full of pain and shock, signifying the loss of innocence.

Tony jumped back from the door. He whirled around to look to Anna. Her eyes were wide, startled.

The city officer started for the door. "What's going on in there?"

"Stay out," Tony ordered.

"What do you see, Kenny?"

The boy cried. Tears poured from the sides of his eyes, over the darkened bruises that surrounded them.

Mrs. Smith managed to pull herself up from the chair. She was at Kenny's bedside, wanting to hug her grandson, tell him that it was okay.

And Whit waited, also entranced, but wanting more than anything to hear a name if the boy knew one.

"I see Missie, lying on the floor. I see blood. I see a man, laying there too. More blood."

"What else?"

"Him!"

THIRTY

TRESSA PRAYED AS her body crossed the earth, over the sharp rock ledge, this time more gently. The light that penetrated the mask increased. Strong hands lifted her. The hood was pulled off. She saw a man's face, red and flushed, his eyes cold and hard. At first she couldn't put a name to him. Then it came to her. The gag came off. She swallowed, allowing the muscles of her jaw to relax.

"Mr. Posich!"

"You all right, girl?"

Her eyes darted around. She saw that she was in a basement. And the rank stench had returned. She turned to see where he had pulled her from. A small door opened into a crawl space beneath one part of the house. She saw moist black dirt and cobwebs. It made her shiver.

"You're okay now," Hank said.

"Where am I?"

"Tim Franklin's house. Deputy Franklin."

Tressa backed away from Posich. "What am I doing here? What are you doing here?"

"Come on, let me get those ropes off you. Your hands are purple."

She danced away from him, almost tripping over something on the floor. When she glanced down, the gaping face of a dead officer stared up at her. Blood soaked the front of the white T-shirt he wore. He stared up at her with dead eyes.

Tressa screamed.

"Easy!" cried Posich. "It's Deputy Franklin. He was the killer."

She was sick. It spewed from her mouth onto the dirty concrete floor near the body of the deputy. Posich approached her slowly, put an arm over her shoulder. "Come on, let me untie you."

This time Tressa allowed him to unbind her wrists. She gasped, her nose and throat burning.

"What's that odor?" she asked.

Posich guided her toward the steps. "Forget that. It's what's left of our other suspect. Franklin killed him too. He's turned sour."

The warm late-afternoon sun blinded Tressa as they exited the small frame house. She shaded her eyes.

"I bet you're hungry," Posich said, supporting her as she teetered down the steps toward an unmarked police cruiser.

"How did you find me?" Tressa asked.

"I finally just put two and two together, which makes me a better detective than your father."

"Do you have any water?"

"I'm going to take you to the hospital. Let them check you over. Besides, your father's there."

"In the hospital?"

"No, *at* the hospital. Leastways that's what they told me."

Posich put her in the cruiser. The rank odor of the house still clung to her, and her stomach almost erupted once again. She swallowed hard as the deputy walked around the front of the car and climbed in.

He lifted the radio mike. "Unit Two to County."

"Go ahead, Unit Two."

Right then, Tressa breathed a sigh of relief. He was really there to help her.

"I found Pynchon's daughter. I'm on my way to the hospital."

"Ten four," the voice proclaimed. "I'll advise him."

"Ten four."

Tressa leaned her head back on the seat. "Gosh, I'm so thirsty."

"It won't be long," he said.

A second, wrenching cry came from the security room. Anna and Tony both jumped at its intensity. There followed a few minutes of silence. Then the door burst open. Whit charged through it.

"It's Posich!" he said as he brushed by them.

Gil fell in behind him. "My car's at the emergency entrance."

Both of them dashed through the emergency room. A feminine voice cried after them. "They found your daughter."

Whit stopped, turned. "What? Who said that?"

A young nurse ran to him. "The sheriff's department just called. Deputy Posich is bringing her here."

"Is she okay?"

"I don't know."

"Are you sure it's Posich?" Gil asked.

"That's who the boy saw."

"Maybe we oughta wait," Gil suggested.

Whit closed his eyes. "I don't know. Maybe he's not coming here."

"Why would he call it in? Maybe the kid saw what he wanted to see, Whit."

"We'll wait. Go call the department and see what you can find out."

Posich leaned down to replace the radio mike. And Tressa took a deep breath of the warm air.

She sniffed. *That odor.* The strange, familiar one she had smelled down in the basement the night before. It came from Hank Posich—his breath, the same odor that she had found so repulsive in the Steak Haus.

"There, we're on our way."

Were they? Tressa's mind raced. Should she just keep quiet? Hope that he did take her to the hospital? Should she try to run?

"Whatsa matter? You look like you saw a ghost or something."

"I'm just cold all of a sudden."

"I haven't even turned the air conditioner on. Must be shock. We'd better step on it."

Tressa sniffed again. Was she right? Or was it just her imagination? She lowered her nose closer to her chest as the cruiser whipped out of the driveway.

"It takes a while for the smell of death to go away," Posich said, noticing her behavior.

"You didn't say how you found me," Tressa's voice quivered.

"Like I said. I'm a better detective than that daddy of yours."

She said nothing else, but she kept her eyes on Hank Posich. He was headed toward the hospital. At a stoplight, he caught her staring at him. The street was sparsely lined with older residences and small service businesses.

"Girl, relax. You're safe."

The stench of his breath swept over her. No doubt about it. It had been him. And again she was sick, heaving little of nothing up from her empty stomach.

"Gawddamn," Hank bellowed. "Not in the car!"

He reached over for her.

"Keep your hands off me," she shrieked. Out the window she saw a vacant, weed-filled lot. More by instinct than thought, her hand went to the door. She clicked it open.

Posich's eyes flared. "You know!"

She was out of the car, stumbling, running. Behind her she heard Posich scrambling out. Then she heard the raspy voice of a man on the radio.

Tressa, weak from her night of captivity, ran in a jerky fashion through the lot toward a row of trees.

Gil hung up the phone and hurried toward Whit. "They tried to raise Hank on the radio. They got no response."

"Oh, my God. Let's go."

It had been a stupid thing to do. Tressa realized it just as she reached the small clutch of trees. There were houses on her left and right, but she saw no sign of life. Posich had held back, waiting for her to reach the trees. It wasn't until she entered their cool shade that he speeded up to catch her. He had no trouble. She tripped over a rock and skidded onto the soft bed of leaves that covered the ground.

He dived on her.

Gil took the most direct route from the hospital toward Tim Franklin's house. Whit urged him on. "Step on it, dammit!"

Posich's cruiser was stopped under a green light. Traffic—what little there was late Saturday afternoon—was going around it. Both doors stood wide open.

"Oh, sweet Jesus," Whit said.

Gil screeched to a stop right in the intersection. Both men drew weapons as they bailed out of the car.

"You brought it on yourself, girlie. I was hoping to take you back all fine and healthy so you could tell 'em how I saved you. Whit Pynchon's daughter would have made a fine witness."

"No," she moaned. "You can't. You told them you had me."

"But I never said what condition you were in."

"Maybe someone saw," she said.

"That's just another chance I'll have to take."

"Tressa!" Whit boomed.

The two men made quick circles around Posich's empty cruiser, their eyes alert for any sign of movement. They both heard her scream.

"It came from there," Gil said, pointing toward the row of trees about thirty yards on the other side of the lot.

Whit wasn't sure.

"Dammit," Gil said. "Let's move."

Posich, sitting astride Tressa, drew back and swung with a vicious backhand. It dazed her. She fell back semiconscious.

He leered down at her. "Keep your fucking mouth shut!"

"Tressa!" came the cry again.

Hank saw the two men charging toward the trees. He drew his weapon.

Gil felt the impact before he heard the sound. It ripped his leg out from under him and he crashed into the weeds. Whit stopped, scurried back to Gil. Blood poured from a leg wound.

"Damn," Gil said through gritted teeth. "The bastard shot me."

Whit glared toward the wall of trees. "It's my fault. We shouldn't have been charging like the goddamned cavalry."

A second shot forced Whit to the ground.

"Hank!" Whit shouted.

He heard loud laughter.

"Give it up, Hank. Backup's on the way."

"I got her!" Hank shouted back. "She's gonna get me outa here. You know it. I know it."

Whit pulled off his narrow belt and made a tourniquet for Gil's leg. "You know what to do with it, don't you?"

The deputy was losing a lot of blood. "Yeah, just go get that bastard. Waste him if you can."

"Lay still," Whit said.

Then he started crawling through the tall, thick weeds. "So help me, Hank. You hurt her," he cried, "and I'll kill you!" It was a feeble threat.

More laughter. "I'm not gonna kill her, Pynchon! You are!"

Behind Hank, Tressa rolled in the natural mulch of leaves. Her jaw throbbed. Her head spun. She heard her father's voice, but she wasn't sure if it was a hallucination.

Whit pushed ahead, hoping he was moving in the right direction. Another shot rang out. The bullet pinged near him. "I know where you're at," Hank said. "Stay put, or I'll kill her."

Tressa's head was beginning to clear. As it did the pain turned worse, but she tried to ignore it. Her vision focused on the back of Hank Posich. He wasn't two yards from her, his head moving back and forth, the gun aimed. Her hand found a rock, small enough for her to lift but big enough to stun him.

The sound of distant sirens confirmed what Whit had told Hank. "Give it up, Hank. Let her go."

"Fuck you!" Hank cried.

"Tell me why," Whit shouted.

"You're all bastards! Every one of you! I bet you fucked

her too!'' While Hank was shouting, Tressa's hand moved closer and closer to the rock.

''What are you talking about?'' Whit said.

''Missie. I bet you fucked her too! Everyone else did. But I got them, most of them anyway. Franklin! Curtis! That gawddamned kid. I was gonna get him for good, too—first chance I got.''

''But you didn't get a chance,'' Whit countered.

''The kid surprised me. When he fell off the cliff, I figured that was the end of him, but even if he lived I figured he was gonna be too scared to tell what he saw.''

Whit lay in the weeds, the pollen tickling his nose. He shook his head at Hank's words. ''Hell, Hank, the kid really didn't remember who it was.''

''I'm gonna walk away from this,'' Hank cried. ''If I don't, your little girl's dead. It's that simple, Pynchon.''

Hank turned around to check on her. The rock caught him just above the nose, sent him flying backward.

''Daaddddddyyyy!'' Tressa tried to get to her feet, but the world seemed to turn upside down. She stumbled and fell. Hank rolled on the ground, clutching his forehead. ''Daddddyyy! He's down.''

Whit heard her voice, her words, and sprung to his feet. He saw Hank rise from the ground, the gun once again in his hand. It was pointed straight toward Tressa, who was backing away. ''You tight-assed little bitch.''

The dense mass of Whit Pynchon slammed into Hank's back. The force of the collision separated both men from their weapons. Hank, his face pouring blood, seemed oblivious to his injuries. He stumbled a few feet, then charged Whit, burying a shoulder in Whit's gut and driving him from the forest and back into the sunshine. Hank's weight came down on Whit's stomach, pinning him on his back. Whit tried to squirm from beneath the man, but he was immobile. Huge, rough hands dug into Whit's face. Thick legs straddled him. Whit's hands came up to lock on the muscled wrists. He tried to pull them away from his head and eyes, but they were like old oak, firm and unmovable.

"Jeeesus!" Whit screamed as his thoughts began to turn muddy.

"Freeze, you bastard!" It was Tressa.

The grip on Whit's head relented.

Still pinned under Hank's weight, Whit tried to look up. His vision remained blurry. And Hank sagged down on him, pushing the very breath from his lungs.

"Tressa?" Whit managed to say.

"I'm here, Daddy."

He forced his head back far enough to see that Tressa had his revolver. Its barrel was pressed tight against Hank's forehead, just above his nose, right upon the bloody contusion.

"You're going to die," she said.

To Whit, it sounded like someone other than his daughter. Her voice was cold, cruel. "Tressa, just back away far enough to be out of his reach. Let me handle it."

Tressa ignored him, speaking instead to Hank. "Beg, you slimy shit."

Hank Posich sat quiet on Whit's stomach.

"Tressa!" Whit tried to shout, but he hardly had enough wind. "Back off so I can get up."

Hank spoke. "Do what your paw says, little girl."

"Shut up!" Tressa snapped. She jammed the gun hard against his forehead.

The movement brought the deputy to his knees. Whit grabbed the chance to pull free. He fought to his feet. "Good job, Tressa. Give me the gun, and you can relax—"

The thunderous explosion echoed over the vacant lot. The blowback of brain and blood splattered both Whit and Tressa. And the gun's recoil knocked Tressa on her behind.

Whit's eyes whipped first to Tressa. Her face and hair were flecked with bits and pieces of Hank Posich. He looked then to the deputy. His huge body had cantilevered back on his knees, and his face should have been staring at the westering sun. But there was no face.

"Oh, Tressa!" He pulled her to him.

"He didn't beg, Daddy. I wanted to make him beg," she said, burying her bloodied face in his shoulder.

EPILOGUE

WHIT STOOD WITH one arm around Tressa, the other around Anna. They watched the first ambulance pull away with Gil Dickerson. A crew lugged the body bag bearing Hank Posich to the second vehicle.

"I think that escaped mental patient is back in the deputy's basement too," Tressa was saying. She hadn't had a chance to tell him everything yet.

"He is?"

"I didn't see him, but he"—she nodded toward the black body bag—"said he was. He said Franklin had killed him."

Whit hugged Anna a little tighter. "You know something? If it hadn't been for that hypnotist, the bastard might have gotten away with it. It makes my knees weak to think of it."

"I knew it was him without any hypnotist," Tressa said.

"I doubt your sense of smell would have been enough to convict him, assuming you were alive. Hell, he could have brought you in dead—like he said—and blamed it on Franklin."

"It seems so senseless," Anna said, "those women dead just so Hank could cover up the killing of his wife. It's the most cold-blooded plan I've ever heard of."

Whit watched them hoist the bag into the ambulance. "There was more to it than that. In Hank's twisted mind, he blamed the wives of all police officers. I think he figured he was doing Dickerson, Linnerman, and Foley a favor. Like Dickerson said, the only killing he probably regretted was his cat.''

''When did he kill Tipton?''

Whit shrugged. ''I don't know. I'd say not long after the picnic.''

''How did he pull that off at the hospital? The alibi, I mean.''

''It wasn't ironclad. He counted on them seeing him arrive and visit the snack bar. Of course he didn't count on Kenny Shaffer seeing him. Because of the hospital gimmick, he didn't have time to make sure Kenny was dead. He had to get back to the hospital. Actually, he was very sloppy.''

''Am I in trouble?'' Tressa asked. ''For shooting him?''

''You saved my life,'' Whit said.

''I'm not sorry I shot him,'' she said. ''Can I go back and see Kenny?''

Whit looked to Anna, who was smiling, then back to Tressa. ''Sure, I'll take you to the hospital. I want to buy Jake Reese the biggest steak in town.''

They started for the car, but Tony, who had arrived at the scene just before the ambulances, called to them. They waited for him.

''I'll need a written report,'' the prosecutor told Whit.

''I'll put it in the mail from South Carolina.''

''Just what the shit do I tell all these newspeople? Anna, talk some sense into this bonehead.''

Anna put her arm through Whit's. ''I'm going with him, Tony.''

''You can't just walk off and leave me,'' Tony said.

''Watch me. Besides, Gil will be up and around in a few days. He'll make a hell of an investigator.''

One of the attendants approached them. He pulled a small white card from his pocket.

"Here." He handed it to Whit. "It was falling out of his shirt pocket." The attendant pointed to the vehicle containing Hank Posich.

Whit looked at it and shook his head.

"What is it?" Tony asked.

"Ferdie Tipton's crazy card," Whit said, offering it to Tony. "You might want a souvenir."

Tony pushed it back. "Keep it. You need it."

ABOUT THE AUTHOR

Dave Pedneau lives and works in southern West Virginia with his wife and one daughter.

Attention Mystery and Suspense Fans

Do you want to complete your collection of mystery and suspense stories by some of your favorite authors? John D. MacDonald, Helen MacInnes, Dick Francis, Amanda Cross, Ruth Rendell, Alistar MacLean, Erle Stanley Gardner, Cornell Woolrich, among many others, are included in Ballantine/Fawcett's new Mystery Brochure.

For your FREE Mystery Brochure, fill in the coupon below and mail it to:

Ballantine/Fawcett Books
Education Department—MB
201 East 50th Street
New York, NY 10022

Name______________________________

Address____________________________

City________________State________Zip________

12 TA-94